ONE
CHRISTMAS,
ONE
MIRACLE

BOB KUCHARSKI

For information about this title or to order other books and/or electronic media, contact the publisher:
Bob Kucharski
Bound Brook, NJ
Bobofbb@localnet.com

ISBN: 978-1-7339703-0-3 (print)
            978-1-7339703-1-1 (eBook)

Printed in the United States of America
Cover and Interior design: 1106 Design

DEDICATION

To all those fortunate individuals who make those quiet miracles happen that affect the lives of others.

TABLE OF CONTENTS

P<small>ART</small> O<small>NE</small>

I remember the sportscaster John Michaels, or was his first name
Lou . . . ? Well, anyway, I guess everyone remembers his broad-
cast line from the hockey game of the 1980 Olympics when the
Americans upset the Russian team: "Do you believe in miracles?" Well,
perhaps that holds true for sports and games of chance but in real life
nothing unusual ever happens for most people. Certainly no bolt of lightning in the sky ever struck me. I never had an intuition or premonition
of any foreordained event. I could be in the running for a nomination for
the world's dullest person leading a nondescript life on this earth. But
it seems that everyone I meet has at least one exceptional, spell-binding
story to tell — tragic, humorous or thrilling, but a story nonetheless.
Maybe I can't tell stories or maybe I'm just oblivious to things going on
around me. I think that everyone has an obligation to tell the one story
or recount one event that has made some kind of impression or change in
his or her respective life. Thus with the proverbial gun (or fountain pen)
to my head, there is only one thing that comes to mind. Just one thing,
and I am scraping the bottom of the barrel for this! What happened
did really happen a long time ago and it was curious, if not downright
confusing. It may have been a wondrous event to all those with whom
I had contact, although I gained no personal benefit whatsoever. The
accountant's tally sheet would certainly verify that! So, miracle may be

stretching it, but it certainly was out of the ordinary — that's for sure! Lives were touched. I never thought of writing anything down, because things were a little confusing, too goofy and just not adult enough to warrant any kind of serious attention, not perhaps until the end anyway. Moreover, it's been at least 15 years since the event transpired; time takes the alacrity off of the way things occur. And as mother was wont to say, just having a sharp knife in a drawer, without any usage, would make it dull. Anyway, it's a story of how I met Santa Claus. Ironically, I did not go out and try to find him but rather Santa found me during a very pressing moment. But I saw that other lives, lives of the most vulnerable, were touched, although no one would ever know the background of activity wherein I became a kind of hot wire or conduit through which electricity flowed. A passive encounter on my part since I only watched, yes, but somehow, someway I still cannot get this event out of my mind. Maybe that was the miracle. Let me share with you some details of the story.

About ten or 15 years ago I was "working" as a communications and development officer for a nonprofit agency that was officially called, by the agency's somewhat esteemed chief and head potentate, the largest agency of its kind in the entire state of New Jersey. That's a most impressive claim since bigger almost always means better. The official agency propaganda claimed that it provided every kind of service to infants, children and adults with disabilities — well, almost everything. All who listened to this outstanding proclamation could not help but be impressed — no documentation or certification was ever called for. Anyone who saw the agency's facilities and diligent staff would become believers too. I was impressed as well, but I never became a whole hearted believer in the official agency proclamations. Too cynical or skeptical, I guess! Maybe I was too close and saw things from the sordid inside. Propinquity does a lot to wreck a romance. But no staff person would openly challenge or question this claim on the inside? Questions were never encouraged.

So everything was unquestionably great. Life was good. Everything, including the economy at that time, was on an even keel. Amen!

Back then, I lived in a small, old house. This was a kind of place that your grandmother or great aunt may have been born in. In fact, I was eventually told that a colleague's relative was born in there during the turn of the century. It had charm, but was small and needed "modernization" to bring it up to comfortable living standards — things like storm windows and a heating system that worked . . . among other things. But I was in this cold, drafty but charming house for the long run. (Anyone who visited said it had charm, although they never experienced freezing that came with regularity with every winter's night.) It humbly had everything that I essentially needed during this time of my life, which was simple stuff. My wife left me years ago with the accusation or excuse that I was oblivious to her needs, although she never quite could define what her needs were or ever asked about my needs. Maybe that's where I learned that asking questions is really a bad thing. Thus I adopted the philosophy that all your questions, and your problems, too, should be kept to yourself. Thus, my life limped on and I was surviving. My social life diminished to a trickle and in its stead I joined a running club which took me all over the state trying to record "PB's" (personal bests). Of course I never achieved a stellar PB but at least I was able to pass physical examinations with comparative ease because of the running. The other hole in my personal life, the other side of the coin, was compensated by working for this nonprofit agency. After all, there is no one out there who would be publicly outspoken against helping someone with a disability. There were all sorts of kids with all sorts of physical problems. And these kids were attended to and cared for by a professional and paraprofessional staff of women who were exceptional individuals, all very competent and caring, and some of whom were very good looking. So that kind of took care of my social and dating life, going into work and having an active imagination regarding staff. Working for this kind of nonprofit became a kind of PB, and I hope that would be brokered into a nice reward in the afterlife since the money and residual benefits were slightly above the subsistence level. I was never part of the inner sanctum of the management team. Money and benefits notwithstanding, you could see the benefits for an agency such as this. A month before any election, the politicians would become suddenly available for tours of the agency's facilities, visits with some of the cute kids therein, and, of course, the photo op, wherein warm and fuzzy pictures would be taken — just before election. Even the most hard hearted would vote for a politician, staged smile and custom tailored suit, snuggled up with a cute, disabled kid hanging, but sometimes, infrequently drooling, all over 'em. Such is life. It never ceased to amaze me just how some patterns continued with an uninterrupted rhythm from season to season, and year to year. Oh yes, someplace in my study there is a collection of photos of these prominent personalities, from presidents to Hollywood stars and those in between. But I keep them hidden. None of them were ever my friends, so what's the point? Some of these politicians looked good as they pretended to have a caring interest in these kids. Great photos!

My life settled into a predicable pattern. Mondays were always difficult for me because I had to break the normalcy and serenity of the weekend to return to the staccato and frenetic discord of the work environment. And this coming Monday was no exception. In fact, it was more than no exception; it was the Monday after Thanksgiving. It was super imperative that I be in and at my desk by nine. Those coming weeks in December, before Christmas and the break before NewYear's, were absolutely frenetic. All proposals for possible grant considerations had to be out because most foundations and a number of corporations would cut their year-end checks then. In addition, there were social clubs, service organizations and individuals who, at this time of year, would willingly open up their respective wallets and give, sometimes generously, to an agency such as ours with cute kids with disabilities. All you had to do was ask. So I had proposals to write and phone calls to make. Eh! That's how I stumbled upon a secret that the deity was keeping from us: coffee with caffeine. Despite whatever the AMA or print media continuously reports, coffee is good for you! Very good. So . . . .

It was always painful to get up and out of bed on a Monday. After a while I did have it timed out to a science. It was seven-ten in the morning; by the time I became somewhat cognizant, the clock radio showed 7:12. Not too bad, only a two minute delay. Kiki, my beloved cat, was not moving too fast either since the sky was somewhat gray and overcast. This beloved harbinger of correct wake up times was not functioning today. Something must have hit her snooze button. Shuffling along with the wake up routine brought me downstairs within 30 minutes. Well almost 30. It was 31. I lost a minute because of the Monday morning factor. (The theory is thus: time accelerates as one gets closer to the weekend. So normally what would take me one hour to do on Monday would take about 54 minutes and 26 seconds by Friday. It's a theory but it has been verifiable for me — most of the time.) Going downstairs I had the typical Monday-morning nondescript breakfast, washed down with tea and a couple of vitamins. Monday's regime included the vitamin especially formulated for males along with a dose of minerals and beta-carotene. And the Kik was not too demanding, getting her usual gourmet food from the can, along with the grits (my name for the hard, crunchy cat food that comes in bags of various sizes and tonnage and erroneously called Kibbles). Going back upstairs to get somewhat perfectly groomed for the Monday festivities at work, I glanced at the clock and found that somehow, somewhere I lost another minute from my schedule. Great! That added some more time to make up on 287 to work. But I could do it! Three minutes is not much when you were a former, part-time race car driver. Went back upstairs, into the study area, picked out the most appropriate tie from my collection of marvelous neck ware, stopped in the bathroom to brush my teeth, and then proceeded into the bedroom to pick a jacket from my marvelous collection of selections and then down the stairs and out the door. Unfortunately, bounding down the stairs I ran into Kiki with a problem: hair ball barf. There in front of the door, blocking my exit from the house and adversely affecting my on-time schedule for work, was a remnant of her breakfast. If it wasn't in front of the door, I could leave it. But no, it had to be directly in front of the door. Moreover, she was mad at me. I could tell in just the way she was looking at me that it was my fault. She was probably thinking "cheap food." Not far from wrong, but if you don't like the stuff, don't eat it — the philosophy to which she subscribed from time to time. This time was not the time, and it could compromise my arrival at work. I went to the kitchen, got one sheet of paper towel and returned to the living room for clean up. I tried to pick up the stuff in one cleaning since time was of the essence. Unfortunately whatever was in the barf mix had a greater thickening agent than most glues that I regularly purchase at the local dollar store. I had to go back to the kitchen for another sheet of paper and a water mister to break this adhesive bond. Yes, the mister always mostly worked, but this surgical procedure added another two more minutes of time to be made up. Barf remnants disposed of, I was on my way out the door, but only after I gave Kik a piece of my mind: "Bad cat! If I get caught by Ferucci, you will be punished." She looked at me, and then calmly went away as if she didn't hear or didn't care. The clock was theoretically against me but I had two aces in the hole: my expert driving and my car, a 528 BMW. That bugger could crank! So I got into my thrill machine, turned the ignition key and it started, flawlessly of course, pulled out of the driveway, navigated through the back streets of town and finally onto 287, heading toward work, at the speed of light, or the speed of sound, or something a little slower like the legal speed limit — no one ever disapproved of the way that I drove. I had to make one of those critical, life decisions, however. Should I stop at Lucca's coffee shop in Metuchen or go directly into work? Here were the variables in this dilemma: I would be at work early but without the needed caffeine that would provide the needed boost for me to perform optimally and almost like my job. Or should I stop, get my caffeine fix that would ensure spectacular performance that would begin my day and, therefore and moreover, benefit the agency and everything it stood for since I would be performing in excess of 100 percent. It was a no-brainer as I directed my finely tuned machine off of 287 and towards the back roads of New Durham Avenue leading to Metuchen and that oasis of all good things to all those of good will, Lucca's Coffee Shop. Amen!

Lucca's was a necessity to anyone with a modicum of civility and sanity. It was an oasis in the sea of turbulence. It was the opened door to a world that only could be provided through caffeinated tranquility. Not to say that this wonderful environment was homogenous. Unfortunately, no! Anyone could and did walk in. There were the cast of characters that I wished would not be there, and at 8:30 in the am would just leave me alone. But this was never my karma. I always had this ability to attract the lost sheep. Why couldn't I attract the tall, good looking, desperate blonde with a million or two in the bank and who wanted a very sympathetic and understanding listener? No, I always get the whackos — from that herd of lost sheep with no money and more problems than a soap opera. But every day with a new sunrise brings a glimmer of hope with another cup of coffee; today had the potential to be better. At the very least, I could enjoy a good cup of coffee, with a bagel or baguette to munch on. Ah, those wonderful executive decisions!

Parking could be a little difficult, depending upon the day and occasion. The main street in Metuchen was almost always filled but that was never a concern for me since I parked on a side street. And today it seemed that luck was finally with me since there were indeed open spaces on the side street. I brought my racing machine easily into the spot and without hitting curb in the excitement of my good luck. Now another executive decision had to be made: how much to put into the meter. The Metuchen police were very enthusiastic about making sure that everyone fed the meter. You never went into Metuchen without change on your person. So, I had to make a quick calculation. It was 8:40 and I had to leave the coffee shop in ten minutes to make it into work on time by nine. So, Metuchen would beat me up for a dime this morning. Almost fair enough! Parked the car but did not lock it as I sauntered around the corner to the coffee shop. I did a quick calculation: the walk coming and going would cost me one and a half minutes round trip, leaving me eight and one-half minutes to enjoy my coffee and bread. This apparently would be quite acceptable. When I finally got into the shop and there was a small line, headed by the loud-mouth realtor. She never just got one thing; she bought for the entire office and probably for any potential clients that she envisioned having that day. This meant more delays, as well as having to listen to her whooping and hollering in the morning. I mean why did I have to put up with her? I was not married, not having sex nor was financially dependant on her. So why did I have to continually run into this loud entity at such an early hour, disturbing my peace of mind? More time off the coffee clock and more aggravation in my life!

What seemed hours took only about another minute and a half in real time. In perceived time, well, it was much longer. During that tremendous hiatus I had the opportunity to look at the selection, now limited because of that big-mouth realtor took everything, of breads and pastries. I did not see my salted bagel. Nowhere to be found; I would have to ask. I hated begging so early in the morning, although the girl (or woman) behind the counter was somewhat attractive. Not greatly attractive, but somewhat. I guess she would look better in a bar at night after a few drinks. But at this early hour of the morning, the appeal factor was not turned on. I had a singular purpose: coffee with a salted bagel. That was it! When my moment came, I ordered confidently a salty bagel with butter — all without looking. Her response was: "I have to look. I don't see any." That's one reason why she could not be considered exceptionally good looking, no immediate response to my pressing needs of a salted bagel with butter. No, yes, she could not find any; all out. She suggested an alternative, one with raisins. No one with good taste would ever eat one of those, as I commented to myself, especially at this early hour. So, I compromised myself and my sense of good taste and ordered a plain one. But I instructed the lovely behind the counter, in response to her inquiry, to butter it well. She did; some satisfaction. So I took the compromised bagel, along with a small coffee and found a seat by the window to watch the world in Metuchen go by — chomping on the bagel, sipping my coffee and just cursorily glancing at the *Post* and *The News Tribune* headlines. According to the Timex, I had about two and a half minutes left of this glorious solitude before leaving and going to work. But for me glorious solitude never lasts long; today was no exception. Right next to me, in the high bar chair that overlooks the main street with people frenetically coming and going trying to catch the train into Manhattan, slides in Enid. She was one of the many town artists, and as artists were wont to go, had her share of eccentricities and opinions that would be doled out to you whether you asked for it or not. She greeted me with a hello as she sidled into the bar chair right next to me. Whether she knew my name or not, even to this day, was an irrelevancy, I guess, to both of us. So here went the peace and quiet of the remainder of the morning on the express track of life. She asked me how things were going, and I responded honestly that I got off to a slow start because of the cat and her fur balls this morning. Her quick response was that I was complaining and negative again, and then she told me about her two kittens and just how wonderful they were. She queried why I was so consistently negative. I kind of ignored her advisement and chomped even more quickly on the remnants of the first half of the bagel. She, in turn, took out some rub away lottery tickets and began rubbing like crazy. In the process she claimed to have won $52 last week. And, "You know," she added, "that when I go to Monmouth Park, I am even more lucky." I thought that a trip there right now for one would be lucky for the both of us, but unfortunately the horse racing was over. The morning lecture continued when she added that she had an art exhibition that would begin soon in some hall, which everyone knew where it was, and I should attend and perhaps even buy one since I like paintings since I looked like that I had good taste or money. I stuffed the final portion of my bagel allotment into my mouth, swished it down with a gulp of coffee, and prepared for my quick departure, claiming that I was late for work. She chortled with her closing "Hee, hee . . . perhaps you'll be more sociable next time." Yea, I said to myself, if I am not sitting next to you.

I took the remaining half of the bagel and wrapped it in a napkin, stuffed it in my jacket pocket, and left the coffee house. This was the end of my much desired morning of tranquility. I wondered if this portended the day and the coming week at work. Between the caffeine (which someday the medical people will determine that it is a necessary vitamin for a healthy life), the unsolicited interrogation at the coffee house, and trying to make up lost time to work, well . . . events just had me a little out of kilter. Got back into the car — no parking ticket, which is a good omen — and proceeded to venture to work on the back roads, off the main drag. But a word of warning to the wise: it is never a good thing to break the 25 mph speed limit on the back roads of Metuchen. This I knew and obeyed, although the clock was against me. And sure enough, just seconds into the second part of my journey, on the back street in the blue and white Chevy, was a Metuchen cop, just waiting like a spider for the unsuspecting. As I drove by in my pretentious car, dutifully obeying the speed limit, I gave the bushwhacker the look. What could he do? No moving violation. Ha! We both knew that he preyed on the unsuspected and the weak to justify a high salary. Some go through life with little class. I thank the Almighty that I'm not one of them.

Passed the Metuchen tennis courts (another speed trap) and into Roosevelt Park. Despite being in Edison and Middlesex County, the park is a pretty place at any time of the year. And around the corner was the agency's main facility, fronting the lake. This lake had about three trout left in it, the result of the state's yearly stocking program, followed by intense fishing pressure day after day. And some 10,000 geese were crowded on the lake's surface — a tribute to governmental oversight and administration. Pulling into the agency parking lot could be a little tricky for a driver of less skill, because of the queue of small, stubby yellow school buses that discharged the school kids in an orchestrated procession each morning. But the BMW maneuvered around and through into my assigned parking spot. Yes, rank does have its privileges, little or large, I will take them all, including assigned parking.

Got out of the car, got my briefcase and closed the door. Since I had assigned parking right next to the building — a large white sign with green letters that wrote "Reserved for the Director of Development" — there was no need to lock it. Looked at my watch and found that somehow, somewhere, I lost three minutes. I was officially, or unofficially, three minutes late. Big deal, who or what's to kill for three stupid minutes. And my luck was getting better — anything was better after running into that woman at the coffee house — the back door to the building was opened. I could just sneak in and slip into my desk. But my good intentions got immediately sidetracked when I ran into Janet. It seemed that my good luck was continuing. As I came into the building, Janet came sashaying around the corner. Let me briefly explain Janet to you: she was head of the speech-language pathology department (this means she had a master's degree — this is good), she was blonde and she had a body that could tantalize and invigorate the imagination of any man. In

11

fact, her body would negate any need for Viagra. If you needed Viagra in the presence of Miss Janet, you also needed your pulse checked so see if you were still alive or very dead. As for me, I was always very much alive in Miss Janet's presence.

As soon as I saw her, I immediately greeted her with an enthusiastic "Hello, Miss Janet." And she immediately responded with an observation that had the tinge of a complaint. "I have been here since eight this morning and already two of the other directors have not responded to the issues noted in my memo. You know, the speech department is always doing its job and yet we don't get the respect we deserve. I just hate being placed on the back burner and being ignored."

"Janet, I just can't understand it how anyone could ignore you. I'll never ignore you." As for the respect issue, I kept that misdirected thought to myself.

"Don't be so fresh! I'm trying to run my department," she said as she tugged at her freshly pressed, clingy red blouse.

Trying to take the edge off the situation and trying to add life to a dying conversation, I added, "I like your red shirt. Looks great!" This was a successful move since her attention was immediately diverted from work issues into the issue of appearance and looking great.

"Yes," she said, "you cannot believe where I got this and at a great bargain, too, but it was such an ordeal. But I like the way it looks."

I agreed and responded that the blouse, indeed, made her look great and, by association, "The entire speech department was great, too."

She smiled, but I still don't know why. Was it my suave manner, the way she always responded to my tawdry flattery, or was it just as I turned around right behind me was Mr. Ferucci, the assistant director, the second in command, in the whole place? He was so close and on top of me — I would rather have been on top of Miss Janet, but as my luck would have it — you could not have placed a match book cover between us. Of course, I was rather startled and somewhat annoyed. Not being a morning person and somewhat more attracted to Miss Janet than to some short, sawed off Italian administrator, I was somewhat taken back since now he was almost in my face. Almost, I should say, since I was about a foot taller, or, more often than not, Italian administrators are by nature short . . . and by nature, somewhat cantankerous.

He grabbed my tie — it was a Jos. A. Banks deluxe model — and started to pull. He snapped, "Great! At nine o'clock you are supposed to be at your desk, working for the agency, not wasting your time and staff's valuable time in idle chatter." He began to pull me towards my desk which was in the common office; Janet began walking away. She had the art of walking down to a science; she should have been a physical therapist or a dancer in a go-go bar. As I turned back so did she and smiled. Was it me, or was it the sight of this rather vertically challenge Italian leading me down the hall to my office desk, punishment for being just a few minutes late. But it was a chance meeting with Janet — all worth it, I guess.

Led like a steer to the slaughter house, I was unceremoniously marched into the main office. Ferucci exclaimed, with a bravado that the ladies in the room could not but hear, that I get paid to be at my desk on time and not socializing with the speech department and blah, blah, blah. Trying to salvage all that was left of my honor, I tried to unknot my tie that was tighter than what any eagle scout could do, while blurting out that it was only mere three minutes late and the Good Book wants us to be nice to others. He gave me one of those Italian looks and waddled back into the private enclave of his office. I had only a desk in a shared common office area with other administrative staff in those days, but he had his own. Whether he was Italian, like the agency's leader, whether his position assistant director was important, or whether he really did anything significant that effectively shaped the form and direction of the agency, I still don't know to this day. All I know was that I was a have-not with a tie in a knot and he had an office — so much for my bargaining talents when I first signed on. I did get good promises and intentions. But that was then and this is now. How quickly and conveniently are promises forgotten and seldom kept

When he left office area, I promptly got up and went to the restroom to salvage my Jos. A. Banks tie. Suddenly, the day seemed to be taking a downward turn. The tie was really racked up. I tried to save this really nice burgundy paisley tie as best I good. Since it was a quality tie, not too cheap by any standard, some of it was returning to pre-harassment form, some but not all. What could you do, really? You can't slug a short supervisor without any expecting ramifications. And what if you lost? It would be more embarrassing getting beaten up by a short person. So, you continue as you were.

Returning to the office area to begin my work for the morning, I immediately went to the communal coffee pot for the first dose of the agency's "finest." It was made earlier in the morning by Ferucci who seemingly never slept because he had nothing better to do than to come into work early and make agency coffee and make staff miserable by wrecking expensive ties. He got these packets from a major discount food, clothing and whatever else is for sale warehouse chain at a good price. Unfortunately the coffee tasted like it was on sale . . . last year. You could stand a spoon in it before it dissolved. It tasted like liquefied lead pencils. I even offered to part with my own monies to upgrade this lethal liquid treat to something drinkable, but my generous, self-sacrificing offer was ignored. No one seemed to understand the real importance of a good cup of coffee laced with a healthy dose of caffeine. No caffeine, no production — it is as simple as that. Yet they never did fully understand.

The commune that was called an office had its cast of characters. Along with myself there were four members of the accounting department, all with a history not to be recounted here. But with four people, you knew that there would be differences and political intrigue, even here in paradise. Mr. Chuck was the latest hire. He had a CPA degree, or something like that, from some institution far away from New Jersey. A cloud of ambiguity hovered over him like a fog on a moor, but this intrigue never made him more interesting or appealing. Carol, the former head and big cheese of the agency's accounting system, was now dropped to a number two ranking because of the arrival of Mr. Chuck. She wore her disjointed unhappiness like a badge of honor that was flayed at the edges at those appropriate times she chose. The other members of the crew, Rosemarie and Marie, were merely bookkeepers who had mysterious reasons for being there, but work was not one of them. So I settled in to get a good morning's worth of work. And it went well, when at about 10:30, Ferucci came in. The ladies of the office adored him. They lit up like dried-out Christmas trees thrown on a bond fire. I could only manage a barely perceivable grimace. As he sauntered into the work area, he casually looked over to me and said words to the effect that he was glad the agency was getting a little work out of me. I responded immediately that I always worked hard; the problem was that I just made it look easy. He did not like that response. Was it the information within or just the delivery? Who cared? Ferucci scooted over to the coffee pot and had a healthy dose of his own poison, although he thought it was a good cup of java. It will always remain a mystery to me how someone could be so scrupulously fastidious about his personal appearance, damned critical about foods and wines in general and yet so oblivious about the essentials of life, coffee, itself. The agency coffee was plain lousy!

I worked, both pretend and real, while Ferucci pattered and made small talk with the office help. He sure knew how to grease the machine that makes relationships. This was not my area of expertise, nor was it a skill that I ever wanted to acquire. I always felt and hoped that my life's history would prove that good work supersedes good intentions and good schmoozing. Ferucci could schmooze with the best of them. And part of his technique was that he managed to say or do something nice for everyone in the office: Carol, Marie and Rosemarie and even Mr.

Chuck. Everyone received his insincere executive blessing this morning. As he was leaving, he turned to me and said, "The Big Ragu left Florida a little late, probably because of business, so he will not be in this morning. But we can expect him in later this afternoon. He hasn't missed a board meeting in 25 years and doesn't want to miss this one, the last of the year. I'm just letting you know in advance so you could be prepared."

I, for one, enjoyed inner peace knowing that the agency's leader was away on vacation. The news of his impending return was about a joyous as knowing that a root canal was prescribed. It wasn't that he was a bad person, just boring, narcissistic, boring, overbearing, boring, and generally shallow and somewhat boring. So this was my all-star morning. It was going downhill faster than an Olympic skier. My only recourse was to immerse myself in my work, which was somewhat of an aid in blocking out the surrounding troubles and tribulations of the soap opera office. I had a potential foundation funding source lined up, and after talking on the phone to them, it seemed like a good idea to offer them a rather copious and thick proposal for consideration. If you can't be good and succinct, then be mediocre and long winded. So that would take care of my morning until lunch.

Certainly one of the most necessary and important high points at work was the lunch break. More thought and meditation ought to be given to this most significant of activities. Lunch is a good. It was the psychological half-way point of the work day. Although for me, I took my lunch earlier just to escape from the prater that always accompanied the members of the office commune when they all took theirs an hour later at one. It wasn't that they were bad people; it was just that we marched to a different drummer. And I was happy with my beat, and sometimes, if face value was any indication, this group was not consistently happy with the music they heard in their respective heads. Anyway . . . the proposal was drawn up — it was a good one — bagged and tagged, and placed into the outbound mail box before the self imposed deadline of noon. Then

16

my attention turned to lunch. Since it was so close after Thanksgiving, there was never a thought of (turkey) sandwiches from home. So I had to go out because I really wanted to. It was a kind of a minnie vacation: an almost gourmet food treat and no hovering presence of anyone from the administration. My decision process, faster than lightning, took me to the pizza shop located in the nearby shopping center, but I was not going to have pizza. Instead, my meal du jour would be their tuna sub complete with the works — everything, including onions! After all, I was working in this oppressively communal office and onion-breath could well be a subtle defense. And, who was I seeing anyway? So, without further ado, I quietly got up from by chair and went to the coat rack to get a jacket to depart, while prying eyes, I'm sure, scrutinized my unceremoniously quiet exit. The further I got from the office, the more elated I felt. Freedom is subversive and addictive.

In less than a five minute driving time, I was at the pizza shop. Parking could sometimes be a little tight, given the limited spaces and the lunch-time crowd. But I never got stuck, being a superior driver. When I walked in and got to the ordering counter, there was always someone ahead of me, but that was alright since I could quickly glance at the specials board. Today, nothing caught my eye, so it would stead-fastly be the tuna sub with the works. The place was always frenetically busy at around the noon lunch break. It was amazing that work staff at the pizzeria gracefully danced around each other without any major catastrophe; the place where I worked could have used a lesson or two from Fred Astaire or Gene Kelley. Paul, the owner, caught me out of the corner of his eye and gave me a loud, Italian hello and then tried to push the daily special. With my mind firmly set on the sub, I thanked him, ordered and waited. One of the workers, some nameless indi-vidual whose permanent address had to be in either Mexico or South America, prepared my stuff and I was out of the place in less than four minutes. So, the math was thus: five minutes to get there, four to order and then five to return. Fourteen minutes from a 60 minute lunch hour makes 46 minutes of enjoying my time. My time would not be spent in a fluorescent-lit lunch room with a TV blaring a soup opera. It would be spent sitting on a park bench fronting the lake that was adjacent to the center itself. Peace and quiet, in late fall — what could be better!

The park in late fall was gorgeous! There was a walking path of six-tenths of a mile — I actually measured it since I was into jogging then — around its entirety with two very small bridges going across its shorter end, connecting to a little island. Somewhat romantic, though, since photographers frequently had the newly married in this area for photos, although the park geese managed to fully decimated all grasses and every other eatable living vegetation around it. I guess it all depends on your perspective of stuff. When the county renovated the lake at the taxpayers' cost of some ten million dollars non-conducive goose shrubbery was planted between the lake and a new boardwalk. But even then you could still see the evidence of their collective evil snacking. But, overall, most of the shrubs there were still intact, especially on the steepest slopes. Not too bad! This is why, whenever possible, I parked myself on a solitary park bench and watched the world go by, knowing that my precious, limited time was flying by. But quality frequently does beat quantity. The scary thought was that thirty-minutes just may be all the time we have in paradise.

The tuna sub that followed so close upon the Thanksgiving holiday tasted especially good. The soda of the day was Dr. Pepper and was up to the complementary occasion. Finally, my dessert of choice was a good book. Let me qualify that: There are no bad books, just some that are more endearing than others. At that particular time I was slogging through one of those heavy theological tombs. Collectively these fit into a particular academic type: the writer has either encountered the deity or some other outstanding but hidden truth and then tries to convey all that insight via longish, polysyllabic words that leaves the reader scratching his or her respective head even more confused and in the dark. But Christmas was coming and I wanted to catch, finally, the true meaning of the season, Christianity and a blessed life. And I was struggling. I have met a few individuals who have claimed to have seen the light and were saved. For me, it became a kind of an esoteric joke, really, like everyone getting in on the punch line of life but me. Likewise with religion. It seems that those lucky few that are assured of their salvation get it with a smugness that seems most ingratiating. I was never one of them. To date, I never had an experience of either seeing or brushing elbows with the deity. Sunset and rainbows don't count! No one who has passed away has ever returned, even for a moment, to give me a special sign or message. I have no degree of absolute certainty for anything spiritual, except, perhaps, for the cleric demanding more for the church's second collection. So my only recourse was to continually stuff myself with this massively delicious tuna sub to the point of intestinal pain, and enjoy my time on this solitary park bench, in this earthly paradise, struggling with my salvation as the days ticked relentlessly down towards Christmas. Maybe this would be the year! So, after eatin' I started readin'. It was kind of a musical pattern. Read a paragraph, sip a soda. Read a paragraph, sip a soda. It was all I could do to break "the whatever's" of the academic text. It was "heavy" to say the least. Long polysyllabic words, abstruse meanings — if you were lucky enough to understand — circuitous thought development . . . . What are these religion people trying to say? Maybe by implication all the laboriously smart people will be in heaven and the rest, well, you know were they'll go. Thus, I read a paragraph and then sipped. And with a sip, I took a momentary break to view the aesthetic beauty of the lake and its surroundings, and contemplate upon sentence after sentence in the paragraphs that I did not fully understand. I wondered if the other place would be a park-like setting even for the unsaved.

So I sipped again and looked around. Lunchtime was a busy place for the lake. Activity abounded. There were always fishermen, escapees from corporate cubicles, strolling hand holders and most of the agency's physical therapy department, whose lunch schedule usually coincided with mine. Sometimes I would read, sometimes I would exchange light pleasantries with the agency staff or a lunch-time stroller. No pressure, no nothing — just catching my breath before the onslaught of the afternoon work regime, and if I would even get lucky, run into the deity. But I learned to enjoy the little of what you can get in this life. The only things I could be sure of on this park bench were a fisherman catching a very respectable fish or a good looking female coming around the bend. Their presence was an unmistakable delight. If you couldn't see 'em, you could smell 'em coming down wind. And I was lord of this little paradise here on earth . . . for one delightful part of an hour. Not a full hour, just a part. I was happy and content with that. But as it was said before, all good things come to an end, and so it was with my lunch hour. With a look at my watch, I had a mere five minutes left to wander back into the office. It's maddening to have heaven, or Oz, but then to loose it because of duty or obligation to return to an environment that is not genuinely warm and friendly. I am still waiting for the religion people to handle this situation. In the interim, I dutifully marched back toward the center, to the office, to begin the second half of my daily penance. As I quietly came into the office space, trying to be unobtrusive as possible, Rosemarie yelled out, "How was it out there"? I responded, honestly, saying that it was simply delightful. She shot back, "So you only eat lunch with us on bad days." "No," said I, "some things are just too nice to pass up." With that annoyance behind me, I went back to work and the office staff filed out to the lunch room to eat and watch the latest installment of the soap opera in the enclosed and confined lunch room. I proceeded to revel in the quiet, dutifully doing my work. The peace and quiet was good.

I actually enjoyed hunting down potential funding prospects. I guess it was a primal instinct that was culturally channeled correctly. It was with society's approval that I sought out the rich to give to the poor — the variation, this time, was that the poor were handicapped and had special needs. I was becoming a hero, a twentieth-century Robin Hood, and, yes, a candidate for potential sainthood. One could not feel bad about oneself from this prospective. And I was working in quietude, just like a monastic. The only problem here was the occasional affinity for Miss Janet or some of the other juicy lookers on staff. Equal opportunity was something I believed in those days. I comforted my slanted theology by saying that it was either lust or rust, and since I was somewhat alive, I could not be rusty.

The peace and quiet was most delicious, save for an occasional roar from the lunch room crowd. They did react to the trials and tribulations of the soap opera drama. I never got into that swing of things, and probably never will. But I enjoyed my collective two hours total of lunch separation from that group. Peace and quiet. Amen!

Peace and quiet do not last forever, at least in this world. With the approach of two o'clock, the staff came dribbling back into the office, one by one. Each one commented upon some segment of the soap opera in such a manner that it was kind of a Cliff's Notes on the entire proceedings. Not that I cared about anything that went on. It was just that they were somewhat loud — just another intrusion and upset to my internal tranquility. But this too passed as they slowly but inevitably settled down into their respective work routines. Thinking about it, however, I guess the soap operas were a kind of opiate for those who lead humdrum, insipid lives. Perhaps when I get older and more sedentary, but for now, no soap operas for me.

Although nothing lasts forever, the afternoons always seemed to drag like the proverbial nun. From soap opera time to now, I got another decent proposal off and ready to go towards another targeted foundation. Yet when I looked at the company clock, it was only two-thirty. Dropping the proposal package into the outgoing mail carton, I decided to make a trip to the bathroom. Not that I needed to do anything but get out of the office and take a little break. There were three in the building, actually four, and I choose the one furthest away from the office. A walk would do me well, and I could check out the kids and staff as well. This job did have certain advantages. The kids, all stuck with problems that would never go away, inexplicably challenged any spiritual malaise, and the staff, some 98 percent female, well, there had to be some "lookers" in the bunch. An appreciation of aesthetics never hurt anyone. And just looking, never buying, never led to bankruptcy. So I looked. Unfortunately, this entire process of going to the bathroom on the other side of the building took less than five minutes. Returning to the office, I decided that I would have another cup of the corporate coffee — the worse coffee in the world — and that process could take as much as five minutes if I played my cards right. This was not to happen! As I walked back into the office there was Mr. Ferucci with that smirk on his kisser. He observed, "You are not at your desk."

"That's correct," I said, "because I was in the bathroom. After all, I may be wonderful but I am only human."

With that Carol blurted out, "That may not be the case!" There was a residual twitter with the rest of the office staff. Ferucci smirked even more. Then came the crushing announcement. "I have some news for you, which you probably will not like. I just got a call from Mr. Rigatoni and not only is he back from Florida but will be in the office later this afternoon. Even as I speak, he is on the way. I'm excited."

You could have put a dagger through my heart, or anything else for that matter, and it would not have made much of a difference. My work vacation was over; the good times were over; the Pax Romana was finished. The most boring individual I have ever met was coming back to put a fresh pall over everything living. The situation was inescapable.

The prognosis was negative. The fact of life was that he signed the pay-checks; and he also determined who got what and how much. To get this dagger in my heart took less than a minute. It wasn't even three yet.

And then Ferucci went in for the kill. "By the way, how are the holiday trees coming?"

I had that apparent blank look, so he repeated himself, "The holiday trees." He must have thought that I was struck with temporary idiocy by my blank expression. "Every year you get the order for the trees for the classrooms and the administration office and the atrium in front. You've dropped the ball again. Do you expect me to remind you of how and when to do your job?"

Actually I did forget but this was so inconsequential to the overall state of affairs that I didn't give it much priority. To save myself, again, I shot back to Ferucci that "I needed the exact numbers. I don't like doing the same job twice." With that he marched me into his office. There, after fumbling through some papers he pulled out a half a sheet of paper with the tree tally. "We need 24 holiday trees for all the classrooms, one for the nurse's office, one for the therapy department, a Charlie Brown tree for our office, and a large one for the atrium."

"When do you need these Christmas trees by?"

"We need the holiday trees yesterday so the teachers can have them decorated by the time of the end of year holiday party for the kids," Ferucci snapped back.

I went back to my desk and immediately pulled out the Yellow Pages and started searching for sellers and purveyors of trees, Christmas and others. I got trees before but I really didn't feel like traveling or putting too much effort into something that I knew would find its way into the dumpster less than a month later. Found one close by, listed the address on a piece of scrap paper, and left the office for the BMW and undertook the first official run in the name of Christmas cheer. It was always fun being on the road for Christmas and getting stuff for the kids, and being out of the office portion was a bonus. I went down Route 1, observing the legal speed limit — why hurry when you are on company clock? — and eventually made my turn east onto Amboy Avenue. I didn't go far when I saw Roses & More. This was not my tree destination that was listed in the Yellow Pages. But they had trees and the prospect of wheeling and dealing invigorated me on this late, crisp late-autumn day. If it didn't work out, it didn't matter since nothing would be hurt anyway, and I could always do down the road and find the place that I was originally going to. So I pulled unto the side street, got out of the car and started to snoop around.

There were trees galore in the back, all looking freshly cut. The more I perused, the more I liked what was on display. I was so engrossed that I didn't realize that I literally bumped into one of the yard workers. Startled, I hit him with my best line, "I am interested in getting a lot of Christmas trees for some handicapped kids at a special school." He looked at me rather oddly and responded in broken English that I had to see his boss inside. Mildly annoyed since I wasted a good opening line on someone who could not understand English, I thanked him with a phony smile and proceeded to the front of the store. Inside, the shop was on the smallish side but with lovely displays and bouquets and the like. It was pleasant enough. But there was no one around. So I went to the counter and rang the bell. A voice out of the back room yelled out, "Just a minute." In a very long minute a woman came out, greeted me and asked for what I wanted. I hit her with my best shot about a lot of trees for special needs kids. After a slight delay she told me that Lorie, the owner, would best help me, if I could wait just a little while longer since she was on the phone. Waiting is a killer for me. I just hate waiting. I just knew that there were some people back in the office that had a stop watch on me and I would have to explain every lost second out of the office. So to kill some more time I wandered around the small shop looking at the flowers, displays and knick knacks for sale. It was a pleasant enough experience but I was on the company clock and the busy bodies were always timing me. Didn't they realize that? Didn't these flower and tree people realize that they were putting my feet into the corporate fire? These few purgatorial minutes, which seemed like a mini eternity, were finally broken by the owner's voice of "How can I help you?" Startled, I turned around quickly, almost knocking over one of the displays in this tightly laid out shop, and was practically face to face with the owner. She was drop dead gorgeous. I was stunned. She was that good. Whatever happened, the last thing that I wanted to happen was to loose my composure or break a knick knack in the process. So immediately I started into my spiel again about needing a goodly number of trees for kids with handicapping conditions, who happened to be in a facility just around the corner from her establishment, blah, blah, blah. Although I may have stumbled, my presentation must have been good, because she smiled and offered to give me a break on a new shipment of trees coming in the following day — all freshly cut and, with some degree of sympathy for my presentation, at a very competitive price. She gave me the total price so that I could write up a project order, along with her business card. She smiled; I left. I returned to my car not knowing whether to be elated or totally depressed. I brought the card to my nose but could not detect any fragrance. Why didn't I pursue the smile onto the next step, I don't know? She was super attractive, personable, and had her own business, which could mean lots of money in the bank, although she did not have a master's degree. Maybe that was it. Why was I so capable of advocating the causes for these special needs kids and so woefully pathetic in advancing only minimal needs for myself? In a funk, I returned to the agency, prepared a PO and presented the same to Ferucci. I gave him the business card and told him that he could make the necessary arrangements with Bill Brown and the boys from maintenance to pick up the trees in a day or two. He inquired why we could not have them today. I responded by saying that we were getting a freshly cut shipment, and it would be better and safer if he could have some patience and wait just a day or two more. Placated, I left his office and returned to my desk to await, with dismal depression, the arrival of Rigatoni. But at least the Christmas trees were on the way. This was at least a small step towards providing a good holiday for the kids and staff. I wasn't getting anything out of this deal. I guess it was back to pursuing the whispy Miss Janet after all. She had a master's degree.

Part Two

The women in the office were in a mild buzz since Rigatoni was arriving shortly and would regale his trip to Florida in painful detail. Almost assuredly he would recount a restaurant experience or two, a variety of beach stories and how he overcame the challenges of long-distance travel with all of his family stuffed into the agency van. I would prefer passing on this afternoon and the waste of vicarious living throughl someone else's experiences. For the interim, I plunged into my work with some degree of mild hope. If I worked hard, really hard, five o'clock would come and I would be free for the rest of the blessed day. So work I did. But every time I glanced up at the corporate clock, nothing seemed to be happening. Maybe the battery was dead. Maybe time was at a standstill just for me and my work. I was doing an incredible amount of work — too much work — in this short period of time. Work was becoming my blessed sanctuary. I felt like Quasimodo, but the corporate office was no spiritual sanctuary like Notre Dame. But for all the bending over the computer, I was becoming slightly hunched like that famous bell ringer and could have used an Esmeralda or a drink or Janet or a trip back to the flower shop. Notwithstanding, time moved painfully slowly. In fact, it seemed like the clock was almost moving backwards. Someone should be contacting Steven Hawkin or someone from the Princeton physics department. The impossible was occurring.

With due diligence my only recourse was to stop work and treat myself to another cup of coffee from the corporate percolator. If there ever was a contest for the worst coffee in the world, this stuff would more than hold its own. Right now, it could hold a spoon straight up. Its taste was more like liquefied lead. But desperation drives an individual to extreme measures, and I was more than desperate. At best this coffee could kill me or at least send me to the local hospital for an hour, day or week or two, and I would have a legitimate excuse to miss Rigatoni's vacation recap. So I pushed back from my desk and sauntered over to the coffee machine for a half-a-cup of Ferucci's finest. I tried to kill the rest with a healthy dose of milk or cream or whatever remnant was in the pitcher. I did offer in the past to bring in some of my good stuff to make a respectable cup of coffee, but Ferucci refused. He preferred buying his grinds in the convenience packets that were offered by the local warehouse discount distribution club. I guess in his mind it was another example of the agency's generosity in taking care of staff and doing the same within budget. I ought to be more grateful. As I took a swig of the stuff Rosemarie blurted out that I wasn't looking too good or too happy, or something like that. I blamed it on the coffee as I trundled back to my desk. The minute hand on the clock was still locked. It looked like another trip to the bathroom was imminent. Maybe I could get a fleeting glimpse at Miss Janet or anyone else to boost my sagging spirits. Anything would be better.

After the coffee and shuffling through paperwork, I made a courageous decision: it was time to go to the bathroom. Of course, I would choose the one at the farthest part of the building. It was cleaner and perhaps I would run into a living body and stall my return to desk duties. So I went. I felt penetrating eyes scrupulously watching me as I quietly exited the office. It was gratifying, of sorts, to know that my personal doings were as important as their work.

The trip down the hall to the other side of the building was, unfortunately, non-descript. The classrooms were empty since the kids went home and teacher and therapy staffs were not present, probably at meetings or something. Another unsuccessful trip, to say the least!

The bathroom hiatus took only seconds. I emerged and began my trek back to the office. But perhaps my luck changed since there in the hallway, with tools of the trade, was custodian Bill Brown with mop in hand. This was good because within seconds we got into a good sports discussion. It was Monday and the previous day was the full complement of the NFL football schedule. Bill and I had a friendly gentlemen's wager on the Sunday games as well as the Monday night feature. There was a distinctive pattern that emerged from all of this activity: Bill most frequently lost. This was a good thing. First of all, it gave me a sense of limited accomplishment working for this agency. At least in one area I was doing something right. I was consistently taking Bill Brown to the cleaners, week in and week out. And the proceeds were directly, or indirectly, going towards funding my coffee addiction at Lucca's. This was also good. It kept a local business flourishing and it kept me happy, in a limited sense. The down side was that Bill was not making a great salary (no one really was unless they were Italian or related to Rigatoni), he had a wife and a couple kids and was their sole support (his life was difficult). But Bill was constantly obsessed about getting one up on me in anything athletic. This did not happen with any frequency, unfortunately for him. So, I asked Bill, "How the heck are you"? He muttered, "Fine." I rejoined, "It's so wonderful to see you. It's unfortunate that you had another bad weekend. But that's life. You have my money"? His head hung down low in defeat, he muttered something inaudible, and reached into his pocket and pulled out a crumbled dollar bill. I reached out and took the winnings with a heartfelt "Thank you." And then I added, "Save for your marriage, some may think of you as a looser." This was to be the beginning of some verbal taunting. Unfortunately, again, for me, just as I was beginning to turn up the heat, Ferucci came flying around the corner. The best part of the wagering scenario abruptly came to an end, like having a meal without the dessert. I was about to beat on a defeated enemy, only to have the battle stopped just when everything decidedly was going in my favor.

"So," Ferucci said, "you are supposed to be at your desk, working for the agency, but you are here instead, taking money from this employee, who doesn't work too hard to start with. You are disrupting the work flow."

"He doesn't need dessert money," I said, "since he's too fat anyway. I am doing him and the agency a favor. No dessert means less weight means more speed and productivity for work." I enthusiastically added, "In fact, the agency should commend me for looking out for its long term welfare and the welfare of its good employees."

Ferucci glared at me. I don't know whether he lacked a sense of humor, could not understand my logic that Bill Brown was indeed in dire need of loosing weight so he could work harder, or just did not appreciate good comeback material. He gave me a backhanded dismissal to the office by saying that he was looking for Bill anyway since "something" came up. Dutifully and obediently I shuffled back down the hall to the office, looking over my shoulder I did see Ferucci giving instructions to Bill. When I got back into the office area I did glance at the clock; it registered just after four, one more hour of nervous anticipation before my escape. I forced myself back into the work routine for the final lap with the hope that if I worked with more intensity time would go faster. Then five would come and I could make my escape. So I immersed myself into my work. I had papers stacked up on the corners. I had papers flying all over. I looked like the real thing. Quietly, I noticed from the corner of my eye, Ferucci slithered into the office, most probably inspecting that I was at my desk and not enjoying myself. He said nothing; I pretended not to have noticed his incursion into a legitimate work environment.

He left. The clock showed 4:21. In 39 minutes I would be free. In theory, yes, but unfortunately things would change, for the worse for me, because at precisely 4:36, President Rigatoni came though the door. I had 24 minutes until freedom, or so I thought.

The office staff welcomed him back as if he were Caesar returning to Rome after a long and successful campaign in the hinterlands. I was less enthused. Either they could see more in the man than I or else they were more pronouncedly adept at sucking up to an authority figure. Ferucci was especially excited. I muttered something (insincere?) about how he was missed, or something like that, and quickly went back to pretend work. Twenty-three minutes remained on the clock. Within seconds of setting foot in the office, Rigatoni began with a quick overview to all in the office about the trip to Florida, which was also spiced with some mention of side trips and diversions and exceptional restaurant adventures. I didn't know if this was a public lecture where everyone's attention was required or just some aimless ramblings or what. So I just imbedded myself deeper in work. Either way, I would be wrong, short term or long term.

Because it was a trip for some sort of tangential activity related to the agency's business, the agency itself picked up some portion of the tab. How much exactly, no one knew. And as long as he was driving to Florida, it made no sense to drive alone. The agency van could hold seven as well as one. So he, again, took his wife and family with him. At the very least, the Rigatoni family got to see the sunshine state at a discount.

Notwithstanding my pretensions to work, I along with the entire office could not help but hear how "wonderful" this was, how "the best" that was, or the food in the restaurant was "not up to" his wife's culinary productions at home. After this summation of his southern diversion, Rigatoni proceeded into his office to reclaim his territory and his alpha dominance over all, open a week's worth of mail and shuffle through a mountain of paperwork. Nineteen minutes left until freedom. I could almost taste it. Since it was approaching departure time, I too began the paper shuffling process to wind down the day. A shuffle here, a pile of papers there, a grunt and/or groan in between, I seemed to be putting on a good show and the clock seemed to be with me and time began to accelerate. Stephen Hawking should have been present and taking notes. With the countdown going into single digits — there was only nine glorious minutes left until five — Ferucci came in and laid the bad news on me: "We have been summoned to the presidential suite. The Big Ragu has requested our presence."

I think I was still alive but was almost sure that my heart stopped or suffered a stroke or something like that. I stopped living with that news, although my vital signs were still there. The most boring man in the world — no, the entire universe as explored by Captain James T. Kirk — was going to encroach on my precious, after work time and attempt to bore me to death. If I was going to die, why couldn't be with a heart attack in bed with Miss Janet, or anyone else for that matter? Why be bored to death with a bore? I just could see my gravestone now: DIED YOUNG BECAUSE HE WAS BORED TO DEATH AND HE DIED AT WORK. What a lousy way to go! No romance, no flair, no style.

I asked Ferucci if I should bring a notepad or something, since Rigatoni assumed that all his words were important enough to record for posterity. Ferucci said that he would never tell anyone what to do but he always brought a notebook since one never knew. So notebook in hand, I followed Ferucci into the presidential suite. I glanced at the clock and it read four minutes to five. Then I glanced on the floor. Although the room was not occupied for over a week, it was a disaster. Newspapers were on the floor, papers on file cabinets, and I think a sock or something dark under the coat rack that was leaning like the famed Tower of Pizza since it was overloaded with shirts and jackets and ties. This is what I could see. Save for one florescent light on, the office was rather dim. Every window was covered with a blind that was closed tightly. I wondered if the CIA operated with more secrecy.

As we walked in, Rigatoni said, in Italian, to sit down, sit down. Ferucci got the first chair and I got stuck with the one with "stuff" on it. I had that uncomfortable look that was painfully obvious when I was told to simply move the stuff. So what do you do with personal stuff that isn't yours? Stuff that may not be clean? Stuff that may have been around since the sinking of the Titanic? This mélange of stuff belonged to the person who decided if you were employed for another day or not. It was awkward. No wonder I was uncomfortable. And this was just another chapter in the continuing saga of uncomfortableness. And the lecture did not even start. The clock on the wall had only a few minutes to five. Unless he was giving us the Gettysburg address, there was no way that I was getting out of this place on time. I could only hope that this would not negatively impact my spirits for the evening.

Ferucci began by asking how the trip was. This was kind of a dumb, suck-up question since those two were in almost daily contact. And it would add even more unnecessary overtime to my stay in the office. But it was another couple favorable points on Ferucci's yearly performance evaluation, under the category of sincere and honest interest in agency activities. Rigatoni, evidently pleased, began: this was the best trip he's ever taken, the convention was great and made even better when he added some of his insights, this was followed by his peers begging him to serve on a few committees, all important, followed the next day by a meeting with a very wealthy agency funder who now lived in Florida, and overall had a lovely time with his family relaxing in the hot Florida sun and collecting sea shells on the beach someplace on the western part of the state. Ferucci interjected and applauded each and every time he could — more favorable points on his yearly evaluation — while I bit the inside of my mouth. Somehow, someway unknown to the commoners, this trip was not entirely financed out of Rigatoni's pocket but billed to the agency — another tuna that would pass through the auditors net. No wonder this trip was wonderful and successful! With all this posturing, the clock now was ten minutes past five, and the lecture was only just beginning. Would I see home and my beloved cat before sunset? Evidentially not, because Rigatoni began to recap what he told us just minutes before, just to make sure that everything sunk in. To compound matters, time was now flying. The clock no longer was standing still; it was spinning like a tachometer on a Corvette. The inside of my mouth was beginning to bleed as I bit harder. Physical pain would always overcome emotional pain. That was one of my theories. It was working. I was suffering in silence.

Rigatoni cleared his voice. This was something that he frequently did when he was going to orchestrate a full set of pronouncements. "I know that your time is valuable, just like mine, so I wouldn't keep you here long." (If he truly believed that my time was valuable, he would not have imposed this meeting at this inconveniently late hour to begin with!)

Ferucci immediately responded, "It's always time well spent when we are with our president." I bit the inside of my mouth again. I wondered if eternity would be like this!.

Rigatoni was well pleased with this show of support. More points for Ferucci's evaluation. He continued by saying that sometimes his wife Rosa comes up with a good idea every now and then. Evidentially the trip and the Florida sun were good for both of them since she supported an idea that he was considering for a while. He looked directly at me and told me his mind was firmly made up, coupled with an affirmation from his wife, that I was going to get a new office mate, someone who could help me with the capital campaign and general fund raising. Right now I was the only development officer or fund raiser or bush beater in the entire agency, and the agency needed several million new dollars to build, add on and renovate. There were growing demands of an ever expanding agency. No money, no mission.

The need for help was a chronic concern that I raised months ago but was only being addressed now, not on company time but my time. No knee jerk reaction here. Rigatoni moved as about as fast as the Catholic

Church. Help would be most welcomed, the sooner the better. But who would it be, where would he or she come from, how much input would I be permitted in the screening and/or the selection process?

But before he came to the conclusion of the meeting, Rigatoni digressed again and asked me how things were going since during this time of year the rate of donations increased exponentially. I responded by saying that those foundations, organizations and individuals that routinely gave in the past were already contacted, and there were some nice hits already. Rigatoni looked pleased. Then I added further that there seemed to be in increase in smaller donations, especially in-kind stuff like toys and clothing for the kids, because of the spirit of the Christmas season. I thought that I was doing well; I thought everyone would be pleased. Rigatoni, instead, put on a frown like a contemptuous Walter. He looked straight at me and said, "We don't use the word 'Christmas' here because it's not politically correct. We use the word 'holiday.' Everyone celebrates the holidays. Personally, I would rather have you solicit for monetary donations, not in-kind things like clothes and toys. The agency could better use the money." I thought I was doing a thorough job, touching all the bases, methodically getting money from the big guys and in-kind stuff from the small guys. So, in my enthusiasm I responded by saying that, "People give what they want to give and what makes them feel good." Rigatoni's blood pressure must have risen a hundred points since he turned an even darker shade than his tan, but before the situation could become potentially very uncomfortable, Ferucci got things back on course by returning to the topic of the new assistant and asked, "Anyone in mind?"

Rigatoni responded, "Yes, I have two individuals in mind. Although I have been far away working in Florida, the needs of this agency are always close to my mind and heart. I have already begun the process even before I got back. That's why I am the president."

Both Rigatoni and Ferucci were pleased. I was less than happy. I had no effective input into anything. The clock showed 5:35. Thirty-five minutes of my precious time was gone for all eternity, never to be retrieved. If purgatory was like this, I would begin repentance now. I have seen the afterlife and don't like it. Amen!

Rigatoni then began to share his vision on just what the new development assistant would bring to the agency and how everyone, including me, would benefit. Ferucci was very attentive and I caught him taking notes from the corner of my eye. I still don't know if this was feigned interest or just another self preservation measure or just trying to further cement his position in the agency. I was not taking notes. Was this a mistake? I just knew that there were some hot, attractive numbers at the professional fund raiser's monthly meeting last November. Maybe I would be asked for my opinion or a contact that I might have. Maybe I would be lucky and get an office mate that looked like Bo Derrick. I had a faint glimmer of hope. Rigatoni continued expounding on his vision. Then the wheel of fortune abruptly turned and I got lucky. His cell phone rang, stopping him almost in mid sentence — if I were listening I could have recounted where he stopped. But whatever! He picked it up and after a curt hello told us that this was an important call that he had to take and we had to leave the presidential palace. This overtime meeting that cut into my free weekend time was mercifully over. I could go home. Ferucci and I left and in the process the last one out was asked to close the office door. I did it since it was my hope that I would get some points for that one feeble act of acquiescence. Returning to my desk I straighten up the paperwork that was all over the place. This careless cleanup took just a minute or two since I was most anxious to get out. Mission quickly accomplished, I exited the building through the side entrance and got into my car. As I pulled out, low and behold, there was Rigatoni speeding off before me. How strange that he would come in for less than an hour just to recap his trip! I gladly let him go ahead of me. Ferucci's car was still in its spot, probably because he lived where he worked, no social life. As for me, it took over half an hour to get home since the meeting forced me to hit rush hour traffic. When I got home and through the door, Kiki was waiting for me in no uncertain terms. She gave me an annoyed meow since I was late by her clock and proceeded to stomp into the kitchen where her food bowl was. I apologized to the cat and told her that it wasn't my fault for the stupid meeting. She was placated for now and I went upstairs to unwind and write-off the rest of the evening.

Part Three

I f weekends are in color, then weekdays are in black and white, with varying shades of gray. The first full week of Rigatoni's return was no exception. It was a monotonous monochrome, throbbing on with an almost numbing dullness towards Friday and the coming weekend. Nothing really exciting happened at work of any note. Even the chance meetings with Janet lacked their usual sparkle. No only was the work load still there, things seemed to have increased exponentially, with Christmas and the frenetic activity of rounding up all the potential funders and their gifts before the calendar's year end. In addition to all the other stuff, I was firmly committed to hitting those small, individual donors for in-kind donations for the kids. Rigatoni be damned and sent to the coldest corner of hell, it wasn't him or his family who didn't have a coat on a winter's day. And kids need toys at Christmas too! Christmas is for kids. That always was and still is my quiet belief. Even the threat of excommunication from the agency could never wrench that from me. So during the weekdays, I worked to make Christmas better for as many as possible. Friday afternoons and the weekend were to live for. In a few days I would experience the glorious exhilaration of the weekend and freedom. This was consistently something to look forward to with joyous anticipation.

My Friday began with the usual daily work regime. Up, got dressed, went downstairs to feed myself and Kiki, then off to Lucca's before work. Traffic on 287 was slightly lighter on Friday, so I made time, which always almost meant more precious minutes at the coffee shop. Unfortunately, this was balanced out by my dawdling out the door on the last weekday morning of the work week and subsequently loosing time. What can I say? Work itself is tiring, which was compounded by an even more tiring environment with those people in the office. Thus, all the more reason for Lucca's and the wonderful effects of caffeine on a worn out, over imposed psyche.

The drive to Metuchen was uneventful. Parking was a little more difficult, perhaps because Christmas was near. There were no spaces available close to the shop, so I had to park way down the road. There were no free meters either. Was this a bad sign for the upcoming work day or just happenstance? Personally, I hate putting money into meters. I kind of viewed these things as a penalty for living in a state with politicians who had no respect for an individual's pockets where the money may be kept. However, I paid the stupid meter a nickel and detoured into the lottery shop. Another bad sign: the tickets I had for the last drawing were worthless; I lost again. So with a sour attitude, I sought out the quiet comfort of the coffee shop. Peace and quiet: a motto that all mankind should live by. Battered but not broken in spirit, I made my way onto the coffee shop's line. There were only two in front of me. Both were realtors and both were getting large take out orders. Not just ordinary orders, but orders that required special attention: like toasting the bagel, cream cheese not butter and extra froth in the latte. And plenty of mindless bantering would be the attendant's tip and my annoyance. All this was needlessly taking away from my quality time and intruding on my peace and quiet state of mind. I guess it was my curse in life or bad karma to be swamped by intrusive people with blatant identity crises. But there is one sorry comfort in this life in that nothing lasts forever, including the line at the coffee shop. The realtors were finally processed, and out the door, and it was my turn for my 15 seconds of glory: a small coffee with cream, no sugar, and a buttered baguette. No bantering, no idle chatter, no special orders and no big tip in the jar by the register as I tried to make my way to the window section to indulge myself in coffee, baguette and peace and quiet. And I had it for about 30 seconds until Edith the artist spotted me and took a seat right next to mind. "You don't mind if I join you this morning? I've picked up some of these rub-away lottery tickets, and I can talk as a scratch off the cards. I won 65 dollars the other day and I just feel lucky this week. So how are you"?

I muttered something almost incomprehensible just to respond, like I was alright or something, under my breath, barely audible. After all, it was still early morning and my peaceful space was being violated by an uninvited guest. That was as nice as I could possibly get. For the remainder of the morning at the coffee house I tried to do two things simultaneously: read my magazine and try to civilly respond to the observations of the raving looney perched next to me. Needless to say, nothing went well. I did about a paragraph and a half — enjoyed and retained nothing from what I read — and she was annoyed since she got only perfunctory attention for her smatterings from me. I excused myself and left early, since I claimed there were important things to finish at work before the weekend. As I departed, she wished that I would be less irritable. Why am I such a magnet for whackos? Why couldn't I be a chick magnet instead? Bad karma!

Being driven out of Lucca's by the artist, I came into work some 30 seconds ahead of the nine o'clock deadline. All well and good, I guess. After parking the car I tried going in through the side exit but the door was already locked, long before the scheduled time for security's closure. So I schlepped to the front of the building and made my grand entrance. Perhaps my luck was changing since I almost ran head first into Miss

Janet as if she were waiting for me. The prospects look so good that I immediately began with a flippantly, playful greeting and salutation. Evidently my material was not too good this morning or Miss Janet was having another bad hair day since I was almost casually dismissed. However, remembering our wonderful repartee of our past meetings, and her great body still present in this meeting, I was undaunted. I pressed my not so honorable intentions. Evidently something was wrong since she was more agitated or in a hurry or something and she blurted out something like "fresh" or something. This was good since it meant that I was getting to her or something. Just as I was about to push the envelope further, there around the corner slithered Ferucci, whose hearing must specially tune to the sound of my voice. His purpose in life must be exclusively to entrap me. He had the look in his eye, while Janet scurried down the hall. It seemed that my potential for any luck was about to fade, and it wasn't even lunch time yet. Ferucci caught sight of the slightly miffed Miss Janet, grabbed my tie and yanked it, and informed me that I was too old for her and that I was late, again. Regaining my composure, I glanced at my watch and saw that it was only a few seconds after nine, thus my response: "If the side door was not locked before it was supposed to be, or if I had the code, like everyone else, I would have been in the building and on time according to your clock. However, a mere few seconds over the course of the day is nothing to get upset about." Ferucci gave me a snide smile and proceeded down the hall but gave me that affirmative injunction, "Get to work!" Lost face, and a lost Janet notwithstanding, I went into the office to begin the morning routine. As I walked in, Rosemarie immediately spotted my knotted tie and blurted out something to the effect about not taking adequate time to get properly dressed in the morning. I responded with one word, "Ferucci," and went to my desk, hoping for peace and quiet at work. Evidently hoping for any kind of a break was not now in the equation. Good ol' Rosemarie. There was nothing ever wrong with her vision. She could spot an ant with a bread crumb walking up a telephone poll some 50 feet away . . . and tell you whether the bread was white, rye or whole wheat. And I guess I was blessed, too, since almost every day I would be scrutinized before I began my work routine. I think I passed most daily inspections. Today it was merely another wrecked tie by Ferucci.

After that bumpy start, I settled into the work travail. The remainder of the baguette helped offset the agency's coffee. On this particular Friday, it was even worse than the usually bad standards for free, corporate coffee. Something should be done before someone lands in the hospital or something. And that was my final thought of the morning until 11 when Rigatoni wisped in behind my desk, startling the ever loving life out of me, to announce that there would be a meeting at two to discuss matters and issues of great importance to the agency. Great! Another proclamation to ruin my joyous expectation of a happy lunch hour and another weekend of freedom. I acknowledged this unwelcomed news with a forced smile and a small bit of the lip. Another assassination attempt; boredom was taking direct aim on my life.

For some unexplained reason, the ensuing hour prior to lunch ran rather quickly, and before I knew it the clock was closing in on twelve. At least this was good news. Thus without any forethought I took myself to the pizza joint again and order the tuna sub special, complete with Coke, for $4.95, tax not included. Lunch with peace in the park! This, too, was good. And, as an added bonus, the weather was with me. It was one of those glorious fall, pre-winter days that was more reminiscent of late summer, warm, not quite hot, without any of that New Jersey humidity. There were some leaves on the trees, but who cares about fall foliage anyway? I was committed to thoroughly enjoying my lunch in surroundings that could be described as only a notch or two below paradise standards. So lunch began: a bite on the sub, a sip of the soda, a line or two from the book, and a glance up to just to check on the surroundings. Yup, the surroundings were still there but hinted of a past glory of just a few weeks ago. Thus it was easy to break into a routine of bite, sip, read and look. This was a great rhythm of the universe and I continued until the end. To top this lunch off, nothing would be better than a short stroll around the lake. So I began. I encountered couples holding hands, fisherman (legal and otherwise) and therapy staff from the school. I kept on moving, uninterrupted, and got to the far end of my stroll and noticed, again, the solitary brunette. We passed; I glanced at her and she at me, and then we quickly passed like the proverbial ships in the night. She was OK. I think she even smiled. This was not the first time that I sited her around the lake. Interesting, however! As I proceeded to the bridge and the end of my quasi mystical experience, my serenity was abruptly ended with an encounter with an upset Kathy who asked, "Did you see it"?

I responded by saying, "Yes, it seems that the brunette just passed me some few minutes ago."

"No," said she, with a trace of irritation, "the duck. The mallard with the fish hook in its bill. We must save the mallard!"

"But I saw nothing out of the ordinary, and I have just minutes left on my lunch. If you need any help, I'll be on the park bench reading this book. But I have only minutes left because I have to be back in the office by one. You know how those people are. But for what time is left, you can count on me." I delivered that bit of insincerity since I knew that she could not cover the distance around the lake and return to find me in that short a period of time. I retired back to the park bench to finish up another chapter, look for the opportunity to have one more glance at the phantom brunette and then return to the punishment of my work station. Things were going pretty well. I got a solitary position on the park bench, saw the brunette although from far away, and was just finishing the last paragraph of the chapter when my serenity was broken by Kathy's voice, "I found him and we have him cornered. Come on!"

I had two immediate thoughts: "Oh brother!" and "Why me?" I could only imagine what was next as I moved rather quickly with Kathy to the small side of the lake. There was Donna, an occupational therapist, standing in front of the bushes right next to the water's edge. I couldn't see anything, but Donna pointed to something moving in the brush and with that Kathy said to me, "Get over there and head him off, just in case he tries to escape." So there I was, some two feet from the water, staring into the undergrowth and seeing nothing. But I was holding my ground. With that, Kathy went into the bushes and I heard a commotion of sorts. She shouted to me, "Watch out, he's coming your way." All of a sudden this enraged zoo escapee came flying out of the jungle of growth to make its move between me and the lake. In split second time I moved closer to the water's edge to thwart the escape. No good, too slow. The duck hit the water, and my right foot starts to sink in the mud before I was fully aware of this unfortunate situation. Notwithstanding the escapee, my reaction time was somewhat quick to mitigate a full catastrophe. Unfortunately, somewhat usually doesn't make it. I had muck and mire up to my ankle. I stormed out of the vegetation to try to clean up, while Kathy went bounding after the duck. Donna looked at my distress and consternation and began laughing. "This is not funny," I said and went back to the center to get cleaned up. Besides being a mess, I was now past my lunch hour and Ferucci would be sure to nail me for being on lunch overtime. But that did not happen. Coming out of the bathroom with a wet sock and a right shoe that could have used some polish, a quick look would not have disclosed the traumatic ordeal that I just suffered. Thus, I went back to my work station, deserted and beaten, and began the abbreviated afternoon work schedule. Besides the wet, uncomfortable feeling of my right foot, something just did not feel right. Something was amiss. After working for some time it suddenly occurred to me that I left my book at the lake. It wasn't my book; it belonged to the library. Thus I scampered out of the office and back to the lake to retrieve property that was entrusted to my care. Luck would have it that the book was still there. Retrieving said property, I turned to return to the office and there saw Kathy, with a blanket, carrying the duck. "We got 'm, with no fumbling the second time around. But thanks for your effort anyway." I nodded, unenthusiastically, and headed back, with Donna giggling in the background. I kind of limped back, trying to minimize the water damage on my right foot. My sock was not wet, just very soggy, and my right loafer was still had some remnants of the partially caked mud that fell off with every step. Any boy scout could have following the trail of mud that eventually would lead to me. As I came through the side door with a look of dismay on my face over past events, I ran into Ferucci — just what I needed! He had no understanding of the ordeal that I so quietly suffered, just the time. "How long do you usually take for lunch"?

"I had to retrieve some personal property."

"Don't leave your property all around and you'll be on time . . . for once. And try to be on time for your meeting with the president this afternoon. It's not good to keep the president waiting. He doesn't have my good nature when it comes to staff tardiness."

I gave Ferucci a cursory thank you for his advice and went back to my desk. As the time got closer to two and the meeting, the mud on my right foot got clumpier and debris of mud and other lake stuff began to accumulate under my desk. (I think this was the way creation started.) But my sock was still damp, and I imagined I was emitting a kind of swampy fragrance. It could be my active imagination. Evidently I had to resign myself to the fact that I would have to wait until I got home to change. This would bother me all through the meeting and until I finally got home. No way around it, I contracted the dreaded Dr. Scholl's damp foot syndrome.

It was somewhat after two that Ferucci came into the common office area, notepad in hand, and motioned to me to follow him into the meeting.

"I'm just finishing up; it will be a minute." With that Ferucci engaged in chatter with the office people discussing the most recent episode of "As My Children Turn" or whatever soap opera was on between one and two. Who knows? I gathered my clipboard, loaded with scrap paper — that's all these meetings were ever worth — and proceed to join up with Ferucci for that final march into the valley of snooze and doom. Of course, nothing ever escaped the scrupulous gaze of Rosemarie who immediately noted, and rather clearly for the entire office to hear, that there was something amiss with my right foot. Not wanting to go into a detailed explanation at all, I just rolled my eyes and ignored her, and went into the office. She responded by noting how unfriendly or hostile or something I was, etc. I just went into the office. The remainder of the afternoon would be troubling enough. I needed nothing more to compound the matter. My irritation level was on the way up and the meeting did not even begin.

The presidential suite was a kind of architectural peninsula, three walls of glass and the one wall connecting the room to the facility structure itself. With all the glass exposure you would think that anyone with any aesthetic sensibility would try to take in the overall beauty of the park environment and the lake. Not Rigatoni. The overhead lights were on and the blinds were tightly drawn. Sometimes coming into this office area your eyes would have to adjust to the lack adequate lighting. In Italian, as was Rigatoni's custom, he welcomed us in and bid me and Ferucci to sit down, which I did, right on top of one of Rigatoni's shoes that was on the chair that, unfortunately, through random selection I had the misfortune to choose since I was first in. I with as much finesse as I could muster in this dark cave placed this smelling artifact on the floor. Rigatoni gave me a smile, but I could not determine if this was generated by my uncomfortable, almost comic, mannerism or his own mental notation that he would get me later for a covert criticism of his own personal housekeeping. Probably both, one never knew.

With a posturing kind of smile, Rigatoni tried to add to the seeming importance of this meeting by stating that we had a lot to accomplish in this short period of time. He hoped that our pencils were sharpened.

Usually there were three phases to these meetings. The parts bonded together like an overly orchestrated ritual. Rigatoni usually began with a digression with something of a semi-personal nature, enough to make you feel that you were part of his "family" but not enough to feel like immediate family. He liked closeness, but not too close. This theoretical propinquity was only one way, his way. Then somewhere, someplace in the midst of these meetings, was the irrelevant trick question to show his overall mastery and insight over us and all situations, and to see if we were paying attention. I was never able to guess correctly and stopped playing a long time ago. I just was never into the full flow. If I wanted to play games, I would do so with good friends and on a playing field that would be level. On the other hand Ferucci could play with the best of them. Maybe it helped to be Italian. Maybe Ferucci had an innate skill to optimize any situation because of some kind of innate ability. He could play along with humor. I just wanted to quickly jump into the business of the meeting and get the thing over with. And my impatience was augmented by a soggy right foot. Added to the third phase was breaking, new news of his recap of the Florida trip. Sure enough, Rigatoni's introductory remarks began with a digression about his trip, again, to Florida and all he accomplished and sacrificed for the agency while he was on this working vacation. The casual observer would believe that this vacation trip was really a business trip. He would have a hard time, though, trying to explain his very dark tan acquired during November. Why the outside accounting firm that audited the agency books never caught on to this or other stuff that got slipped by remains a mystery to me unto this very day. After additional rambling remarks about something inconsequential or other, he digressed about this trip to Florida, again, and about some skewed observation or insight that was important to him and therefore should be noted by us after he so perfectly explained. I didn't get it, so I tuned out, concentrating on my soggy right foot and how Kathy and the rest of the unappreciated world were not entirely cognizant of my salvable efforts to save the quacker. Some 20 minutes later Rigatoni managed to get my attention on to a matter of some concern to me, wherein he decided to add to the staff to help out for the capital campaign. This news, out of the blue, did startle me from my slumber and stopped Ferucci from taking those copious notes for which he was famous. I usually never asked questions, either in public or private meetings, since Rigatoni did seemed uncomfortable with anything from my direction. However, Ferucci had a kind of immunity wherein he could say almost anything and get away with it. He did, thank goodness, ask "Who do you have in mind"?

With a smile and a bobbing of his head a pleased Rigatoni responded by saying that he had two individuals in mind. We knew both, but beyond that he would add nothing more at this time. He would explore and determine who would be the best fit. Stupid me, I could not resist, asked if I would be part of the interview process. Rigatoni piqued and said that I should be concerned with raising more money for the agency, especially with the holidays almost on top of us, like a 42d Street hooker. Christmas was the best time of year for people to open their hearts and their wallets. He wanted to save me from any unnecessary distractions or worry. That's why he was the president, to make the big decisions. (He never mentioned big bucks that he was raking in, but he knew what everyone else was making.)

And then came those words that would have, in the future, a lasting impact upon my life, although I did not realize it at the time. Rigatoni looked at me and Ferucci and casually mentioned that, "It seems that Henri will not be around for the holidays, so I am leaving it with this team to come up with a suitable substitute for Santa Claus. Henri has a personal matter to take care of and will not be available." The team concept notwithstanding, Rigatoni was looking at me all the way. Not only was I responsible, I would be liable. "Some parents and board members come to the annual Santa visit, so it's important to get it right. Right?" I nodded in agreement. Ferucci picked up his pencil and began to write.

Ferucci assumedly took this one down. I kind of thought here we go again, another straw for the camel, or donkey in this case, to carry. I was more concerned with my soggy right foot. The clock on Rigatoni's wall had barely after four on it, so this meant that there was at least another hour of the agonization to endure in some state of physical distress. Lord, have mercy on me! This must be what purgatory is like.

The meeting lurched onward. In addition to the soggy foot problem I realized that I would be missing Bill Brown and our weekly football prognostications wherein the end result would be depriving him of his beer money. Bill usually departed at four to take on another job to support his family. On some days of the week he had an 18-hour day. Certainly one could admire his devotion to family but not a wage or salary system that required him, or anyone else for that matter, to work long hours with such uncomplaining consistency. However, I felt no remorse in taking his money, on a regular basis, in our petty wagering ritual. I felt it was kind of a good mixture of a test for manliness and intelligence and building up of his flawed character. I won week in and week out; it almost lost its excitement. But any feelings of pity were quickly offset by the personal gratification to see Billy grovel as I beat the bucks out from him. The irony was that Bill was physically strong and solid like a rock. He could have passed for a linebacker. And yet to have him grovel with regularity before my slender body was very uplifting. In fact, it was reason enough to come to work on Monday in the first place. On the other hand, Ferucci was shorter than me, but he was higher on the corporate ladder. Plus he was wise in the ways of the corporate world, at least that of the agency world. So doing to him what I did to Bill would be significantly more challenging and be a definite coup d'etat. Baiting him or catching him off guard would be an almost impossible task. Getting back at Ferucci was becoming an agenda item that would be moved from the back burner at the most opportune time.

A thought did occur to me — the first good one of the afternoon — that I would excuse myself to go to the bathroom and then bound way down the hall into the custodial room and place my wagers with Mr. Brown. Should I risk it or not? Spontaneity does have its virtues and rewards . . . in normal situations. But was this the right environment to pull a risky move? That thought reverberated again and again in my mind as Rigatoni droned on and on, and my damp sock became progressively more distracting. Nevertheless, with Ferucci perpetually hovering over me and waiting for opportunities to turning me for a bounty, I decided to go for it: the bathroom break. I raised my hand. Rigatoni gave me that look: half stunned, half annoyed. I butted into his territory. I was interrupting his meeting. I wrecked his train of thought. (It was a small train, though.) He looked at me and said, "Yes." Evidently he thought I was going to ask him a question about the last this and that he posed. But instead I said, "I guess I had one cup of corporate coffee too much. Can I have 60 seconds to go to the bathroom? I'll be right back." Ha! I caught him off guard. With a request so short, sweet and innocent, so incongruous to what was going on, by surprise he could only agree. But there was no simple "yes" on his part, he just had to add that "We could all use a little break. Some fresh air will add zest and sparkle to the rest of the meeting." With that I quickly stepped out of the office and bounded down the hall, to the other side of the building, looking for Bill Brown. I covered the eighth of a mile distance between east wing and west wing in less than 20 seconds. There is no substitute for speed. I bypassed two rest rooms and went right into the custodial office, which was the facility boiler room with some storage racks and four beat up desks that the custodial team used to mimic the executive administration when they had they had their meetings to talk about cleaners, tools, sports and the women on staff. Luck was with me on this one since Bill was delayed by some work project and just leaving.

I said, "I gotta be quick since I just got a brief time out from a boring meeting. This weekend I'll let you have the Giants, and I'll be more than generous and give you four points."

Bill said, "No, I lost last week. I need more points."

"Look, Mr. Ding Dong, they are at home and absolutely need this victory to have a chance at the playoffs."

"I need more points. Right now, I am working two jobs to pay you off. I have no money for gas. My wife is mad, too, about all this loosing."

"Look. You have to control your wife better. And accept reality, you are a looser. But, since I am a nice guy, here's what I'll do. I'll give you six big points and the Giants are at home. How 'bout that?"

Bill took the bait and the bet. I was giving up six points. But the poor guy didn't know about the Friday injury to a key Giants' player that would have some affect on the game.

It looked like I had this big, fat fish hooked again. Now to quickly go back to the office and resume the meeting, I quickly exited the custodial office and turned up the hall. Briskly walking, I moved quickly around the last turn into the great hallway when I quite literally ran into Ferucci coming the other way. I don't know who was more surprised by this chance encounter. It should have been Janet or some other attractive staff member that I ran into. No such luck again!

Ferucci looked at me and, after a slight pause, said, "You had to use a bathroom on this side of the building?"

This time I was ready for him with the response, "The others were unacceptable for normal, human usage. You are really too nice and ought to make clean bathrooms a priority with your custodial staff. So this was my only option."

He paused again, although this time the interval was less. "Normal is not the word for you. By the way, did you notice if Bill Brown was in the building?"

"I don't know. Doesn't he normally leave by four?"

"We'll see." With that Ferucci zoomed around the corner and almost ran head-first into the departing, in an extreme hurry, Bill Brown. That sparked a slight smirk on Ferucci's face. He quickly turned his attention to the exiting custodian and asked, "Was he the reason that you're late getting out of here?"

Brown moving toward the door yelled out, "He hasn't been good to me this week." The door closed as he left.

Ferucci had that exasperated look. We both knew that he had me, but there was no hard evidence that I excused myself from the meeting to place a gentleman's wager with Bill Brown, unless I incriminated myself and confessed. Unlike the Spartan youth, I was not going to take the honorable way out on this one.

"So," he said, "you left the meeting to bet?"

"No, I left to go to the bathroom. Weren't you listening? Unfortunately, the only clean rest room facility was on this side of the building. You know, you just can't get good help anymore." With that I started to quickly walk away, leaving Ferucci searching for a good retort. Ferucci always had two consistent work issues: cleanliness and getting some modicum of work out of the custodial department. This time, like most, the quick strike was best. I did get halfway back to the office when I heard Ferucci's footsteps gaining on me. My long strides were offset by the pitter patter of his short, little feet trying to catch up to me. I knew that what he lacked in size he would make up in crusty determination. With that, I increased my speed, soggy foot and all, to try and separate the distance between us. Without looking back, I could hear the pitter patter of his little feet furtively gaining on me. At least I could take some satisfaction in punishing him, since he would do same to me. I always lived my life with an adaptation of the golden rule: do unto others before they do unto you. It wasn't until the last turn into the long hallway that he caught up with me, slightly out of breath.

"So you made another bet with Billy? You're depriving a working man of money to feed his family."

"Just looking for a clean haven, like most of us." I deflected his baited question and, in the process, moved closer to the office to resume the meeting. This, of course, was a momentary victory that would be paid back, by me, later with interest. Little victories, though, must be fully savored, even for their respectively brief moments and dire consequences that expectedly follow.

I was first into the office, followed by Ferucci. We both sat down and our presence was acknowledged by an expressionless Rigatoni who cleared his throat and began, without loosing a beat, where the lecture was interrupted. His discourse rambled on like the winding, muddy Mississippi. From comments on apathetic board of director members, staff apathy to county officials needing to do something about whatever. I found my attention quickly drifting away as I wistfully looked toward the clock, which was moving ever so slowly toward five and the magical dismissal time. I started to think about how I was going to spend the money won from Bill Brown when Rigatoni turned to me and said, "You were not writing much and taking notes during this important meeting. Hopefully, you job performance in the coming weeks will be better than your note taking."

"I always take my work seriously," I said.

And then came Ferucci's comment, "I think he takes his work almost as serious as his football bets with Bill Brown." Just when I was almost off the hook, with the clock showing just minutes to five, the theoretical time for dismissal, Ferucci got his cheap shot in. Damn and Rats! Rigatoni's expressionless mannerism began to turn, ever so slightly, into a grimace. "Yes. We are going into this critical phase of the capital campaign and we all must get focused without distractions. That's why I am getting you help in the development office."

Rigatoni had me there. The capital campaign and other fund raising activities needed help from day one, but the implication that I was on perpetual vacation was both inaccurate and offensive. How could I respond to this personal slight? Given the circumstances, with only a Charlie Brown kind of response, I said, "I take my work seriously." Rigatoni looked at me, cleared his throat, and began to drone on, without looking directly at me. You could never know with Rigatoni, because he would selectively hold evidence of personal affronts forever on the back burner. Ferucci was different. He got his zinger and then moved on. With him, nothing was ever that personal. He lived for the moment of the great zinger; I kind of admired that since I was always left things simmering on the back burner. I never let anything out, including the cat. And here I was left looking bad, holding the bag, and with a very damp foot to boot. It certainly was a dismal end to the work week. The meeting concluded — after five and late — with Rigatoni's tag closing line: "You all have your marching orders. There is a lot of work to be done and the year's end is closing fast. Let's work hard to make it a . . . ." Before he could finish, his cell phone rang. He concluded with the word "success" and bid us to close the door as we left as he attended to his personal business.

As we left the office, our respective faces must have showed the effects of this meeting. Ferucci was effervescent. He had pages of notes and I must have looked like I was dragged through a combat training session at Fort Dix. Maybe it was an act of sympathy but Ferucci looked at me and asked if I wanted to stop for a drink and a light snack. The ordeal left me too exhausted to refuse totally. "As long as it's local, it'll be fine." Ferucci, as if it were well planned in advance, suggested the new California-type restaurant in the mall. "Fine! See you there in ten minutes." "Ten it is," said a smiling Ferucci.

I returned to my desk, arranged my work in semi-neat and somewhat organized piles, and prepared to leave the office. After five on a Friday, the office became devoid of life like a graveyard, save for Rigatoni being locked in his own personal crypt. I shuffled off down the hall, into my car and went straight to the mall. Parking was no problem at this transitional hour and I had no trouble finding a good spot by the entrance. When I got to the California Café, Ferucci was already there. He saw me and looked at his watch. The gesture was rather obvious. He said, "I thought you said ten minutes." I could only shake my head. Sitting down I changed the subject to what to drink and eat. But luck was with me a little since we hit the café during happy hour. We ordered a glass of the house (cheap) red and then perused the site and menu. Happy hour has to be one of the top ten greatest creations of all time. Putting the menus down we both descended upon the bar area where there were free appetizers. Not having eaten in hours, I took on the persona of the defeated convict in *Dead Man Walking*. My first move was on the bowl of mixed nuts. One generous handful from bowl to mouth. My cheeks puffed up like a rogue chipmunk. Munching away I slid down the bar to the pretzel area. Again another handful into the mouth. Since it was only 5:30 or thereabouts, the café was only sparsely populated, giving me incredible mobility and unobstructed snacking opportunities. Witnessing my passionate attack on the snacks, Ferucci was both astounded and amused. He called out something to the effect about embarrassing him in public. He may or may not have heard my response that I was just beginning, although it is most difficult to speak clearly with a mouth full of free food. But I always felt that free supercedes embarrassment any day of the week. The attractive barkeep looked at me, smiled and said something to the effect that happy hour at the Café was a "happening," or something like that. With my puffy checks, I managed a truly forced smile and muttering something unintelligible. I couldn't pick her up since I was more intent on snacking and she had a tattoo, which was taboo in my neck of the woods, which was exactly where she had hers.

I returned to our table which jutted out almost in the mall itself, and took a goodly sip of the wine. This house red was not bad. I leaned back in the chair at the same time that Ferucci accused me of belching. In disbelief I just shook my head and said, "Life can be pretty good at times." With that Ferucci began recapping the recent meeting with Rigatoni and other agency business. Mostly, I nodded in agreement and took in some more wine in the process. Even with the alcohol going into my delicate system, I could never be fully sympathetic with Ferucci's unequivocal support of his Italian boss and the way things were run. Others who worked there did come to me with their respective complaints, issues and problems. I guess some rubbed off. And Rigatoni was rough on me, almost all of the time. So I guess I had a job, while Ferucci had a commitment. I finished the wine and was looking for more. My wish was answered since Ferucci got up, took the two empty glasses and went to the bar for a refill. He quickly returned with two more glasses as well as two menus. Handing one to me he said, "It's time to see if they make serious food here. I saw someone get some pretty good ravioli at a back table."

"Why pay for food when they're providing the stuff for free during happy hour?"

"Start living and enjoy your money. I wish I had your money. Life is too short to be wasted on handouts." The irony of his last remark was that he was making triple my salary but always claimed to be living hand to mouth: too many family commitments draining his lifeblood.

With that, Ferucci got a waitress' attention and order three items from the appetizer portion of the menu. "Life is good," he said. He took a sip from his wine, held the glass up to the light and solemnly stated, "I'll give this cabernet an 86. It needs to breathe. In fact, it may need a respirator. It lacks body, strength. Yes, when you're Italian, you appreciate and need things with strength and character, like a good red wine. In fact, that's the only kind of wine there is. No one with any sense of taste would ever drink a white or rosé. That's all there is to that matter." With that, Ferucci took another sip. Shortly thereafter, the appetizers came. Ferucci looked at me and simply said "Manga" and began eating. I ate out of protest since I wanted to snack on the free bar stuff which was coming out from time to time. But Ferucci wanted what he wanted and when he wanted, and that was that. I was thinking about the unnecessary bill that was just run up. Before I could think too much longer, Ferucci took my plate and began to apportion my share of the treats. He smiled in the process and gave the entire presentation a B−. "Life is good," he said, while all I could think about was the forthcoming bill. In the interim, we talked about agency business and he recalled some of the issues during the meeting with Rigatoni. I couldn't care less, save for the new assistant for the fund raising position. I tried to wheedle some additional information from him since Italians do stick together (this is something my father always preached as gospel to me); however, nothing was forthcoming. As the waitress was coming with the bill, Ferucci mentioned something about the Santa Claus project. Taken off guard, I must have had a blank look on my face, which Ferucci immediately noticed. He said that, "The trouble with you is that you don't pay attention. You were told that your responsibility for this year is to get a Santa for the kid's holiday party. Were you listening? Apparently not!" I guess I wasn't still listening since I was more intent on finishing all the stuff on the table. Daddy always said waste not, want not, so I was determined to finish everything in front of me. With my mouth full of food, Ferucci was taking care of the bill. I tried to mumble words to the effect that I always listen. My response was barely intelligible; Ferucci looked exasperated, but I was almost full so I didn't care about his or any other's feelings at the time. With the bill fully paid, Ferucci left a generous tip on the table. He saw a look of disapproval and replied that this is all the money the waitress may make working today. "Too many cheap suits around," he said looking directly at me, and then with a quick grin said that he was running to Thom McCann's since they were having a going out of business sale that was too good to pass up. Since he was on a budget, purchasing stuff on sale was a good way to save money. With all the food off the table and out of my mouth, I was finally able to intelligibly reply that "If you're truly on a budget, then don't shop at all."

But he bounded across the mall courtyard, heading directly and quickly toward the shoe store. I tried to follow but got farther and farther behind. The enthusiasm of a sale added a spark of adrenalin to Ferucci's gait. I barely could keep up. The signs were plastered all over the Thom McCann window blatantly announcing going out of business, last days, incredible savings and the like. Most were in red lettering, so you assumed that this was very serious. Ferucci dashed into the store, like a kid jumping into a lake during the first hot day of summer. I was more deliberate, preferring to stalk my bargains before any buying blitz. Eventually we met some place in the middle, sat down and began the methodical process of trying on selected shoe bargains and driving the poor clerk crazy. It was almost embarrassing since my one foot was still somewhat damp from the afternoon escapade. I glibly remarked to the store clerk that I sweated a lot because I was under a lot of tension at work. Ferucci did not notice that remark since he was in a state of euphoria sparked by the buying frenzy and the boxes of soon-to-be purchases began piling up at his little feet. Maybe it was the energy of the situation, maybe it was the full moon or some other psychic event but I started to amass my own collection of shoe boxes too. The discounts were very good, and the shoe styles were not limited. I stopped at three; Ferucci had five and still counting. Common sense, a dissipation of energy, a terribly soggy foot and/or a shortage of inventory finally brought our selection process to an end but not before we both took a financial beating. Using plastic, we checked out with Ferucci going deeper into debt than me. He had two very large bags of merchandise to show for his efforts to my one. When we got to the door, he said matter of fact, "I'm going to Macy's since they have a sale on something that I need." I didn't know if this was an invitation or merely a statement of health or being or something, but my shoe purchases were weighing me down both physically and financially. "I'm going home," and with that I began making my way toward the mall exit. I did by chance glance over my shoulder and saw Ferucci bounding through the mall's courtyard and heading toward Macy's. The evils of drink, compounded by too much spending cash and free time — maybe that explained Ferucci's condition. Who knows?

I trundled back to my car in the mall parking lot, lugging my newly acquired treasures with me. I felt victorious but exhausted. The soggy foot was as dry as it was going to get. The ride home, going the opposite way on 287, was uneventful. Within less than a half hour, I pulled into my drive way and carried the packages along with my brief case to the front door. Kiki was in the front window, waiting for my delayed arrival. Key in the door, there was a loud, impatient meow greeting me. I apologized to the cat. I told her I was delayed by uncontrollably forces as she determinedly marched into the kitchen and sat down in front of her food bowl. Packages and bad foot notwithstanding, Kiki was immediately fed. Thereafter I moved immediately to the bedroom to finally remove the irritant that plagued me all day. It was almost seven o'clock already, a kind of funny hour, too late for me to go out, but who would want to go out, and too early to go to bed. The several glasses of wine were having their tranquilizing effect. My only option was to go down stairs, watch TV and doze on and off before bed time. Kik joined me on the opposite side of the couch, purring softly, as I watched some PBS account of saving some kind of exotic species in some exotic place that I probably will only visit in my wildest dreams. Friday and the work week were officially over, and my credit card took a minor hit. I had two glorious weekend days to recharge my batteries for the anticipated work week to come. But anticipation was not going to wreck my weekend respite.

P<small>ART</small> F<small>OUR</small>

T he weekend was less than exciting. The high point was going to the local place of worship and almost hearing a sermon on how the unprepared were missing out in building up treasures in the afterlife. Once upon a time in my earlier life, I was so prepared for getting the good stuff promised in the next place that I would reach for rosary beads whenever anyone would pound on a Bible, but trying to maintain that perpetual state of readiness and preparedness left me emotionally exhausted. I couldn't keep up being that ready all the time. So the more I tune out, either at work or in church, the better I feel in the short run. The Sunday afternoon pro football game promised to be better than the sermon and I had monies on the outcome with Bill Brown, but the temptation of a day that was sunny and warm for this time of year was too great. So I racked the mountain bike on the back of the car and went off into the country for a commune with nature. Despite overdevelopment, the western part of New Jersey still is able to retain a portion of that pristine beauty that in any time of the year one remembers what was and how little was done to protect what was truly precious. (Now why couldn't that be the topic of a sermon on some Sunday?) Being opportunistic, I was determined to hold on to this fleeting moment in this end of year cycle. Every warm day during this time of year that broaches winter is truly a gift. Normally with a few weeks before Christmas people would be shopping. But what the heck, my Christmas list was rather small and my shopping could be done at a liquor store, a lottery store, a dollar store or the like during the cover of darkness. Why waste the gift of a beautiful day.

Inevitably, like death, taxes and politicians on the curvilinear campaign trail, Monday mornings do come around, which means back to the grind of work. I was not exempt. The proverbial bell was tolling, this time in the form of a clock radio. One of my bedroom windows faced east and the sunrise with all its promise for the coming day. If daybreak were any indication, the omens did not look good for this Monday; the sky was an ominous gray, almost nondescript. The glory of the previous day was most definitely gone. It was with a sense of foreboding that I got out of bed. Kiki was sleeping on the opposite side and did not move. I struggled with bathroom regime and dressing routine and went downstairs to have a light breakfast. Halfway through and in the process of taking a couple of vitamin pills, Kik thumped down the stairs and marched into the kitchen. She went over to her food bowl, sat down and looked at me, and gave me a decisive "wrack" for her food. It was just one; no meows here. So I had to stop in the middle of my meal to give her breakfast immediately. I am admitted a weak person when it comes to most animals; she was happy. I quickly finished, got cleaned up and left, as she was still eating. No emotional, long drawn out goodbyes as I snuck out my front door. The drive on 287 was not bad since not too many cars were on the road. It must have been another holiday or something. Since I was way ahead of schedule, I convinced myself to stop at the coffee shop again for a bracing cup of caffeine. I had the feeling that the upcoming day would require all the caffeine I could possibly imbibe. Some days you wake up and just feel that the other shoe is going to fall. This was one of those days.

I was early at the coffee shop. Parking was tight, which was rather unusual since the traffic on 287 was light. My usual convenient spot was not available so I had to practically circle the block before I found something behind the train station. Passing by the lottery store, I stopped in to buy a few tickets for the millionaire drawing. Maybe this would challenge my foreboding sense of bad luck. The counter guy from New Delhi gave me my tickets and wished me something or other. Just could not understand him and no desire to do so at this early hour. With the potential for a million dollars in my pocket, I trundled down to the coffee shop to take my rightful place in line for Lucca's best. Only one person in front of me and a salty bagel was available. I placed my order, took my treats and got a quite spot by the window to watch the world in Metuchen pass by. The rhythm of coffee, bagel and glance out the window had a soothing, hypnotic effect that make me progressive oblivious to my surroundings. This was the peace and quiet that mystics write about. Unfortunately, mystics never encountered the artist who had that moment came into the shop and dropped three different newspapers next to me. Maybe this is what is called magnetism. If it is, I didn't like it. In staking out her territory, she startled me from my meditative respite. Some coffee spilled on my pant leg. Great! I soiled myself, at the work day's beginning, and she thought it was hysterically funny. I gave myself less than a minute to conclude my stay and be on my way before I was subjected to her review of the weekend and my personal life. I stuffed the remaining half of the bagel into my mouth. I looked like a deranged woodchuck with an eating problem. I took a final gulp of my coffee just as she slid the window chair uncomfortably close to me. She looked at me and asked in her raspy voice, "How is it going?"

"It's going out the door. I've got one of those days at the asylum . . . you know what I mean." I wrapped the other half of the bagel in a napkin and stuffed it in my pocket. Evidently I didn't lie well or my delivery was off. It was the morning and I never claimed to be a morning person but she did not appreciate my leaving just as she was arriving. She grunted and wished me something or other. I wasn't paying much attention since I didn't care as I exited the door and out to hunt for my BMW, if I could remember where I parked it. Notwithstanding time spent trying to find a forgotten car, the bad news/good news was that I would be early or at least on time for work. Well, perhaps that would give me some extra, relaxed time to work my magic on one who seemed to have no long-term memory of our respective flirtatious activities. There was no past with this woman. Every time was kind of the first time with her. Did this mean that my best lines were lost on this blond with a perfect ten body? Life can be so frustrating when you want it to go right. Janet and me, perfect together?

The trip from the coffee house to the park was uneventful. Since it was mid December, there were few leaves on the trees. If I drove slower, perhaps I could count what was left, just a remnant of the past fall's former glory, another possible sermon topic?

Getting in early, I sought the side door, which was the quickest way into the office. I kind of strolled in since I wanted to kill time and increase the odds of running into Miss Janet. Even the most inconsequential tête-à-tête with her would brighten up another lousy Monday morning that began another grueling work week. But with my luck, no such luck. All I saw were some staff running around and teacher aides wheeling in the kids in their chairs. No Ferucci either. I shuffled into the office and as I took off my coat to place on the rack Rosemarie saw me and started, with great enthusiasm, shouting out her recap of the weekend. She went to a Grateful Dead concert or a re-creation of some sort. Was this some cult dealing with Halloween? It still was early in the morning for me, and up to this day I was not familiar with this group. Don't know if I could recognize one of this group's songs. Certainly could not sympathize with all the hoopla, especially at this early hour. My drowsy morning reaction evidently had a stifling effect on Rosemarie's remembrance of her weekend activities since she shifted from screaming enthusiastically at me to simply screaming. She even took time to notice the smug on the pant leg from the coffee. She proceeded to get the office into her buzz. It was early Monday morning and I did not know, or care, who the Dead were. At this early hour, I felt more dead than alive. It wasn't my fault. Why can't they leave me alone at this early hour?

By 9:05, a litany of grievances flew about. The chorus accused me of being unfriendly, unsociable, not a team player and dressing in the style reminiscent of the '50s, or thereabouts. I'm sure there were other charges as well. I threw my hands up and exclaimed, "Whatever!" just as Ferucci came into the office. He picked up on the tail end of all this hubbub and a slight flicker of a smile came upon his face. He added to the verbal morning madness by loudly claiming to be the executive director, not a referee. After that proclamation, he asked me to accompany him to his office. This was almost a good thing to do since it got me out of the roaring hen house and into the tranquility of a tranquil inner sanctum.

Although they both were Italian, the contrasts in office decorum between Rigatoni and Ferucci were striking. The former look like a disaster struck about a week previously and the chief resident was still waiting for an insurance adjuster to assess damages. Not only did it offend the eye, the olfactory sense was compromised as well. It smelled like Secaucus. Ferucci's was different. You could eat of the floor; it was that clean. The desk was orderly. Books and binders were shelved and in the upright position. On the walls there were some photos of family members. And this office had a slightly antiseptic smell of some kind of Lysol or similar cleaner. Overall, not a bad place to recover from surgery, or to have another meeting or just terminate an employee.

The meeting with Ferucci did not go as I expected. After casually mentioning something about getting along better with Rosemarie, he babbled on to other things: his weekend, his family, antiquing, his car, the agency, the staff, and on. I nodded my head in complete acquiescence since I was on the clock and getting paid, no matter what, and it gave me a respite from the office hornet's nest. So after about some

20 inconsequential minutes, I went back to my desk in a more subdued office. That day, and the following day, followed upon that meeting since nothing happened of great consequence. We were two more days closer to Christmas and the holiday break, something I'm sure we all needed and would welcome.

What also would be most welcomed, and it was much closer to Christmas, was Mr. Brown's money. He lost another one. Unfortunately, not running into Janet this morning but into the office buzz saw, followed by the impromptu meeting with Ferucci, distracted my focus for the morning, and perhaps the entire day. Discretion being the better part of valor, I went back to my desk and postponed my all important meeting with Mr. Brown until lunch time. It was a seemingly wise decision. An uneasy quiet descended upon the office's western front. Rosemarie became quiet like a dormant volcano, the other office ladies had their respective heads down in work, Ferucci evaporated into his office, and no one heard from Rigatoni, who never came in that day.

Sometimes tracking down fat Mr. Brown, even at lunch time, could be an undertaking in itself. My plan of action was going to be a two-for-one hit. Lunch would be leftovers in the school kitchen and then a chance run in with Mr. Brown. For a mere dollar donation, one could have access to the lunch of the day, the stuff the handicapped school kids were having. Dora, the school cook, would almost always have remnants of the meal available. Somehow, someway, despite logistical safeguards and administrative oversight, there were extra meals available most of the time. The meals themselves would never make any Zagat recommendations, but there was plenty of the stuff and, for a dollar; you couldn't beat the price. So for that Monday, my meal du jour was macaroni and cheese, some exceedingly well cooked string beans and a container of peaches in a sugary syrup. The stuff was edible but needed salt or some other missing ingredient for taste. Mr. Zagat would have raised an eyebrow or two. No Bill Brown however. Thus I began the hunt for my justly won winnings. After some minutes of searching, on my lunch hour time, I found the deadbeat in one of the back hallways on a ladder examining some kind of pipe or cable in the ceiling. With my prey in sight I got excited and yelled out, "Hey deadbeat, how'd you like the weekend?"

"It was OK. I worked my second job on Saturday and then on Sunday I took my old lady to see the kids play a basketball game, and then had dinner that night at the in-laws. Not too bad, the free food and all."

"Did you see the game?"

"Yea, my kids played well. Matt almost killed somebody that got in his way. That's my boy!"

"No, no, no," I said, "I'm talking about the pros. It was a dynamite game, and, unfortunately, you were on the wrong side of the betting curve . . . again. When can I collect your just debts that you owe to society?"

Bill, poking his head out of the ceiling, looked a little sheepish and told me that he spent a significant portion of this weekly allowance on taking his old lady out on the weekend and on some breakfast on the way in to work. Could I wait until later in the week? I agreed since that permitted me the opportunity to verbally beat him up again; it was kind of bonus. I shuffled away, enthusiasm slightly dampened, to the atrium to finish up my lunch hour by reading a book. Just didn't feel like going outdoors to read; the weather was definitely changing to reflect the oncoming of winter. On my way to my spot in the atrium, I spotted Miss Janet and could not help but blurting out, "Hey, I had peaches for dessert today and thought of you." She gave me a strange look and kept on going to wherever. I thought it was a great, spontaneous line for the moment. Evidently not! The moment faded like the sun behind the increasingly rolling clouds that were descending upon the school that afternoon. At least I had my book to cozy up to in a snug corner of the atrium.

The rest of the afternoon was quiet and nondescript. When I got back to the office, the rest of them were at lunch and at the soap opera. I buried myself in the mound of paperwork and without the luxury of looking at the clock. Afternoons on weekdays seem to fly by more quickly than the same slot on a Friday to signal the start of the weekend. The end of another work day came quickly and when five o'clock came, I went. Kiki was waiting for me in the bay window when I pulled in less than a half-hour later. There was no meow to greet me, just a quick march to the kitchen to signal that it was her turn for attention and eats. I complied.

Tuesday was only marginally different from Monday. The same gray, cloudy weather was still hanging on. The parking situation at the coffee shop was the same. I had my same fare, without much of a crowd. The quiet was appreciated. Got into work early, for the second consecutive day, saw nothing of Miss Janet, and Rosemarie wasn't even acknowledging my presence. This could be what is meant by life balancing the good and the bad out, or maybe I just was invisible today. Ferucci was not lurking in the halls, and Rigatoni was lost somewhere in the endless commute or in another phantom meeting of no consequence. The paperwork tedium that was work was broken by a few phone calls and the promise of a business appointment that was scheduled for Thursday. Five o'clock came and I promptly departed for home. Kiki was waiting in the bay window. Without a meow at my entrance, I methodically went to the kitchen to give her some eats. She purred. Another day down and one more closer to Christmas and the glorious holiday break after a frenetic year-end finish at the agency.

Another marginal sunrise! Wednesday morning began like the previous two days. The sun was pathetically weak, signaling that the serene days of autumn finally lost out to that inhospitable companion that would be winter. The process of getting out of bed, getting dressed for work and then going down the stairs for some breakfast food and a handful of vitamins seemed somewhat tedious. I motivated myself by repeating that this was Wednesday, or hump day, and marked the half-way point in the work week. Only two more days until the weekend! I was on my third or forth vitamin pill, sloshed down with some tea, when I heard Kiki thumping down the stairs. She came into the kitchen with an annoyed look since her food was not ready. Without her characteristic meow, she just sat down and stared at me, knowing full well in her impertinent way that her stuff was on the way. Within a minute I complied, being the weak person that I was and still am. After this minor skirmish of nerves and will, I left on my way to work. First, however, was the stop at the coffee house for my morning jolt of caffeine before facing the onslaught of whatever was waiting for me across the other side of the lake. Parking this time was easy, so it was a convenient hop, skip and jump into the warmth of Lucca's. The windows were steamed because of the interior warmth of the place clashing with the cold outside. It felt snug and good. There was no line so I got my coffee and treats and took my customary chair by the window, gazing out aimlessly on the Main Street traffic. My mind kind of wandered off and I became totally oblivious to the individual who invited herself to sit next to me with an audacious bang of her newspaper and other paraphernalia; it was the artist again! Evidently the law of balances operated over the long term as well. She accosted me with a gruff good morning and began immediately began haranguing something or other about Metuchen and small town politics. My tolerance level was quickly tested and was found to be inadequate, and with that, I placed my other half of the buttered, salty bagel in my pocket and focused on the exit, which was close at hand. She chortled something and I responded that I had to go, and that was that.

But having *café interruptus* had its blessing. I would be early and could wander the agency hallway and maybe run into Miss Janet having a good day. If that failed, I could seek out Mr. Brown and collect his just debt of honor. I did come through the park early just as the sun was weakly breaking through the overcast. This I interpreted as a potentially good sign. With an assigned space reserved exclusively for me — the only perk I ever got at that place — parking was easy. The side door was unlocked, so for once I had easy access to the back hallway. Strolling through the building toward the maintenance office, I casually glanced as Miss Janet's office but she wasn't there. All well and good, I could catch her on the rebound. I went through the boiler area into the maintenance room feeling especially elated, knowing that my dollars were coming at the expense of slightly beating up Billy. Walking into the area the wind was taken out of my sails. Bill was dejectedly drinking his coffee and blankly staring straight ahead. I knew that my presence would just have to cheer him up. In a loud voice I said, "How is my best buddy Bill doing today?" and gave him a hard pat on the back. It was like hitting a sack of unresponsive potatoes. With very little coaching, I was able to find out that he had another disagreement with his "old lady." He had my sympathy; but I wanted his money or should I say my money. It was the principle. He was 48 hours late. It seems I was faced with a moral dilemma. Give my buddy Bill sympathy and support, or challenge his moral fiber with my demands that he meet his just debt of honor. The nuns always stressed moral fiber, thus I asked, "Where's my money?"

Bill gave me that distressed look, like one of those pathetic basset hounds, and after a slight delay, reached into his pocket and pulled out three crumbled dollar bills. Normally, I would be concerned if this were his last three bucks for the week. But what is right is right. So I took the money, my money, from the poor dejected Mr. Brown. This was almost the same moment when Ferucci came bursting into the office looking for someone from maintenance. He struck pay dirt, two for the price of one. He found Billy and me. Ferucci had that look of serene happiness, like a cat with a cornered canary. "So you are not only late but gambling on agency property and agency time!"

"It's not gambling," I said, "but mathematical applications to predict probability and outcomes. I am really helping Mr. Brown so that he can get his retirement portfolio in order. The money you see is just a fee for my advisement services."

With that Ferucci got red in the kisser. It looked like his shirt collar button was going to pop. Quickly exiting the maintenance room, I turned over my shoulder and said to Bill, "See you tomorrow for another financial lesson." Sometimes a good zinger is worth the long term consequences. This one was worth it. I bested Bill again and Ferucci was most annoyed with my finesse move. This was my two for the price of one.

Ferucci did not go into cardiac arrest that day. I always felt that his karma was to induce others into some kind of heart problem. I'm sure, though, that my comments registered negative points which most assuredly would be paid back later with interest. But sometimes, good material must have its due. I felt happy, although rest assured a payback would be coming with interest. So what?

I made my way to the office, through the hallway that connected with Janet's office. The good news, bad news. Things were kind of balancing out this week. She was there but appeared to be engaged with a serious discussion with one of her staff members. This was an opportunity to test the power of my magnetic attraction. Passing her office I said in a louder than normal voice, "Good morning Miss Janet and Miss Laura." Their conversation stopped, they turned and looked at me. I think Laura smiled, and then they resumed their discussion. One thing about Miss Janet, she was intense. If it weren't for her good looks and dynamite body, she would have been an interesting match for Ferucci.

The office had that ominous quiet to it. The ladies were busy at their respective functions. The greetings that are usually exchanged in the morning, because of either habit or custom, were done. All well and good! I didn't have a problem with that. I just wanted the peace and quiet that comes with a personal life that has well defined borders and boundaries that carry over into a business environment. Unfortunately in this environment this boundary was crossed almost daily. It made me feel like being admitted into a family that I would rather not join, even on a good day, even after a few drinks stronger than coffee.

I took advantage of the break in the corporate storm to plunge myself into the work of the day. There was stuff to do and having full undivided concentration was good. The paper mountain mess on my desk was attacked with some degree of enthusiasm and I was on my way to greatness. The morning began to roll. With what seemed to be my first glance at the corporate clock, lunch time was just approaching. Taking a momentary break, I stretched back in my chair and began to contemplate my options: a cheap lunch in the school cafeteria, a trip to the pizza place (which was on my Monday and Friday schedules) or perhaps the takeout at the Chinese restaurant. Sometimes critical decisions can be delightful. It was just passed 10:30 in the morning. Even at that hour, I found myself leaning toward my third option. However, their luncheon menu was extensive. Chicken, pork or shrimp, what would be best an hour from now? This potentially could be my most important long-term decision of the week. I was getting excited about my menu choices and reveling in the joys of the simple life, financed, in good part, by Mr. Brown and my excellent football picks. Life felt good.

My feelings of well being were slightly dampened with the late morning arrival of Rigatoni, who lumbered into the office. He was all smiles as all the office staff bid him a jolly good morning. This was in contrast to my more reserved response. He went into his office, leaving the door opened. The office buzz died down. I went back to my work, while simultaneously contemplating my lunch options. Things were seemingly going back to an even keel, although the open office door was a distraction to me, like a buzzing fly. Mind over matter. If I focused and immersed myself into my work, all distractions would be meaningless. This began to work and lasted for about several minutes until Ferucci came in and summoned me. "We have a meeting with the president."

"When?" I asked.

"Right now! It's not good to keep the president waiting." Yea, I thought to myself, this is the guy who would be late to his own funeral but everybody else has to jump to keep him happy. Yea! I asked Ferucci if I needed a note pad and I got the standard response that he always took a note pad because everything Rigatoni said was important. This was beginning to spoil my lunch date with myself.

We dutifully trundled into the office. If the agency still had a cleaning service, the presidential office was not affected or it was off limits. Whatever the reason, there was no changes from the last time we entered this sanctum sanctorum. Even the trash basket was overflowing and looking like a volcano but this time spewing crushed up balls of white paper. Rigatoni gave us a smile and bid us to sit down. This part was always a challenge and an adventure, and today was no different. After a few seconds of uncomfortable fumbling and moving office debris, we both took our usual seats, Ferucci on the right and me on the left. I looked up and saw that the blinds were more opened than normal, letting the late morning light in. Was this some kind of omen? Given the early nature of the meeting, something had to be up. Rigatoni began with giving us his politically correct smile, a nod of the head and began with his customary clearing of the throat. That gave way to the introductory small talk of insincerely inquiring our respective weekends were, how work was going and whether we had anything of an exceptional nature that we wanted to share. Like bumps on a log, neither of us could admit to the exceptional. That provided Rigatoni the opportunity to get up to speed and take charge completely. "You are probably wondering why I called you in this morning," he said. I immediately had three quick thoughts but if I shared them out loud, any one of the three would have lead to my immediate termination. "For some time," he continued, "there has been a need for a development assistant." He looked directly at me when he said this. "And today we are going to meet the individual who has decided to accept this position from the agency. We will do this over lunch. We'll depart around twelvish, if neither of you have anything more important on your schedules." (A sucker question: What could be more important that a business lunch with the president?) There goes my Chinese lunch as the law of balances struck again. My own personal quiet of a Chinese lunch special was being compromised by a compromised but free lunch on the agency. Such is life in the business world, I guess! Rigatoni was in control; he called the meeting, selected the candidate, would drive to the appointed restaurant and would have the event expense billed to an agency account. Despite all, I promised myself that I would enjoy the free food. Maybe the candidate for the new position would be good too.

We left the agency just after noon. The power alignment was such that Ferucci drove the company vehicle, a mini-van, while Rigatoni pontificated in the front passenger seat. Throughout my long history with the agency, I would never be asked to drive, although I had a big BMW, nor would I be asked to sit in the front seat, unless I was the only passenger. On paper, the trip was a short one, some 15 minutes or less to Perth Amboy, to a Portuguese restaurant. It seemed much longer, though, since in the bucket seated chair of authority reviewed agency history and events of the past month. Not that it was overbearing but if it weren't for the prospect of a free meal and finally meeting someone who would assist in the difficult and thankless task of raising monies to benefit handicapped kids, I would have jumped from a moving vehicle. Cowardice being the better part of valor, I stoically remained in the back seat nodding and grunting to affirm all of Rigatoni's salient points and observations. Just as I was about grunted out, we arrived right in front of the restaurant. Ferucci had that careless abandon of an Italian race car driver, but he never got into an accident. Parking was a tight squeeze. It wasn't Ferucci's car so he could bang a few fenders to the front and back. "Who's to know, who's to complain," he would say again as we departed the vehicle and went in. Rigatoni was first out of the van and into the restaurant where he got the attention of the wait staff. He requested a table in a quiet corner so that he could discuss agency business. All agreed, we marched to the rear and took our seats. The candidate was not there, so we all ordered cocktails to alleviate the stress and anxiety of waiting. Rigatoni ordered a Bloody Mary, while Ferucci and I followed with, what else, a glass of the (cheap) house red. Delivery came quickly since the restaurant was not that crowded. The initial sip of wine tasted good. However, the law of balances began to take effect again as Rigatoni began talking about the individual who was selected to come on board and his justification for the hire. The more he talked, the more the ominous cloud of disappointment began to gather on the horizon. I took another sip of wine and began wishing for an entire carafe. I knew of this individual and she had no experience in raising monies for anything. She was some kind of administrator for a local politician who had connections to the agency. The future looked distressing. I wasn't getting the help that I thought I needed. I was getting schmoozed. I took another sip to dull the pain. But there was one principal of survival in corporate America that applies equally to a nonprofit. Never show up your supervisors in anything, even in social drinking. I wanted more wine but my survivalist instincts prevailed. I gauged my level of remaining wine to Ferucci's. Loose lips sink ships, it is said, and careers as well. Before I could get further depressed, she came in, Astrid Kosnowski, the local township administrator. We all got up and greeted each other with that artificial, forced smile that social decorum demands. Seated, she ordered a club soda and Rigatoni took control of the meeting. Everything on and off the menu was his choice.

The ensuing conversation took on the spectra of a ping pong match — a lot of back and forth but I lost interest in the outcome even before the sparring began. Kosnowski evidently could schmooze as well as Rigatoni could rap, so at least there was the beginning of a sympathetic relationship between them. Most of their conversation dwelt upon elected officials and the political climate within central New Jersey, but not upon raising money or public relations. I feigned interest, while my attention was focused upon the amount of wine left in Ferucci's glass. More wine would be especially welcomed to drown out the talk of politics and back room intrigue. I always had a problem with anyone seeking public life and approval at the expense of compromise. I would have preferred to be compromised by another glass of wine in private. This was not to be today since the waiter came and recited the menu options and specials. The most amazing thing was that the waiter did all this from memory and took our orders without writing anything down. What was even more amazing was that I didn't remember where Ferucci parked the company car. The one glass of wine was taking me over. All I remember was that I ordered exactly what Ferucci ordered. That way I could not get into trouble by ordered an expensive item like a very thick steak or twin lobster tail or something more exotic like the super chef special of the day. In short time our food did come and the order was correct for all four of us. The waiter got it right; I don't know how. The down side was that I had to go through the entire event on one glass of wine since Ferucci did not order a second. I was almost sure that a second glass of wine would have made the meal better and the present company more appealing. I made up the discrepancy with the dessert; it was a calculated risk. I went big time. I ordered a frothy cappuccino, not just a plain coffee. I figured that if it were non-alcoholic, they couldn't find fault and complain. I do like coffee in all its many shapes, forms and manifestations. Notwithstanding that a second glass of wine would have made the entire situation much better, I did order a cappuccino. Under the circumstances it was like kissing your sister, but sometimes you have to roll with the family punches.

Kosnowski threw us plastic verbal bouquets as she left. She had to attend to some kind of important business or something or other. We all got a smile, hug and some kind of word of endearment. I was never a warm and fuzzy person so this was a kind of an Emily Post breach or something. I always considered boundaries as good. If Robert Frost thought fences made good neighbors, then who was I to argue? I put my reservations on the back burner for the time being. Rigatoni picked up the check from the waiter and reached for the company credit card. He was glowing. He thought his introduction of a new member for the executive team was a success and he did not have to personally pick up the bill for the lunch. The agency would be billed. But nothing comes free, as daddy told me oft times. The trip back to the center was a lecture on wheels. Rigatoni repeatedly listed the virtues and the perceived strong points of his choice. Ferucci asked polite questions, seemingly to acquiesce to this decision which was in all reality and finality made in stone. I said nothing since nothing that I would say would make any difference except to annoy Rigatoni. Never try to teach a pig to sing; it wastes your time and annoys the pig, as the saying goes. I was in the beginning stages of learning this life's lesson that hitting your head against a stone wall doesn't crumble the stone wall, it just gives you a headache.

As we were approaching the center — this was after everything was signed, sealed and delivered — Rigatoni asked me what I thought about the new development assistant, as perhaps kind of an afterthought or probably more of an affirmation of his excellent decision making. Not wanting to be dishonest, but also knowing that honesty is never the best policy with your employer, I used the word "interesting." "She's not quite what I expected, to be honest." Rigatoni took this as a compliment for his selection and proceeded to lecture about how important it was, especially for administrative and executive types, not to think within the box. "I got where I am today by thinking outside the box, et cetera, et cetera". As we pulled into the driveway, he asked how things were proceeding for the coming holidays. "Were there any good things coming from development?"

"Yes," I quickly responded. "We have one or two cash donations coming in as well as multiple sources of in-kind donations of clothing and toys for the kids. Notably, AT&T's 'Pick an Angel' program looks like it's been super successful this year. That's the result of a meeting I attended a couple of weeks ago in Basking Ridge to help set up this event." I had to tell him that since he thought that just sitting in an office, waiting by the phone with some kind of title, would be enough to have gifts and donations coming in. Rigatoni responded by saying that "I'd rather have money for the agency programs. That would make a better difference." I could not let my hard work and appreciation of the Christmas season go totally slandered and said, "People decided to give what they wanted to give." Rigatoni grimaced. Apparently he was not happy with my response, but I was saved at this point when Ferucci chimed in, "How is the hunt for a substitute Santa Claus coming?" That took me by surprise since I was preoccupied thinking about more important other stuff. I lied when I said, "It's coming along. I have a couple of leads." Actually, I did not give any thought to this added burden. Why should I worry? There just had to be some poor soul, some social service group wanting to do a good deed at this time of year, some senior citizen group somewhere with nothing to do but with the mission to provide me with a retiree who wanted to feel good and be Santa for one day and be the center of attraction for a party for handicapped kids. I just could image the scenario: a bus load of senior citizens arriving at the center and taking turns playing Santa because a few minutes of work would be too much for one octogenarian. This could be the easiest addition to my increasing work load, getting a Santa, a run-down Santa, any kind of Santa, on short notice. Who would notice? Would the kids notice? So I wasn't too committed to this Mickey Mouse assignment, then or now. So what!

The entourage in the van got back to the center just before two. We got in just as the ladies of the office staff were getting back from their lunch and another soap opera chapter. Ferucci enthusiastically quizzed them about the opera's suggestive racy events that he missed and if Alice or somebody was getting back with Ted or somebody. He knew the plot as well as if he wrote the script himself. The ladies loved him for it. I couldn't care less, especially given the previous hour or two, I lost my enthusiasm for almost anything nonsensical. Ideally, I wanted a tall blonde with some experience in delightfully wheedling money from old, fuddy-duddy donors. This was not to be. Astrid was neither tall, nor blonde nor experienced as a fund raiser. She was a city administrator who rubbed elbows with politicos and handed out paychecks on alternate Fridays. Somehow the law of balances stopped working at lunch time after one glass of wine.

Stoically I went back to my desk and pulled out the yellow pages, just to see if there were any listings of agencies under the generic category of social services. There were lots. I also found a couple of local party stores just in case I needed a uniform. I grimaced and put the yellow pages back. The Santa Claus assignment seemed easy enough but I put the yellow pages away since I had more immediate needs. December always proceeds with the speed of an express train and in all the activity I forgot to tell Ferucci that I needed a company van for next week. I had an appointment at AT&T's headquarters in Bedminster to pick up a truck load of presents for the kids. The "Pick an Angel" program was a success, again — thank you very much — this year and I needed something larger than my BMW to make the pick up in just one run. Bedminster was over 40 minutes driving time, one way, and I could not envision myself running up and down all day, although that would have been a good excuse to get out of the office and kill a day. Any other time of the year when it was less hectic and I would have taken the day off. But December was different. So, with all the fortitude I could muster, I got up and went to the office Mr. Coffee machine for a half a cup of caffeine and get the necessary vitamins and minerals and resolve to face Ferucci.

The coffee, even diluted with a generous dose of milk, tasted especially bad since I still had the memory of the cappuccino from the restaurant. Strong the agency coffee was but I needed it to face Ferucci. Two sips were more than enough as I placed the mug down on my desk and went out of the administrative office and down the hall to his office. The door was opened, but I knocked anyway. He was on an unimportant phone call to a family member and gestured for me to come in. He hung up on his eldest brother but wasn't too upset. "That was my brother John who wants to change some of the plans for the upcoming holiday. Why can't he and his wife get their act together, and why am I the go-between in the family? And as my life isn't difficult enough, what is your problem?"

You could never be sure with Ferucci whether he was completely serious, or if this phone call with all its attendant problems just added to his sense of cantankerous humor or puffed up importance. One thing for sure: he loved his family. Maybe the accounts of family intrigue just added to the overall mythos. I kind of got the feeling that he slightly exaggerated all accounts of his family dealings. It certainly sounded interesting, this large cast of characters who were not singularly inter-esting of and in themselves to be made into a daytime soap opera. It certainly spiced up his life exceedingly well. More often than not, after these phone calls he was usually in a good frame of mind. The present situation looked like good news for me.

Standing, I made my request for the company van. "I have to go AT&T in Bedminster to pick up a large order of presents for the kids. I was told that there was so much that I could not make it in one trip. So . . . ."

Ferucci paused for a moment and said, "You should have told me sooner. Everything is tight for Friday. Why do you wait to tell me at the last minute? You think I am a miracle worker? Why do you always do things the last minute? Plan better; this is a multi-million dollar agency that I have to run!"

"But I just got word their official word this morning. I didn't want to disrupt or upstage Rigatoni's lunch extravaganza."

With a slight smile almost breaking on his face, Ferucci bade me sit down, picked up the phone and got Billy on the line in the maintenance office. After a brief exchange, he hung up and looked at me and said, "It's done!" I was going to have Billy drive me in the company van all the way to Bedminster and back. This was great. Not only would someone else do the driving and help with the loading, but I could badger him about the upcoming week in football. A chauffer that would pay me, I relished the thought!

"By the way, how is the hunt for a Santa coming? The kids' party is next week. You have eight days." I looked at him straight in the eye and said, "It's coming well. I'll have something definitive for you by Friday afternoon."

"Good," Ferucci said. "Then it's a done deal."

I got back to my desk feeling good about myself and the strategic victory over Ferucci. I even treated myself to more agency coffee. It's a hard phenomenon to explain, but as the day wears down, the coffee got even more offensive to the taste buds. Awful wasn't the best word. But I needed a drink to celebrate my small victory. Getting back to my desk I pulled out the phone directory and started thumbing through the yellow page portion looking again for social service agencies in my hunt for Santa Claus. Immersed in my work I was not aware of Rigatoni behind me. When he cleared his throat in his idiosyncratic manner, I nearly jumped out of my chair. I felt bushwhacked. He wasn't smiling as I came down to earth. "I forgot to mention it to you in the car, but I think I asked you when I got back from vacation, that I needed your list of addresses so I can send agency holiday cards. I'm still waiting."

"Sorry, but I don't recall your request for any lists."

"I shouldn't have to ask you by now; you should know the drill. I'll be in my office." With that he turned away, and I put the yellow pages aside, so much for finding the ersatz Santa for now. Turning toward the computer, I began going though those individuals, groups and organizations that provided me with support during the past year. I included everyone I thought important, save those very personal connections to me. I wanted to spare them from Rigatoni's privacy invasiveness.

I wasted more than an hour on this tedious assignment. When the list was completed — some eight pages with names, titles and addresses — I gingerly went to Rigatoni's opened door, meekly knocked and went it to present my good work. He looked at me and the paperwork, pointed to a vacant spot on his desk and said, "Just leave it here." No thank you or anything, just leave it here. Thank you very much. I did and quietly left. Going back to my desk I retrieved the yellow pages and started looking again at the listing of agencies and organizations that could possibly provide me with a Santa on short notice. I paper clipped those pages that I thought had the potential for great leads and then put the book away with a firm resolve to begin in earnest on Thursday morning — this time for sure! The rest of the day dragged on like a nun teaching religion class to public school students after regular school hours. Stillness hovered over the office the entire afternoon. I didn't mind that. When five came I left promptly. The agency never gave rewards for heroic duties after hours, or for work during normal hours for that matter. I drove home on 287 into a sunset-less, dismal gray sky. But things brightened considerably when I got home and was greeted by Kiki who had many meows to tell me about her day. The irony is that a cat was more comforting than the entire work office. The evening concluded with me conking out on the couch after dinner with Kiki along side me purring quietly. I dozed off between nondescript TV shows, planning my next move the next day at the office.

Another gray sky greeted me through the east window as I arose Thursday morning. Kiki was lightly sleeping on the far side of the bed and I arose gingerly as to not disturb her comfort. I quietly got cleaned up, dressed and proceeded downstairs to have a solitary breakfast. After, I went to the rocking chair to read. I did not have to be at work on time this morning since I had to make a stop on the way for more Christmas presents for the kids. I didn't tell Ferucci that I would be late. My best strategic plan was to let him rant and rave until he got a stroke and then I would pull the rug out from under him, after he contracted his self-induced medical malady, and start piling presents and his desk and disrupting the order in his office and in his life. If he didn't die of a stroke on the spot, then embarrassment would do him in. It was a good plan that filled me with the smirk of anticipatory pleasure. Just about as I was getting ready to leave, Kiki came down the stairs and proceeded to a spot in the living room to stare at me. She stayed there for a few seconds and then proceeded to the kitchen for her expected morning meal. Weak person that I am, I complied and thereafter left the house to proceed, via the long route, to work but wearing a smile all the time in joyful anticipation of my impeding victory over Ferucci. Life may be good if you have a well executed plan. Today felt pretty good.

The long and winding road took me to Rutgers Prep. The Delaware and Raritan Canal and the Raritan River ran through the school's back yard. Aesthetically, the campus and the school was a pleasing place to visit and I did not mind waiting in the school's atrium to be announced. For a short time that I waited, a small, steady trickle of students and staff passed by, some giving me a quick, curious glance. I was saved by the arrival of a jovial Judy. She asked if I were waiting a long time and then asked if I could follow her out of the building to her car to pick up the stuff she had. She pointed to where her Toyota was parked and thought it would be a good idea if I could bring my car next to hers; it would make the exchange easier. It was. There were several packages, all nicely wrapped. With the last one, the biggest, Judy said that she and Harriet were touched by my story of one of the kids coming to school without a jacket or coat, even in cold weather. She then took it upon themselves

85

to go to Nordstrom's and take care of the problem. They left the receipt inside, just in case it had to be exchanged for a more correct size. Maybe I laid it on too thick. I like fleecing people out of their money, but just small amounts. I guess I had more of an affinity to pickpockets than bank robbers. These gifts were most generous. With that I thanked her and went on my way back to work. But driving on 287, temptation began to get the best of me. Straight in to work or Lucca's for needed coffee? As I wrestled with this ethical dilemma for about 30 seconds I came to the selfish conclusion that the victory of a car load of good presents certainly merited a mild celebration of sorts. Lucca's it was. I would waste only a few more minutes; how scrupulous could you get?

With some degree of guilt because of an excessive parochial background, I arrived at Lucca's. Parking was not a problem since the pre-work morning rush hour was long over. Although no salted bagel was available, the baguette was very acceptable. Service and seating were not problems either. Peace and quiet along with several morning newspapers that were left behind, his would put anyone in a good frame of mind. And a car load of pretty good presents for the kids. Somedays I am better than good; I'm very good. After some short minutes of wallowing in my victory, and eating all of the baguette so there would be no evidence that I did indeed stop on the way in, I departed the coffee shop while depositing a quarter tip to the attendant on the way out. Got to the car and proceeded to the center, arriving some time after ten. I quickly found Billy to fetch me a cart so I could bring all the gifts in on one trip. Since the side door was long locked, my grand entrance would be through the one of the front doors. Sometimes it's great to toot your own horn. Of course the cart that I got was the wrong type and size but I felt that a major production was in order. So I rolled the loaded cart around the building, up the walk, through the doors and into Ferucci's office. I knocked before entering and before hearing any response proceeded to roll in just as three precariously placed top packages came down. "Where do you want these?" I asked as the packages came rolling to a halt on the floor.

"If this wasn't a respectable place, I'd tell you what to do with the lot of them. As it is, get them out of my office. They belong with the social worker. You should know better."

I did know better. But this intrusion into Ferucci's privacy because of the success of working for the common good was a double victory. The annoyance had to force him to recognize that at least on some occasions, I was doing OK. I stacked the cart, offered Ferucci a phony apology for not knowing better and proceeded to roll down the hall. I gingerly wheeled around the corner and almost ran Miss Janet over. This near accident had the potential of being turned into my favor if I played my cards right. Since chance encounters are usually of short duration, I immediately began tooting my own horn in a semi-subtle way. I peered out over the top of the cart (leered would be just as appropriate) and exclaimed in a very triumphant, jolly tone, "Just look at all these wonderful presents for the kids? Aren't people just wonderful during this time of year!"

Janet must have been impressed because she even smiled. This was a good sign. Then she spoke and the law of balances took over. "These kids deserve everything they can get. But last year, the holidays were really depressing. I don't want a repeat this year."

"If there is anything you want to talk about, just let me know."

"Sometimes it's just too much." With that comment, the smile left her and she turned and walked that walk down the hall. Why is it the better looking the woman, the more baggage? Dumbfounded, I rolled the teeter-tottering cart down the hall and into the social worker's office. There Maria gratefully accepted them and was especially delighted to hear of a new winter coat, among other things, for one of the kids. She smiled and it was genuine. I turned and went out of the office. The cart was left in the hall for Billy to pick up when he had a chance. I went to my desk and after taking some time to settle in, pulled out the yellow pages for my hunt for Santa Claus. It was well after 10:30 and I scheduled my lunch hour for 12, so this gave me about one hour and a half. Getting a Santa should not be a problem since there were lists and lists of agencies for social services, clubs and the like in the book. I was no longer concerned with the law of balances but the law of averages. I just needed one score before lunch. With over 50 entries in the book, if I couldn't get just one hit before lunch I must be pretty bad. So to celebrate my victory even before the battle begun, I arose and treated myself to a half-cup of the agency's coffee. I winced at the first sip. That one sip was enough to get me going.

I did not start my quest alphabetically but went immediately to those groups that were comprised of senior citizens. I methodically made a check in the yellow pages for those that did not answer the phone at 10:45 in the morning. Those that I did get seemed either lethargic, confused or angry. "Our members are too old to drive." Or "We serve only the older members of our community." Or "We have barely enough money to provide for our own members Christmas party." Collectively, in disturbing their equilibrium I was able to deduce that they were social groups only and would cater to the old, local and burnt out farts of the community, and had no intention or desire to look beyond their momentary festivities. Under my breath I wished them all a lump of coal that would burn along with them where they deserved to go. Imagine, turning down kids at Christmas because it just wasn't convenient or would require a little effort to take them beyond their collective limitations. This initial round put me into a feisty frame of mind and made me all the more dedicated to getting a Santa, any Santa, for the holiday party. I refused to be deterred. I needed more agency coffee. So I got up and got another half cup full. I was so god-awful that I made a face that the office staff picked up on. And the comments followed, all unappreciated by me. "What's the matter, our coffee isn't good enough for you." To which I snapped, "Not today it isn't."

So I went back to the yellow pages and branched out to other social service groups, like the Elks, Knights of Columbus and Masons. Although the clock was approaching 11 a.m., more than half did not answer the phone. I came to the gradual realization that the members were probably still in bed or working at their normal jobs at Walmart or school crossings and would become available only in the evening. I began making notes to call these missed groups at night from my home.

I did get one Elks group, out of the county, which was kind of nice. The unnamed individual who answered the phone, he was probably the bar tender or custodian, listened patiently to my appeal. After he listened politely to my scripted spiel, he asked me to consider making a donation to his lodge so they could have an even better party for their constituents. I didn't know whether to get angry or laugh. All I did know that I was on the express train to nowhere. Some 25 to 30 calls made and nothing to show for it except two cups of sampling the world's worst coffee. The prospect of having lunch without a victory was not inspiring either. Just then I looked up and saw Ferucci standing over my desk. He immediately noted my distress look and asked what was the matter. "The agency coffee, notwithstanding, I've gotten nowhere with this Santa Claus project that you saddled me with. I can't get a Santa for the kids."

"You put everything off until the last minute. You should have started much sooner." With that admonition, Ferucci began to turn and walk away.

"Do I have the van for tomorrow?" I tried to mitigate the effects of the impending Santa failure.

"I've got you covered again," he said as he walked out the door. This is what I needed, more knee-jerk, scripted responses.

I made a list of those organizations that I could not contact by phone, with the intent of calling them in the evening from my home. There were around eight. Putting both yellow pages and lists aside, I left my desk and went to the other side of the building to get a cheap dollar lunch, the leftovers after the school kids had theirs. Normally I would go out of the building but the disappointment of not getting one interested party to play Santa to these kids had me down. What's wrong with people anyway? The good news/bad news was that there was plenty of food left over, but it was macaroni and cheese, with a side of very soggy salad. The macaroni looked good on the plate but lacked any semblance of taste. It had to be heavily salted and even that did not help since it tasted more like salt. I felt like a prisoner in a concentration camp. But that was OK since the meal matched my emotional state, which was flat as flat could be. I ate the macaroni, tasted the salt but not the cheese, slithered down the salad, and left to spend the remainder of my lunch hour reading a book in the atrium and trying to collect my composure and thoughts, and devise a new plan of action to acquire a Santa. I parked myself in one of the atrium's corners and began to read ever so slowly, trying to catch my emotional breath between pages. As I looked up between turning the pages and regaining my composure I was aware of a small but steady stream of individuals moving through the building: kids, therapists, teachers, custodial staff, delivery persons and the like. I felt more like an observer watching a film than an actual participant in the agency's daily life and activities. Toward the end of my reading lunch break, Miss Janet trotted around the corner in her unique, inimitable style. She stopped, smiled and inquired about the book I was reading or something. At this moment I was too withdrawn to enter into prattle with her. I guess that was the irony of the entire situation with her. When you wanted to get to the next base, she wasn't there, and when she wanted to get more engaging, you couldn't care less. Was this another variation in the law of balances? Thus she went on her way and when I finished another chapter, I closed the book and slowly shuffled back to my desk to attempt to find a Sucker Claus, AKA Santa Claus, for the upcoming Christmas party. As I got to my desk the office ladies were just leaving for their lunch break, so I could expect at least a quiet hour to sulk and execute my next planned move.

I took out the yellow pages again and started looking for other clubs, groups, social agencies or anything that could fall out of the classification system of the directory. I looked under children, kids and even parties. Under this last grouping I found the name and number of a party store on Route 1 that I used once in the past to purchase some Halloween stuff. I called and went through a thorough but brief spiel on who I was and what I wanted. Their reply was that I could rent a Santa suit for about $600 and play the old man himself. I did raise my voice a little: "Six hundred dollars to rent a Santa suit for one day for a party that would benefit handicapped kids?" The voice on the other end responded in a matter of fact manner that "It's the time of year and it drives up prices because everyone wants to play Santa. But you'd better hurry up since the bookings are very tight and you may not get the costume for the day you want." "I'll see," I responded and practically slammed the receiver down. In the quiet of the office the sound of my dismay echoed off the walls, perhaps making it much louder than it actually was. I proceeded to make a note of the $600 fee and began to mutter something or other as I shook my head in disbelief. The quiet was broken again when Rigatoni cleared his throat right behind me. After my heart started beating again, I jumped a couple of feet off my chair, shocked to find this hulking presence about to mug me. With no apologies given, Rigatoni immediately went into this agenda about the Christmas cards. "I am about finished with writing my personal wishes for the holiday cards to all our benefactors, although I got the list late from you. Are there any cards that you would like to send to your people?"

"No, not really. I think that you covered everything."

With that he threw the list on my desk and asked me to check again, just in case someone he thought important was missed. "I didn't get where I am today without being thorough. No mistakes or bad surprises. Look over this list now and we should be finished by this afternoon." With that he went back into his office and closed the door. Diverted from the Santa project, I cursorily went through the list again. I had little enthusiasm for holiday cards that had an inscription that offered the recipient to have a good year with the tacit implication that the agency would like to hear from them and their money next year, if not now. It had such a tacky, non-personal touch. Why would any agency care if I had a good year, unless it was to wheedle more money out of me? But comply I did, which necessitated putting the Santa search on hold for the remainder of the afternoon.

With half-hearted interest and little enthusiasm, I looked over Rigatoni's list and compared with to the entries on my computer database. The political reality was that if the list were to be handed back without any modifications or additions, then Rigatoni would accuse me of this, that and the other thing. So I did the politically expedient thing: I added two insignificant nonentities to the list. I threw this holiday curve ball back at Rigatoni. It was worth a modest smile. In addition, I did not immediately hand the list back; I waited until late in the day just to make it look like I was very diligent in doing this assignment. Thus near the end of the work day I timidly went to his door, meekly knocked and, after being officially permitted to enter, placed the paperwork on his desk. "Here's the list with two minor additions."

Rigatoni looked at the two additions, furled his forehead, and said, "It took you a long time just to come up with these two additional entries."

"I wanted to be thorough."

"I didn't see anything for my brother who made a sizeable contribution this past year."

"I never saw the letter coming in, nor did I write the follow up thank you."

"It's your job to ask. We're all family here in this agency."

"Sorry about that. I just didn't want to step on anyone's toes, especially when it comes to family." With that I left the office with the feeling that my curve ball took Rigatoni off guard. If he wanted his family members on the list, he should have put them on that months ago. Anyway, I thought that holiday cards from any business were kind of a waste of time since they sounded so phony. Be that as it may, I went back to my desk and wrapped up the activities for the day. I got my own list of clubs and groups that I would call from home that night. Contrary to opinion, my job occasionally went beyond the hours of 9 to 5. When five came, I did go home but I brought the hangover of an uncompleted assignment with me. Kiki was dutifully waiting for me. perched in the bay window and greeted me loudly, in the tone of asking "Where have you been all day?" After she was fed, I went for a four-plus mile jog, showered after and had a marginal dinner. All these things helped pass the time until I made that final telephone call from home that would eventually land me one Santa for the kid's party. Should I call at seven or wait until eight? Thinking this whole scenario out, and it killed me since there is an impulse in me that detests waiting, I concluded that the later time would be preferable since it would give club members a chance to settle in, have a few drinks or something, and settle their respective business before I disrupted their peace of mind. I had about a dozen listings, comprised largely of Elks and Knights of Columbus organizations. I buoyed my enthusiasm by telling myself that anyone should be able to get one right out of 12, like shooting fish in the proverbial barrel. At precisely one minute after eight, the campaign began, fortified with a cup of my own home brewed coffee in hand.

The Elks was the first group to get my call. For whatever reason, the bartender answered the phone. There was a lot of background noise — evidently a spirited discussion of some sort — and I had to repeat myself several times. Eventually the barkeep gave me the home number of one of the group's officers who handled this kind of community outreach.

When I dialed this number I got a pool room or bar or something of that sort. I hung up and redialed the Elks. Explaining my wrong connection scenario, I got another number, which I promptly dialed. I did get a residence, but the woman on the other end said that her husband was not at home but at the Elks or he should be there shortly. I placed this name and number on the back burner and moved on to the Knights of Columbus.

The agency had a pretty good rapport with a number of Knights councils since two board members claimed membership in that organization. With some notes to give me guidance for a smooth pitch, I dialed and waited and waited. No answer, another number for the back burner. So I dialed still another Knights council. I got a voice on the other end that sounded that he witnessed the first days of creation. Departing from my script I quickly stated my need. I was told that the council was comprised of older members who physically were not able to take on any additional community endeavors this year or the next year for that matter. So much for the board connections! As I progressed down my call list, the distances between the home base of the Knights councils and the school became greater and greater. When it approached the 30 mile range, I said good night to the Knights and returned back to the Elks listing.

The Elks seemed to be a more spirited group since most of my cold calls were picked up by someone tending or near the bar. And there was always some background noise, so I had to repeat myself loudly and slowly several times. There was another thread of commonality. More often than not I was reminded that the Elks did actively undertake their own initiatives which included special needs children and individuals. But good intentions and public pronouncements only go so far. It seemed that they had the same script: they've all been booked for this coming season and could not be expected to take on any additional assignments now. Their respective time and monies were all expended and accounted for. My plea for just one individual to be Santa for just one hour went was filed for consideration for the very distant future.

Distraught and desperate, I called back the first Knights of Columbus council and specifically requested to speak personally to the individual whose name I was given. After a pause since they must have been searching for this member in transit, he came to the phone. With mildly sweaty palms and a prep sheet in front of me, I began my pitch for his very special organization to provide a Santa for one hour. (I felt that I was back in high school unworthily asking the best looking cheerleader for a date.) My presentation was very good: clear, concise and a slight pull on the emotional heart strings. It must have been effective since there was a pause on the other end when I finished. Good, I must have made a hit! I did make a hit but not the one that I wanted. I was complemented on my presentation, my work for the agency, dedication for the kids, and on and on. After a momentary pause, the voice on the other end offered me a membership in his council. "We need a few good men like yourself." Stunned, I diplomatically concluded the conversation, not knowing whether to be flattered, annoyed or just plain distressed. All I knew was that the emotional high point of the evening left me flatter than a pancake chasing down the will-of-the-wisp.

I guess a dozen is not a lucky number. There were originally 12 disciples and collectively they did not turn out too great either individually or as a group. Maybe I should make one more phone call to break the jinx. But I exhausted the list that I brought home from work. There was nothing else to do but to reach into the fridge and bring out a 12 oz. bottle of beer to wash my troubles away. Since I was so unsuccessful, I could not really reward myself with an exceptional label. Instead I opened a can of the "No Frills" brand sold next to the local Pathmark. Actually, it wasn't so bad and on a night like this anything would be sufficient to assuage my disappointment. The evening concluded with some nondescript TV programs and a dalliance with a snifter of brandy.

This job with these stupid, nonessential assignments was driving me to drink. On this night, the drive was short! Everything unceremoniously ended several hours later with the evening's high point of going to bed somewhat early before 11. Kiki came up about five minutes later and we both snoozed into the morning with the hope that the new day would bring its blessings of good fortune and good stuff.

We both awoke the next morning to a sunrise that fought to get its precious rays of warmth and comfort through a thick cloud cover. So if the sunrise was a portent of things to come then today would be another fight to accomplish anything. But I took comfort in the fact that at least in the morning I would be on the road with Bill Brown and out of the office for half a day. This was most certainly a plus in my favor that the coming day could go my way. Thus, in measured time I dressed, took care of Kiki's breakfast needs and made my way to work, via Lucca's coffee oasis. Undeterred by the distractions while getting my coffee and baguette, I managed to make it through the agency's side doors on time. With no Miss Janet to distract me, and totally oblivious to the chatter of the ladies in the office, I took my desk, with coffee in hand, and shuffled some papers around on my desk. It didn't make much sense to start a project and then having to leave it to go on the road with Bill Brown. So, I played busy and enjoyed finishing my cup of good coffee in the process. But before I was able to finish, Mr. Brown ventured into the office area and asked: "When are we going?"

"Anytime that you are ready. Did you get clearance from Mr. Ferucci?"

"Then we're all set. Just let me tell him that we're going."

With that, I put on my coat, walked around to Ferucci's door, and after a polite knock, informed him that we were departing to Bedminster and points beyond. He muttered something or other, and Mr. Brown and I were on the way to the large van in the parking lot. "I need something big for all the presents," I said to Bill, but loud enough for Ferucci to hear it.

96

"Don't worry, I've got you covered. I got the biggest one the agency has." With that we walked out the west door, into the lot and got in to old number 52, an extended model with a bubble top that certainly could hold everything in one trip. As Bill put the key in the ignition and started the engine, a look of dismay fell across my face. "Bill," I said, "am I going to have to stand for this entire long trip?"

"No problem," he said, "I got you covered." As Bill was already at the speed limit, if not above, on Parsonage Road, he reached around and handed me a folding wooden chair.

"What in heaven's name am I supposed to do with this?"

"You sit on it, unless to prefer to stand."

Bill Brown must have taken driving lessons from Ferucci since neither observed posted speed limits. To make matters worse, the van had a red inspection reject sticker on the windshield. It groaned, rocked, swayed and everything else uncontrollable as Bill was moving down the highway. For wild man Bill Brown, the numbers that signaled the legal speed limit were thought of as only suggestions, like a waitress offering you the specials of the day. There is no obligation to follow any of that stuff. So too with Brown at the wheel. I sat on the wooden chair and held on to the thick metal bar in front of me for dear life. This seemed better than the alternative, which was standing all the way to Bedminster. I don't think that this was legal because I thought that all vehicle seats had to be permanently attached to the floor or something. But if something works, it works. I never thought that any vehicle could make that much racket moving down a highway without disintegrating in flight. The irony of the situation was that what would have taken me some 45 minutes in my BMW, observing legally posted speed limits, took Mr. Brown only 38. As we pulled into the AT&T parking lot, and my breathing began to return to normal, I asked Brown if he ever got a citation for speeding. He replied, "Yea, just once. Some bitch Edison cop gave me a ticket for doing 45 in a 25 mile zone. I told her that I worked for this nonprofit, handicapping agency, but she still gave me a ticket. She had no sympathy for a working man."

"But you were speeding."

"Signs, signs, who needs signs to distract 'm while they're driving? Don't need 'em!"

In the midst of that brief exchange of information we approached the security gate, got immediate clearance when I told them who I was, and proceed to the loading dock to meet the AT&T staff angels with their presents. They were awaiting me. They remembered me from the pizza dinner earlier in the year when this program was discussed and reams of paperwork handed out to match the giver's present to the child's need. Oh yes, I ate pizza like that was my last day on earth — pepperoni, mushrooms, plain — until I got almost sick. I did it for the kids! But they forgave me, and my stomach did too, as we loaded the van to capacity and beyond. Bill Brown was even impressed. I smiled and thanked the AT&T people profusely but it was sincere. I waved out the window with a "See you next year" as the sagging van rumbled away from the loading dock and banged its rear bumper on a speed bump. It felt good. As we proceeded down the highway, I gently reminded Bill to try to observe the legal speed limit because we were in no hurry to get back to the agency. Bill replied that I was in good hands and immediately hit 65 and beyond on the highway. The van rumbled, groaned and made noises that even a mechanic could not identify. The ride back was so bad that when we got back to the agency, I almost kissed the ground like the pope. I was going to rant and rave about Brown's driving to Ferucci when I got into the office, just for special affect. Scene making can be advantageous. But when I got into the hall, there was my desk on dollies. They were moving me out! Was I getting fired, despite the big haul of presents for the kids? So I did what any normal person would normally do in this time of crisis, I went storming into Ferucci's office. One knock, and without waiting to be admitted, I went flying in. He was unperturbed by my grand entrance, and he just may have been slightly amused by my apparent discomfort.

"What's going on in this place? I leave the office for little over an hour and you're moving me out?"

My unhinged emotional state evidently pleased Ferucci since he was suppressing a slight smile. "You have a new office and a new room mate. Astrid Kosnowski is starting Monday and you two will share the same office. Any other questions?"

Ferucci had gone two up on me: he had inside knowledge and knew that I was somewhat rattled with this unannounced move. Quickly I changed the subject as I quietly tried to regain some of my composure. I asked a question that we both knew the answer to. "I got a van load of presents for the kids. Where do you what the stuff delivered?"

"Give it to the social workers and they will match up the presents to the kids for the holiday party next week."

"What about my desk or lack thereof? I can't work in the hallway."

"Take an early and long lunch and you should be ready to go in the afternoon."

"But where is my new office?"

"The boys in maintenance are cleaning out the storage room next to the boiler room."

"The storage room in the back of the building? Is that an executive location?"

"Now it is. There is even a window. And with a little TLC and creativity, the place could look great. I know that you're not good at home decorating, but perhaps your new roommate can give you some pointers . . . if you are paying attention. Have a great lunch and be ready to go at one."

In the mist of scoring a barrage of zingers with machine gun accuracy, I was dismissed and kind of lost and homeless for the interim. The agency was making decisions affecting me without even consulting and advising me in advance. Was I a family member that was assumed to go with the flow, or merely a lowly pawn in some kind of comic, low-grade chess game? So I met Bill Brown waiting for me outside the office and instructed him to take all the stuff out of the van and deliver everything to the social workers. I also added the question, "Did you know I was being moved?"

"Yea, Ferucci mentioned something to us but I didn't think it was a big deal. Look on the bright side, you will now be closer to the men in maintenance and we can discuss sports and other stuff on company time."

Under my breath I said something like "Great!" "And I wonder if I needed a black seal engineering license in case the furnace broke down." I put on my coat, again, and started thinking about lunch. On the way out I almost ran over Miss Janet who asked what was wrong. I mumbled something to the effect that you couldn't take care of it anyway. With a strange look on her face, I bolted down the hall and took shelter at Menlo Mall to kill some time as my desk, and my future at the agency, was being wheeled away down the hall by the custodial department.

The hour and a half spent in the mall felt like a year and a half. Most normal people would welcome spending time shopping, on the company clock, during the Christmas season. But this was not enjoyable. I don't remember where or what I had for lunch but I do remember taking three full trips around the mall shops looking into all the windows. I lacked the spark of holiday imagination to look beyond the window displays to dream how the respective items would perfect for me. As my watch approached one, zombie-like I began the journey to my car to return to the crucible that would now and forever be termed "my office." You would think that after that massive haul of presents for the kids I would be lauded. No, I was being moved out, without any forewarning or advisement or consultation or anything. Maybe I should be looking for another job.

Upon my return I immediately went to Ferucci's office. He told me my new office was ready and that he would drop in after his lunch to see how I was doing. I made my way down the hall. The last time I walked anywhere with this kind of feeling was when I was in the Little League and the coach came to the mound and replaced me with another pitcher. You can't cry or anything like that; you just have to carry the burden, inside and alone. So I did. But it was starting to seem that I was methodically working my way down the ladder of success — next to the boiler room, with one window, and a roommate coming that I had no part in choosing. I tried to comfort myself with the thought that arranged marriages most often were successful, especially in India and China. This was New Jersey. Small comfort!

As I got into the monastic cell, the first thing I noticed was that there was no place to hang my coat. So I threw it on top of the file cabinet. The next thing I did was to go to the window and see what kind of view I had; it wasn't much. The window was not even at eye level, unless you were seven-foot tall. I couldn't see anything from my desk. To make matters worse, things were kind of jammed in there so the possibility of moving a large, clunky, metal desk for any kind of view was next to none. Like a prisoner, I went to my old desk in the new space and got my disorder out from the boxes to be placed on top of the desk or in the drawers. It would take about an hour to get comfortably in the flow of corporate confusion again. Methodically, my stuff began to be returned to its respective place of origin, but in the process it seemed that it kind of multiplied and reproduced itself while being rolled down the hall. I collected more superfluous stuff than I knew I had; some stuff just may have to be discarded. Each empty box was placed in the hallway, marking my arrival unto the new territory. But there were no visitors. I was quite alone, in exile, lord of my own little empire. I was Lord of the Kingdom of Empty Boxes.

When the last box was emptied, I mindlessly began to shuffle papers. From on top of the desk into the desk drawers and back again, paperwork was flying around. Needless to say, my spirits were sagging, close to rock bottom. And three more hours of this monotony until five. Would the afterlife be like this?

After moping around mindlessly for another couple of minutes, it seemed like hours, I glanced up and saw Ferucci standing in front of me. Coming in as quite as a snake, he scared the daylights out of me that I jumped about two feet out of my chair. Because of the slight smirk on his kisser I suggested that "It would be nice to knock sometimes."

"I didn't want to distract you from those few moments when you do some actual work. But I really came by to see how you were settling and adjusting to your new, private office suite."

When I was first hired, they promised me an office. Unfortunately, I was getting one now but with corporate strings attached. I couldn't resist, "I think the best term is semi-private with limited views."

Ferucci smiled and said, "At least you're moving up." With that he was about to depart, when he acted like something from a Columbo episode, he turned around and said, "Who did you get to be Santa for next week's holiday party?"

"Uh, I am encountering a severe problem with that one. I meant to tell you about that. I made about 50 to 60 calls, and the only thing that I accomplished was getting a personal invitation to join two groups, which I don't want to do. And the party store was going to charge some $600 for a costume rental since it is the season."

Ferucci, not too comforted by my excuse for failure, said, "You had over a month to go out and get just one body to play Santa, and you dropped the ball. So guess what? Since you could not get a Santa, you will be Santa next week. I'll talk to Henri and get his Santa suit. Just make it a point to be here on time, for once, next Friday for the kids' party." With that, he walked out the door and down the hall.

So, I was going to be Santa for a day. Great! Somewhere there must be a job description wherein it would absolutely forbid anyone from being enticed or coerced into embarrassing situations. Honestly, at this late point in my career, I don't ever recall ever seeing a description of my duties and functions. So here I go again, another imposition and embarrassment and whatever else! Santa for an agonizing hour? I consoled myself with the thought that it was for the kids, so it would be alright, somehow, and I would be in costume so no one would ever notice that I was making a fool out of myself. I went back to work, dispiritedly trying to kill time by shuffling papers from the drawers to the top of the desk and back to the drawers. What seemed like an hour took only a few measly minutes. In frustration, I got up from the chair, walked around the cell of an office, stretched, and then sat down. I stared and stared at the papers on my desk. Unlike Kreskin, they did not even stare back. They just were there. Nothing moved, not even an inch. I began to feel like Bartleby the Scrivener; in fact, I was becoming Bartleby. Even that dark knowledge did not change anything. I just stared at the paperwork and then the wall. The energy level and the enthusiasm level was about zero. Some more minutes of nothing. I decided that perhaps a cup of coffee would change the situation. So I got up and made my way to the secretarial office, which was just around the corner. Went up the ramp and saw them there, typing away on their respective computers doing all sorts of reports. The state required copious amounts of paperwork for each special needs kid, so the agency complied. The ladies were typing so furiously that the place sounded more like a garment manufacturing shop than an office. Quietly, with cup in hand, I made my way to their coffee machine. With my luck, it was empty. Flo looked up from her typing and noticed my distress. "We ran out about a half hour ago. Do you need some more?"

"Thanks but I was just killing some time." With that I went back to my cell with only a cup of water, hoping that it would do the trick.

It didn't. There still seemed to be a lock on the clock. It was frozen in perpetual purgatorial afternoon. The only apparent way of getting out of this morass was to undertake some work related task. So I began searching my computer data bank for a willing source to approach and ask for money. I searched up and then down and then all around. I finally came upon one improbable listing. So I had nothing to loose by sending them a canned proposal. Maybe that would do it and kill the remainder of the afternoon. Thus I began my semi-diligent preparations, almost pleased with myself since I kind of found an answer to my afternoon dilemma, when there was a knock on my door. It was Flo from the secretarial office. "I made a pot of coffee."

"You shouldn't have done it on my account."

"It was no problem at all. We were out anyway and you reminded me."

"Thank you for thinking of me. I'll be right up."

I didn't need much encouragement to remove from the cell. Now I knew why there were prison breaks. And the prisoners did not shuffle out; they ran. Now I knew.

Triumphant, I marched to the secretarial office with cup in hand to sample their best. The good news/bad news was that it was better than Ferucci's coffee, but not by much. It still paled in comparison to Lucca's. But the thought and effort was better than any saccharine sweetener. It was appreciated on this particular afternoon.

I returned to the cell with a slight smile on my face. At least some of the office staff liked me. I savored every sip of that coffee. After that, I returned to my work, but this did not last long when Flo knocked again on my door.

"I didn't want to bother the main office, but there is someone in the lobby who wants to speak to someone here about the holiday party. Could I bring him in to see you?"

"Sure," I said. This distraction would most definitely make the day go by faster and get me out of here relatively sooner. Since I was doing nothing, I could have immediately jumped and went to meet this uninvited visitor. But, through my observations with other administrators, I learned that it's best to keep any appointee waiting because in his or her respective mind it makes the visit an intrusion and it beefs up your own relative importance. So I looked at my watch and purposefully counted down a full 60 seconds. I was determined to be important in somebody's eyes before the sun set today.

After the full count down passed, I casually strolled out of the office and down the hall. There in the lobby was a middle aged guy in the plaid shirt, jeans and sneakers. He lacked a tie and a sports jacket — so much respect for my visit. He was not bad looking, but he would not stand out in a crowd like a Hollywood movie star. How important are first impressions, and do they count in the long run? Very casual and not much of a business sense — my first impression concluded. Initially, this looked like one of those dead-end, unproductive chases that were so typical of my job. But you had to smile, if for nothing else, the overall futility of it all of a possible lead going nowhere.

He was already standing when we exchanged the customary greetings with the oblgatory handshake. It was a firm but not overpowering grip. He told me his name was Joe Something or Other. Ferucci was right, I don't pay attention sometimes. From there, I wanted to get immediately into the heart of the matter and get on to other things in the office. So with honesty being the best policy, I said, "They just moved me into a new office that's not even organized or tidied up. Do you want to meet and talk in the atrium or in my new office?"

"Maybe the office would be better since I have some paperwork to show you to support my offer." A bad case makes waste, in my mind; this was going to be a lost cause.

I lost out on that one since I preferred the atrium. So like a mother duck leading her chick, I marched him up and around to my cell, or should I say office. Embarrassingly, there was only one chair there. Joe may have sensed my discomfort when I excused myself and bolted out, after quickly excusing myself, to find a folding chair. I almost ran head first into Billy as I went flying out the door. "I need a folding chair, quick."

Billy, unruffled, pointed to one that was right behind me in the hall. (The maintenance crew was never known for being tidy. Stuff was left all over the place because the excuse was that work was always in progress.) I grabbed the chair, thanked Billy, and sprang back toward my office, not wanting to keep my guest waiting. In my haste, I banged the chair on the door frame, announcing my re-entrance with a loud clang. Score one for finesse! And I picked up some more points since the chair did not open. I fumbled with it like someone wrestling an alligator. No luck. Undaunted, my guest, offering to help, calmly took the chair from me and opened it. It was not a problem for him. I must be getting weak or it was too much job stress or something. He took his seat and I sat in my swiveling executive chair, turned it around and faced him. The guest began with, "Hi, my name is Joe (Something or Other, I didn't catch the last name the second time. He said it too quickly or I was not paying too much attention again). Every year during this season I donate my services to a nonprofit agency and this year perhaps I could help you."

I interrupted and tried to shut this door quickly. "We have a large and dedicated staff since we try to respond to the special needs of each and every kid here. (This was almost verbatim the corporate party line. This I got straight.) Through experience we were not too successful with volunteers, although we have a small handful here. We usually found this group a little unreliable since they quickly have problems dealing with the special needs that our kids present day after day after day."

Joe Somebody or Other smiled and said, "I certainly can sympathize with that but that's not the volunteering effort I was offering. It's just a one time deal. You see, every year I play Santa Claus for a nonprofit group. I was looking through the phone book and came upon your name. I thought that you could use my services. I know I am a little late in the scheme of things. But perhaps you could use me. Even if you already had your Christmas party, I will be more than willing to come back again. I know from experience that the kids respond to what we do."

I was stunned. Here I was on the hook and this guy was saving me from Ferucci, Rigatoni and the rest of the sharks. This was an offer that I couldn't refuse. But like anything else, especially in the worlds of business or dating, you couldn't be too eager or anxious. This would show weakness or vulnerability. So, on the exterior anyway, I had to be nonchalantly cool. Like a poker player, I didn't want to give my hand away, although I was seemingly holding a pair of nothings. All I could say was, "Sounds good!"

Then he reached into his bag and pulled out the first binder. It was one of those three-ringed things, in white, that was pretty thick and somewhat heavy. He handed to me and said, "If you could look at this, just for a minute. It shows some of my past appearances."

I took it. Its weight almost knocked me off balance in my chair and I casually ran through the pages. It showed some photos of Santa Claus with kids, adults, some kind of unidentified dignitaries, along with newspaper clippings, some yellowed by time, commending this here Santa candidate. My chair needed a seat belt because I could have fallen off. This was the answer to my search effort that went some endless days and got me nothing but frustration, criticism and dead ends. Now, I was seemingly getting salvation on a silver platter. What did I do to deserve this? I never considered myself a lucky person. But this was not the time for thinking or conferring with administrators, it was the time for action. Before I could respond, he took the second binder out and presented it to me. "Here's the second part," he said. "When can I come? And when I do, I'll bring Mrs. Claus and the Snowman with me, if that's alright."

Here I was, getting three for the price of one. I wasn't so stupid as to negotiate or discourage this deal of a lifetime. So, without consulting

Rigatoni, Ferucci or the school principal, I committed to Joe Somebody, AKA Santa Claus. In the most authoritative posturing I could manage, I confirmed the deal. "It sounds like something that could benefit both you and the kids here. I left the me out of it; it would sound selfish and self-seeking. Without any further discussion, you're on for next Friday at 10:15 in the morning. Is that OK by you?"

"There are just one or two minor things, that's all."

I almost choked. Too good to be true! I knew it, I knew it! There is always a catch that ruins a deal that is too good. "What is the bump in the road that we can smooth out?" I asked. (When there is a potential problem, always use the word "we" because it equally distributes blame when things go wrong.)

"I need a place for me and Mrs. Claus to change."

"That's no problem. There are plenty of rooms here. We can get you something. Is there anything else?"

"Yes," he said. "When I play Santa Claus, I bring my own presents to give to the kids. It's just a little thing that I do."

Once again, I started having this conversation with myself and this guy at the same time. It's a wonder I didn't get confused and mixed up. "Our social worker and her team make up a list months in advance and then we try to get those gifts most appropriate to the child. Some of these kids are in need and a coat or gloves would normally be on the top of the list."

"That's OK. I usually add something extra nice. For example, the boys will get a remote control car and the girls watches or something like that. I've been pretty successful in my present selection for the kids. No complaints so far."

In an instant, I started doing the math. The school had over 160 kids, and the presents he was allegedly distributing came to six to eight thousand dollars. This was out of his pocket, unless he was robbing a bank or a toy store. Too good to be true? Out of his mind or mine? Not wanting to back myself into the proverbial corner, although this office cell was beginning to get claustrophobically small, I said, "That's OK if all the kids get something, either from our warehouse or presents from you."

He looked at me with a benevolent, almost condescending smile, and said, "Good. Then we are on?"

"Yes, I said. See you on Friday at 10:30."

"Friday it is." Then he scratched out his phone number on a piece of scrap paper and gave it to me and said, "If you have any questions or problems, please feel free to get in touch with me. If you can't get to me immediately, don't worry. I'm pretty busy this time of year but I will get back to you."

"By the way, what about these two binders with the stuff inside?"

"You can keep them. You probably may have more use for them than I have."

With that, he got up, shook hands with me and I proceeded to walk him through the school toward the front door for his exit. His parting words to me were: "You won't have any regrets. See you soon." With that he went through the double sliding glass doors and out of the building. I wish that I hung around longer to see what he was driving because I always believed that you are what you drive. I had the BMW. That proves something. But I was so excited with this unexpected event that I almost ran back to the cell. There I got the two binders and proceeded, with very firm step, to fly toward Ferucci's office. I was off the hook, with a big ace or two up my sleeve. I intended to milk this windfall for all it was worth and if I could make Ferucci suffer in the process, all the better!

The kids were just in the process of leaving for the day, so the march to victory was not as quick as I would have liked. I felt more like a salmon going upstream. Nevertheless like this migratory fish I too finally got to where I was going. I firmly knocked on Ferucci's door and went in just as he was getting off the phone. I think it was one of his family members again since he had that perturbed but amused look on his face. They were not my family, however, so I sashayed in, somewhat confident and vindicated, and somewhat loudly placed the two binders on his desk. Two of his papers went flying off into somewhere. He was not enthusiastic but I didn't care.

"You know what this is?"

"It looks like a loose leaf binder. What is it to me?" With that he bent down to retrieve his paperwork.

This was good since I managed to annoy him and add just a little bit of inconvenience to his work load.

"I've managed to get us a Santa Claus for next Friday. Just in case you and Rigatoni ever doubted me, here are two, not one, of my candidate's portfolio binders. It's pretty impressive."

"Fine" was Ferucci's only response. He took the two binders and placed them on a file cabinet behind his desk without looking at a single page. "How did you get this guy?"

Without missing a beat, I said, "Through hard work, which is it's own reward. And for the record, he's also bringing some expensive gifts for the kids, like remote control cars, clock radios and watches. I can't wait!"

Ferucci rolled his eyes. After a slight pause he said, "I'll keep Henri's backup Santa suit handy, just in case. I have to finish up some important work that you interrupted. Close the door when you leave."

Ferucci had a way of deflating even the most joyous of situations. Here I was giving him and the kids' Christmas on a silver platter and he was talking about backup scenarios. I gave him great news with super documentation and he was anticipating, or perhaps hoping, that I would fail somehow. Still I absolutely refused to let him get the best of me. With a triumphant walk, I went back to my office cell to celebrate in quietude. Along the way the kids were getting ready to go home for the day and the coming weekend. I felt happy for them since they were going to get a moment and day of hope when Santa would come next Friday. There was no Janet around to share my triumph of good news, but it didn't matter. Not only was I off the hook, my star was shining a little brighter. The weekend was beginning to look good too.

Perhaps for this explained reason, the rest of the work day flew by. In my cell of an office I got a little work done. I also got my schedule set for the coming short work week. I had to be on the road Monday to pick up some more stuff for the kids, so that at least was a positive thing: time out of the office, away from those people. So things were good. The only disconcerting thing was that the clock was approaching five and there was no call from Ferucci to stop after work for a quick bit to eat and a drink. Was I going to hold out or just call him? As I pondered deciding to not decide, the magic hour of dismissal came upon me. There was no phone call. It was a sign of something. I left the building at one minute after five and went home. Meeting the ersatz Santa put me in a good frame of mind. I took the blessing and was determined to enjoy it . . . all weekend long. The ride home was a little faster than normal since less cars were on the road; their drivers were probably at the mall Christmas shopping or having cocktails with Ferucci. I was absolutely determined to enjoy the peace and quiet of the weekend respite in the oasis of my home. As I pulled into the driveway, Kiki was waiting for me in the window. Better than a wife! A good sign!

PART FIVE

ince I wasn't at work, the weekend was wonderfully relaxing. I accomplished a few things too but at a slower, more relaxing pace. Christmas shopping for the office had to be wrapped up. It was a "forced" custom to exchange gifts within the office, so I had to get something since we all became "Secret Santas." I was determined not to break the bank for any of the office people . . . and I didn't. From thrift shop to the dollar store to Target, my final stop was Marshall's and I got some kind of porcelain figure purportedly largely discounted. Good wrapping does go a long way towards covering gifts with large discounts. I also got something for Ferucci since a good gift now would hopefully lessen the punishment for the coming year. For Rigatoni, since he was the ultimate supervisor, a packet of cigars that I got earlier in the year on sale. If they were a little stale, so what: I didn't smoke and he would likely be more impressed with the cigar bands anyway than the actual flavor. He would feel macho, the toxicity of the gift could be a blessing in the long run for me. That was how the business of Saturday was handled. Sunday was culminated in the afternoon by landing in Princeton for an Advent choir service celebrating the season and that profoundly elevated my spirits. Sometimes life can be beyond good; it can be glorious!

Late Sunday evening was spent wrapping the remainder presents for the office people. Just to get into the proper frame of mind, I put some Christmas, not holiday, music on the stereo. I kind of got into the spirit of the thing and wrapped in time with the music. My wrapping skills were not the best and the paper itself came from a stash of stuff in the attic, an environment that subjected the wrap to heat, humidity and scrunching. The paper was not handling well. The rectangular boxes all had a roundish look. Something was not right here. I did find solace in the music selections which were pretty good, if you like early Baroque. With the presents finally taken care of for the office unworthies, I turned to the final stage of Christmas preparation for the office. Years ago, a former neighbor gave me the recipe for a winter grog comprised of a base of powdered ice tea mix, with some Tang added along with a pinch of cinnamon, cloves, brown sugar, and other stuff. Add water and serve hot. So I made a trial run that evening and found that this elixir wasn't too bad. Just as an experiment, I decided that it would be nice to add a little zip to the recipe. I got lucky since I had some brandy in the house. Tried my second warm glass, this time spiced with brandy! It was marginally better; it had a nice warm, spicy effect but too sweet. So another experiment was in order; this time the secret ingredient would be a little vodka. Couldn't taste the vodka; it seemed like nothing was added to my holiday mixture. So a fourth glass was in order, this time with gin. This experiment didn't seem to be working too well either. I guess I was not made out to be a chemist or scientist or a bartender, and I was getting a head ache in the process. So I put away the stuff in the butler's pantry, and after patting Kiki on the head, and fought my way upstairs and went to bed earlier than I had anticipated. All this experimentin' was difficult work that just tired me out. There was always tomorrow and the rest of the work year was going to be extremely busy. Lots of rest would do me a world of good in anticipation of what was to come.

Monday morning began in a rather glorious fashion; this I took as a good sign for any and all undertakings of the week. The sunrise for the first day of winter was beyond nice; it was almost spectacular. The sky was lit with a veritable tapestry of colors on the red end of the spectrum. And the sun was following triumphantly behind in a few, long minutes. Kiki, curled up tightly on the bed, was totally unimpressed. I had to get ready a little quicker this morning since the week would begin in with a wildly hectic pace. I had to be ready for all challenges.

Usually I look forward with great anticipation to my stop at Lucca's for coffee and a brief respite of sanity. Not today, however, since the adrenaline of the final days before Christmas had already begun to pump in my veins. I did stop to pick up my coffee and buttered baguette but I did not tarry this morning; it was one of the very few times that I was quickly in and out of this haven of peace and sanity. There were a number of regulars there that morning, including the artist, but good luck was with me since I was practically invisible and went about my business unnoticed. From the coffee house it was just a short trip into the office. All the leaves were expectedly off the trees by now and the lake in front of the building was steaming in reaction to the cold air; its vapor snaking its way toward the sky. I beat the buses out this time and zoomed into my assigned parking spot. Looking at the car's clock I was somewhat surprised; I was very ahead of schedule for once. I had to make a decision, however. Would it be two trips into the office or just one? Would I try to carry my briefcase, coffee and baguette, along with the cumbrous package of presents, all at once, and become a Christmas hero, or would I wimp out and do it in two trips? Why not a Christmas hero? So I got out of the car and placed my briefcase on the ground, then got the package of presents out, and then back into the car for the coffee and baguette, which I stuck in my side pocket, closed the door. Then began the balancing act wherein everything was collected under my arms like a mother hen with her chicks. At this moment, I could have been a good candidate for the circus. If I could have seen myself at this moment, would I be amazed or amused? Was I Hercules cleaning out the stables or Moe from the Three Stooges making a delivery? Undaunted I went forward wanting to make a scene and calling attention to myself, but after all it was very close to Christmas. Everything is forgiven at this time of year. So slowly I made the long way towards the front door, through the hallway, and took the longest route possible to my office cell. My strategy was good since I did want to catch the attention of staff who sympathized with my induced labor and had to be intrigued with the pile of presents that were jutting forth from the top of the bag, which started to show some signs of fatigue and stress. One side was starting to rip. Undaunted, I moved forward and hit the bonanza. There was Miss Janet who, when she saw me in my holiday struggle, instantly flashed her smile that would have lit up New York during its famous blackout. This was my golden opportunity not to be missed.

"Anything for me? Any girl would love jewelry." With that she pointed to that finger on her left hand.

That almost made me drop my packages. Recovering as fast as any mortal could, and without loosing face since she did get my vulnerable side on this one, I said, "Not on this trip. The junk in here goes to the office people that I made me suffer throughout the year. However, I could make a second trip and take up your case with special, immediate attention."

"No, that's OK. It seems I've been forgotten during the holiday season again." With that, she turned and walked away. I couldn't tell if she was smiling or crying. One just never knew with her. That was part of the intrigue.

With that initial morning shock, I proceeded to the office cell. Along the way, there were repeated inquiries from female staff about any of the presents in the bag for them. Sad to say, I was either oblivious to them or too cheap or too grumpy to spread my limited wealth and good cheer around. I did enjoy my triumphal march through the building, garnering attention from staff. Much head turning and no Ferucci pulling on my tie , was something wrong? Perhaps luck was finally, unequivocally on my side.

In my smug, self-congratulatory mode, feeling good about myself, I forgot the law of balances, of how things level out for me in this life. My feel-good mode quickly dissipated when I stumbled into my office cell and found the new office mate there greeting me with a smile and a hello. I almost dropped the bag. In fact, I did drop the bag, stunned beyond surprise. No one quite told me that Monday would be the day that I would loose my privacy and surrender my domain to an intruder. But I should have known better that this day was coming, I just wasn't ready for today to be the day. I guess it was. Maybe this was some kind of spiritual discipline or message: endure suffering now and postpone pleasure until later . . . much later, if ever. This would be a lesson for me to learn about coming to work early.

She was gushing and effusive with her compliments and offered to help. Being independent in nature and feeling that my privacy was someway violated, I declined her offer to pick up my Christmas presents. Undeterred, she gushed on about how delighted she was to leave her political life behind and how great it was to be with a nonprofit such as this and how she was sure to love all the kids here and how she would do anything to help advance the agency's welfare and how warmly she was already received by those she met on her first day and how sure she was that we would work well together since she's heard all sorts of wonderful things about me. Her gushing, like Old Faithful, continued for a while, so much so, that if you could get diabetes from the incessant sweetness. I would have been terminally dead from saccharine poisoning if I were a totally gullible person. Politely, before I could be settled into my morning routine, I excused myself to get a cup of coffee and to regain my composure. Since the secretarial office was closest to my cell, I inflicted this group with my presence and morning traumas. Unlike the crew in the administrative office, this group was genuinely agreeable and less concerned with politics, policies and personality. I drew a half cup of coffee and could not honestly inflict my agitation upon them. I took just one sip of coffee, exchanged morning greetings and pleasantries, and went back to the cell to plan my next move. Astride was all smiles to see me and bombarded me with questions. It was only five after nine but it with the continuing interrogation it already felt like a full day. I had to get out of this place. And what was that smell? I excused myself saying I had to go to see Ferucci on some business. I took my bag of Christmas presents and with a deliberate pace went to the other side of the facility to let Ferucci have a piece of my mind. I was not a happy camper.

Usually I was differential and would always knock before entering anyone's private space. Not this time. Halfway between barging in and falling through the front door, I landed within inches of Ferucci's desk. He was just getting off the phone, probably with a family member again , and the suddenness of my apparition had to be at least mildly surprising to him, but he didn't show it, as my Christmas bag broke and presents went tumbling all over the place.

"These phone calls early in the morning from 'ma familia' are driving me crazy. You're lucky you're not in my family." Then after a very brief momentary pause he said, "Please refrain from littering my office."

In response to this cheap shot, I responded with "These Christmas presents, because of their weight, broke the bag. Perhaps I should return yours to the store for a complete refund, if they are accepting litter."

"I told you to save your money in buying me presents. Take what's left of the bag and any unbroken stuff and put it under the tree in the administrative office. Thank you!"

"I have another issue," I said. "She's here and in my office. When I started I was supposed to get my own office. Now you've given me a telephone booth and she's in it. It's barely big enough for me, I can't breathe and she is taking up lots of space. This ain't right."

"You wanted someone to help you getting more money from people. You should have been more careful in what you were asking. Further," he pounded his closed fist on the desk, "you knew she was coming. Today is your lucky day. By the way, I hope you have a present in there for her."

I almost passed out with that one. She wasn't here an hour and Ferucci had me buying presents for her too. "I'm not the Bank of America or a social welfare agency getting gifts for all of America."

"It's a nice thing to do and in keeping with the spirit of the season. And she will be your office mate and co-worker for life." Before he could continue his phone rang again. He picked up the receiver and then looked at me and said, "I have to take this. It's another family matter. Just put your first delivery under the office tree and try to enjoy the rest of the day."

"What do you mean for life?"

"Again, did you get anything for your new office mate?"

"What! She's been here for less than an hour and I have to spend money on her too?"

"I'm sensitive to other people's needs and trying to make Astride feel at home. But do what you want to do, which you do anyway. I'm a man of the people trying to give you good advice."

With that I would have stormed out of the office, but I have presents scattered all over the floor and he had me on that round. I didn't want to give him satisfaction that he bested me so early in the morning. Thus I fumbled out of the office, carrying a teeter-totter of presents, while he picked up the phone. It was one of his many brothers, probably trying to adjust their respective holiday schedules for series of family get-togethers that would be coming up. Two humiliating trips into the company office did it as I laid my packages down under the Charlie Brown tree. There was some good decorating on this pathetic evergreen, and despite its physical shortcomings, it looked as respectable as it could possibly get for the holidays. I placed my presents in the back and tried to do so unnoticed. The women lit up and almost in one voice exclaimed, "For me?"

With a semi-annoyed voice I responded, "No, that's why God gave you husbands." But even that could not distill their holiday spirit, which seemed to be especially at my expense. Quickly I scooted out of the office and back to my penitential cell. The hall was quiet throughout the school since kids and staff were in classes or therapy sessions. Not even a Bill Brown in sight to beat up for money. All this cavorting around the building took less than a half hour from my work day. It wasn't even 9:30. I had to contend with the rest of the work day, for the rest of my professional life, with the intrusion. It looked like I would be drinking even more coffee just to escape the confines of the office cell.

My return was greeted with a smile and a couple of seemingly polite, non-intrusive questions. But I gave polite but curt answers since I valued my privacy and independence above all. The interrogation did not end. Kosnowski branched out to seemingly inane questions about the Rigatoni, Ferucci, staff and the like. I gave one word answers like one was "difficult," the other was a little "strange," and some were "fumbling." I thought they were honest responses without putting myself in jeopardy with anything seemingly critically quotable that would probably be held against me in the future. I guess the less said to someone you didn't know the better. I had to excuse myself again for another cup of coffee, anything to get away from the confines of an ever enclosing cell of an office. It was already late in the morning and I was already on the way to my second or third cup, depending on the count. Since the secretarial office was closer, plus the fact that I never ever felt warm and fuzzy all over in the administrative office notwithstanding all the time I spent working in there, I took the shortest distance. This shortness of the trip did not kill too much time, but the secretaries always greeted me with a little more enthusiasm. I was told that the coffee was a fresh pot and then asked about my new roommate. They had me with that one since I didn't want to be initially negative — let time take its toll and be the jury — I responded that she surprisingly did indeed show up today. The collective chat went on about this and that stuff but eventually I had to return to the cell, killing only three miserable minutes. I wasn't even mid-morning yet when I realized that I was running out of excuses to be out of the way of the office intruder. My creativity was being taxed to the max. I couldn't think of any more diversions or excuses. I looked like I had to get back to the cell. I wanted but found myself incapable of trying to converse with the secretaries all day. I ran out of things to say that were of mutual interest. With coffee cup half empty — it was almost as awful as Ferucci's office specials — shoulders drooped downward in a defeated position and head bowed, I made my way back to the cell. There I was hit with a double whammy: the window was opened although it was December and there was this sweet but overpowering aroma in the air. I guess I was destined to freeze and like it. As I shuffled in to the area of my suffering, Kosnowski turned quickly to me and said with a smile, "I've taken the liberty to open the window for a little fresh air. I hope you wouldn't mind. We just don't want this small room to be stuffy."

Of course I did mind. She just did it and then asked my passive permission after the fact. I salvoed back, "As long as you didn't break the window or anything." Then I said to myself something if the perfume wasn't so overbearing, then the window could have stayed shut. Maybe the door should have been shut earlier too.

"Oh, you're so funny. They told me that you had a sense of humor and there it is."

I rolled my eyes and quietly took my chair and began to shuffle through some paperwork and my calendar schedule. But between shuffling her papers, or whatever she had, there were more questions. The interrogation did not stop; it just had lulls and valleys. All I needed was a single, overhead light. I was as polite as I possible could be, but was not warm and fuzzy. The torture was killing me slowly but surely. And what was that overbearing scent? Even with the opened window and an outside temperature just a few degrees above normal, I was being suffocated again by this overbearing sweet smell. My nose began to twitch like some kind of giant hare that escaped from Alice in Wonderland.

In the midst of the morning interrogation, Kosnowski could not help noticing my nose that beginning to twitch incessantly. She looked at me and said, "What's wrong with your nose?"

"Besides being too big, nothing at all."

"No, your nose, it's hysterical. You're twitching like a rabbit." She began to chuckle.

I was not amused. I didn't think it was that funny. I didn't scowl or anything; just held a straight, emotionless expression. Nevertheless, she was still giddy at my expense. And my nose was still irritated. Saying nothing, I went back to work, or pretended to do so, anything to get out of the morning interrogation session.

The questions decreased to a trickle, which was almost a blessing. And the morning dragged on, while the room remained cold and the irritation plaguing my rather large nose continued on a slightly abated level. Work was not a distraction since I could not fully focus on what I had to do. Just when I was getting into a rhythm, there would be another question or comment. The intruder cell mate was proving to be disruptive on a short-term basis. Maybe long-term would be better, if I could survive the short term. The events of the morning were going super drag when, only a few minutes past ten, my phone rang. It was Rigatoni, summoning me and Kosnowski to a meeting in his office. Was this a blessing, to go from the cell into the warden's torture chamber for more interrogation? Because his office was larger, it would give me the illusion of having more space without the walls closing in on me.

I conveyed the subpoena to Kosnowski, who was apparently very delighted with the message. She immediate took up her note pad and was literally bounding out the door.

She turned in the process and saw me still at the desk. "Aren't you coming?"

"I have to finish some stuff up. I'll be there in less than a minute after you."

This was a good move on my part. I didn't have to walk the hall with the intruder, thus giving her the credence and blessing of my presence. And secondly, it would send a message to Rigatoni that I was busy and could not easily drop my doings just to respond to another one of his knee-jerk meetings. Finally, I just may catch a glimpse of Miss Janet and her smile would brighten up this miserable day. Who knows?

I begrudgingly waited a half a minute, shuffled some papers on my desk, and then got a note pad and began the long, dead-man-walking trek to Rigatoni's office. The kids were in their classrooms and therapists were doing their thing, thus no Miss Anybody. Before I knew it, I was knocking at the door, awaiting his permission to enter into his inner sanctum. Kosnowski was there, notebook ready with a beaming smile. Rigatoni looked up and said, "Come in, no need to knock." After I took my seat, he added, with a smile, "Astride beat you out getting here."

"I had to finish a little thing up." I gave him a forced smile back.

"You shouldn't let little things hold you up when you have a chance to meet with your president. Now that we're all here, let's begin." With that he cleared his throat and began. I could see that this was going to be another one of those.

He looked at Kosnowski first and said, "I hope everything is comfortable in your new surroundings and that you are adjusting well."

"Oh yes, everything was so wonderful and welcoming. One of the secretaries even brought me a cookie and put it on my desk as a welcoming gift."

With that Rigatoni turned to me and said, "I hope that you also extended a warm welcome to your new office mate and have done everything to make her feel at home with our family here."

"I didn't bring her any cookies since it slipped my mind that today was the day. But I try to do my best later."

Apparently Rigatoni was not overly thrilled with that response either but after a slight pause, moved on to his agenda and went over his points over and over again. Even someone like myself who tried very hard to tune out every thing when he spoke could not help but to remember the stressed, high points of his bumbling sermon. I was supposed to open up the family vault and expose Kosnowski to everything I knew to benefit the agency and improve its fund raising and gathering capabilities . . . blah, blah, blah. I was steadfastly committed, there and then, not to divulge anything that would jeopardize my peace of mind or survival. Do people tell their spouses everything? My survival in this life could very well depend upon that something in the vault of a secretive or specialized information that could save me in my time of trial. No way was I going to tell her, an intruder and someone that I had no hand in hiring, or anyone else for that matter, everything that I knew. Was Rigatoni naïve or just plain crazy? Nobody ever shows all of his cards to an opponent in a poker game. Did Rigatoni ever consider that she may be a spy or a hindrance to my and the agency's mission? Confidence comes with performance; trust with the passage of trial and time. No way was I going to jump into a corporate relationship! I bit the inside of my mouth again, made my resolves more steadfast, and watched the clock tick slowly until that inevitable time when Rigatoni finally at last finished and I was permitted to return, with the intruder, to the cell.

The remainder of the morning dragged on. There were occasional questions that interrupted my work rhythm. And there was that lingering aroma that, not as overbearing in the morning, made sure my headache was firmly in place. With the window opened while we were away, the room seemed to be even colder that in the morning, although the odor abated. Lunch hour would be my daily furlough for warmth, fresh air and quiet, if only for a while. I began looking forward toward this momentary respite.

When that faithful hour finally came for lunch, I politely tried to excuse myself saying, "It's time to put on the feed bag."

Kosnowski turned and looked at me and said, "You're going to lunch this early?"

"Yes, I usually take it at this time. It's one of my many bad habits that I refused to break. And the PBA is coming this afternoon to play Santa, distribute presents to the kids and get a photo op, so I have to be back here before one."

"Do you mind if I come with you? You could show me one of the good, hidden spots and we can talk about this agency, the board, kids, money — everything — in a warm, chatty environment."

I bit the inside of my mouth again. She had me there. I had no appointments or anything like that on the schedule to get me out of imposed invitation. So I had to say, "Sure. Let's leave before noon to avoid the lunch rush."

So that was my first morning in the cell, practically claustrophobic, to put it mildly. We are supposed to revel being communal, social beings; but I value my privacy. In this place it seemed that my privacy and my person was invaded in every conceivable way. I just could no longer catch my breath. Call me anti-social or not a team player. With every meeting with Rigatoni, with every lecture from Ferucci, I was becoming more detached. The wheels were falling off the BMW, the ultimate driving machine. No one seemed to care.

We left before noon on this mixed blessing: it was great to be out of the office, but at a compromise. We landed at the nearby Italian Grill and since we were early there was no problem getting immediate seating. Immediately I ordered the house Italian red, while Kosnowski ordered a diet Coke. She was personably chatty but there were those seemingly innocuous questions that, if they were added up, could prove very compromising, if I answered honestly. Believing in that old adage that loose lips sink ships, I became even more cautious and reticent in my responses. A casual observer would think that I was a clean shaven caveman since I was grunting and nodding my head in acquiescence. Ordering from the menu proved to be right in step with the conversation. I had a nice veal dish (it was on special) and she ordered something vegetarian. Even with a mouth full of vegetables, she still continued with an occasional question. I didn't know where all this was going, but I had to admire her probing tenacity. As she munched, crunched and lunched, my answers began more and more cryptic and innocuous. Perhaps she sensed that there was no more information to be gleaned; perhaps she just ran out of oral gas. The questions stopped and we concluded our meal along with our other pleasantries and returned to the office cell.

We got back to the office at about 12:45; this was enough of time before the arrival of the PBA and their version of the holiday party. I wouldn't use the term Christmas since it lacked something. Perhaps it was their version of Santa. Their ersatz version was about six-five or six-six and easily could have played linebacker for the Giants. It was like a Santa for the state prison, more intimidating than warm and fuzzy. The kids were not bothered by this discrepancy. I guess that even they knew that this was not the real thing. It bothered me more than them. I accompanied the police force, joined by Kosnowski, from room to room as presents were handed out to each kid. My duties for the moment required that I take as many pictures as possible of each and every member of the PBA alongside the kids in every classroom. The flash attachment ate the rechargeable batteries and the camera ate film. It was not unusual that the energy guzzling flash would consume at least four batteries during this afternoon and the camera would burn through four to five rolls of film. Basically I tried to capture every moment, spontaneous and otherwise. The grand finale would the group photo shot in the lobby with the entire force, Santa, a couple of cute kids and an administrator from the agency. Rigatoni removed his candidacy from this photo shoot years ago, probably because he thought it wasn't worth his time or that it wasn't that important of an event. Thus we had to send for Ferucci who made it a point to be exceptionally well dressed for the occasion, which always included a very well starched, pressed shirt and a holiday tie for the occasion. And during the final two weeks of the school year, he would frequently don a festive tie, just to prove to one and all that he indeed was setting the pace for all to be in the proper frame of mind.

Despite this exhausting activity that had the lot of us chaotically tumbling in and out of classrooms like refugees from a Marx Brothers comedy, everything was concluded by 2:30, with enough time to place all kids on their respective buses for the journey home. I wasn't so lucky. Knocked out, I had to survive three more hours before my vehicle would take me home. Mercifully enough, there was no call to have still another meeting in the presidential office. However, the rest of the afternoon was interminably long. The only item of note was that I set a personal record for drinking coffee that day, some seven cups of the agency's worse. When five o'clock finally came, I had an upset stomach, probably from all the coffee acid, and a case of the caffeine shakes. If anyone by the name of Guinness kept a record, I would have been the proud holder of "Most Cups of Agency Coffee in One Day." At the moment, this looked like my dubious claim to fame in my long career with this nonprofit. By my standards, nothing much was accomplished for the rest of the afternoon.

But the work day did not end at five since I had to buy a Christmas gift that evening for Kosnowski. I was pressured and shamed me into it. Reasonably speaking, one would assume that purchasing just one gift would be a simple matter, especially with Menlo Park Mall close by. Somehow I had the feeling that luck, Kosnowski and me were not the best of ingredients for a mix. The blessing of Rigatoni seemed to be turning into a curse.

I bid a perfunctorily courteous good bye to Kosnowski and left for my theoretically short excursion to the mall to buy her something. It was the last shopping Monday before the Christmas break but I anticipated that during the pre-dinner hour, the crowds would be somewhere else — at home, work, school or on the road — and I could use my speed of foot to get this additional problem settled in no time at all.

Initially my luck appeared to be good. I left work without any delay and was not slowed down by traffic getting to the mall. Then things got a little sticky. The place were I normally parked, in the back under the protective canopy of the first floor of the parking deck, was filled up. This was most annoying, since it wasn't a rainy day or anything. So, since I was already in the back, I decided to take the ramp to get to the upper floor. Just as I pulled out, some old lady in a Ford got in front of me and thus began the procession. It was like one of those funeral convoys. She had her lights on and was moving very slowly, at an almost meditative pace. Slowly her car moved up the ramp. So slowly that I thought she was experiencing motor problems or some-thing serious like a heart attack or a stroke. I decided then and there that no emergency medical aide should be given to someone with that kind of driving inability. I wouldn't save her if I had to and I wasn't that kind of doctor anyway. So she was a goner if she was going. And with my luck, she still wasn't going just now. She was in front of me moving very, very slowly with blinkers going left and right and left again. I was enduring this all for a two dollar gift that would be com-ing from an obligation and not from the spirit of the season. All these outsiders to my own personal life were making me a sourpuss during what should have been the most joyous time of year. Obligation and duty can certainly kill the holiday spirit.

After what took too much time, I finally parked my car on the third, or was it fourth, deck level. Because I was rather ruffled, I parked it outside. It was already dark and getting colder. Those in the spirit of the season would have found the weather invigorating; I found it another hurdle to jump over, crawl under or just plain circumvent.

There's between 100 to 200 stores in the mall, too many to count. That's a lot of stores or choices just to make one measly purchase. If I went into ten shops for one purchase, it would mean a ten percent rate of success. If it took 20, it would lessen the rate to five percent. At five quick minutes per store, the entire shopping spree would take less than 100 minutes, given the worse case scenario. The odds seemed to be incredibly good for me getting out of this place by 6:30 at the latest, home by seven, and the remainder of the evening being saved. These projections were most comforting, given the circumstances of the duress of this trip. All these numbers whirled in my mind as I left the car and sought the mall entrance on the upper floor deck.

Unfortunately, even for the best actuaries on this planet, theory and reality never quite mesh. There are always those unexpected, unaccounted quirks that occur for no apparent rhyme or reason and skew the best of plans. So it would happen to me. As I walked into the mall I was stunned by the number of fat people, old people, individuals with walkers and canes, and mothers with screaming brats in strollers blocking everything. If they could have been hanging from the ceilings, they would be there as well. My blazing speed notwithstanding, I could not move. It was like having a high powered sports car and being caught in New Jersey rush hour traffic . . . with a lot of seniors and a few cement trucks in front of you, just to make sure.

Although the top floor was packed, I decided to stay there since it should, in theory, have fewer shoppers than on the first floor which was at street level. I methodically shuffled along. I skipped the clothing shops altogether: too much money to spend on someone whom I only knew for one day, for a too personal gift. In my entire life there were very few people with whom I would ever desire to get intimate and close and spend lots of money on. Cruising through the mall, there was the bath shop. Why I went inside didn't make sense, except to ogle at the attractive help. The inside smelled good too, but getting perfumed soap for an almost stranger didn't do it for me. But I made a note of the asking price for the sale stuff in the barrels, just in case I got hung up. I left the store and according to my action plan made a right turn to proceed towards the Macy's end of the mall. I got sidetracked by of those gift and accessory shops that sell far out, crazy things that were great for momentary gags but not long for anything meaningful or lasting. Honestly, I did not feel like doing anything funny or wasting my sense of humor, along with my money, on someone I really didn't know. One should only joke around with someone that you're close and comfortable with, because there are unfortunate consequences when your best punch line falls flat or gets misinterpreted. More often than not, the recipient of a good one misconstrues the intent of the joke, gets his/her respective nose out of joint, and then demands reparation or rehabilitation or something like that. So why bother with giving a stranger your best, right from the start? It sets up unnecessary expectations for the present and paves the way for a future of unreasonable entitlements. It's nice to be nice, but too nice? — that's not the way for me! So I moved on and went past the Macy's end of the mall to the part that looks like an annex. I stuck my nose into the candle store, but candles never excited me as a gift. I have three drawers at home filled with candles; it seems like a copout gift: a flame with no flare. I cruised by Radio Shack and went across the way to the pretzel place where they again were giving out free samples. The chipmunk in me resurrected and I proceeded to stuff my kisser, first with an ordinary pretzel and then with one doused with honey mustard. Some day I had to come back to this place and actually spend some money to buy one and keep this enterprise in business. Today was not the day. I was still under the influence of getting all the free food during my latest happy hour experience and could not bear the thought of paying for something that I could get for free a little later in the day. So with some discipline, comforted with happy thoughts of a free happy hour in the future, I pushed on in my furtive quest for an appropriately cheap Christmas present. I continued my wanderings in the desert of insignificant plenty. I couldn't even cross the threshold of Macy's; I just looked at the displays from the lobby. As I spent more time in my search, the crowds kept on increasing and a claustrophobic feeling akin to panic began to set in. Nothing good was happening and, in the process, the shopping crowd was beginning to bump and push me, violating my sense of privacy and person. I had to quicken the pace to get out of this place. The only thing preventing me from bolting was the lack of a present. My mission was not going well. I felt like the modern equivalent of Ahasuerus. I covered one half of the mall's upper floor, wasted 45 minutes of my precious time and showed nothing for my efforts. Instead of feeling great with holiday cheer, I began to be filled with feelings of negativity because I was stuck doing something that I was coerced into doing and I wasn't successful at that! There were times such as this where I sincerely believed that the best occupation of all would be that of lighthouse keeper because of the minimal interaction with people. Thus half annoyed and half determined, I proceeded toward the other half of the mall, but this time I was determined to run my route in ten minutes or less. I've wasted enough of time, and have gotten bumped too many times by rude, oblivious people.

The march, perhaps sprint would be a better term, to the other end of the mall, went quicker. There were less shoppers because the stuff here was more high end, and I was not want parting with much of my hard earned money to buy a costly gift. This whole thing just didn't make sense. By the time I got to Nordstrom's far end, my head was bobbing from side to side, like I had Parkinson's or something. I had to get out of this place, but I had to get something first. I gave myself one minute to make a decision — good, bad or indifferent — just decide on something now to end the torture.

I glanced at my watch and saw the second hand move ever so slowly around the dial. Still no decision. I was paralyzed by some unknown force or perhaps it was just stupidity. There was no enlightenment, no epiphany, no hunches — nothing, just plain nothing. I watched other shoppers scurrying to and fro, all seemingly happily on a mission with clear objectives, and I just stood there like I was made of stone. Nothing! My 60-second deadline was up and still no solution. Mindlessly, I began slowly walking back to the side entrance where I originally came in to begin my epic shopping expedition. There was no guardian angel with a road map to gently suggest a direction or option. There were only frenetic shoppers, bumping into me, doing their holiday business.

With shoulders slumped in the defeated position, I was within inches of the mall's side door when I made my final glance at the spectacle prior to departure. That glance caught the lovely creature in front of bed, bath and fragrance place distributing what looked like free samples. And I think she was looking in my direction. That was the sign I was looking for. My gift would be here after all. I bounded down the stairwell, no poky elevator for me, and with joyful expectation closed the distance between myself and this angel of all fragrances and hopefully all other good things.

She greeted me at the door and sprayed my slightly lecherous out-stretched arm with some kind of sweet smelling stuff. With a smile she asked me how I liked it. A double entendre intended, I told her that I would like more, and she did. I got blasted on the other arm. I guess at that point I would become very attractive to an amorous skunk, although I was beginning to get a headache. But because she was attractive with a great smile, I took it in with all the good spirit of the season. I went into the store, again, but this time with the intent of buying something, anything, just to get it over with.

They had a variety of stuff. There were some interesting items in baskets at the ends of aisles with prices that were seemingly marked down. (I really wouldn't know since this was the first time I ever consid-ered buying stuff in this place.) In mid-aisle and at the register counters there were packaged items all ready to go, but their respective prices had to be much higher. What to do? I did both. I got a packaged item since no one could accuse me of being cheap, and I got some odds and ends from the baskets, just to add to the quantity of the gift. This gift could be good since I got some soaps, creams and other smelly trinkets. And maybe this stuff would benefit me in the long run since it would counteract the aroma that pervaded the office cell. This turned out better than I thought since I got a present to get me off the holiday hook and benefited myself in the day to day operations. Good job!

The clerk checking me out asked if I had any coupons; unfortunately, no, which put a slight damper on things. But overall, the price was right . . . and if this stuff just could potentially counteract the mystery stuff that was offending my olfactory sense and my peace of mind. I got my merchandise, some of it was holiday wrapped already, and headed towards the door where the angel of fragrances and glad welcomes was stationed. I tried to make eye contact with the possibility of small talk on the way out, but the tart was looking in the opposite direction trying to entice other big spenders into the establishment. I had to console myself that she wanted me only for the potential of my money. With this sad but true observation on the human condition, I departed the mall and made my way to the car and home to the quiet and warm of Kiki Pussycat.

As I pulled into the driveway, I glanced up and saw Kiki in the window waiting for my arrival. I have never been able to figure out if she was waiting there all afternoon and into the evening, or she could sense my arrival when I was in the immediate vicinity and perched in the window out of curiosity, joyful anticipation of my arrival, or the base desire just to be fed. Whatever the why or wherefore, I heard her thump when I inserted the key in the door. The opening of the door was greeted by one, loud meow and the impatient march to the kitchen to be fed. I complied. Later, after changing into more casual and comfortable clothing, I treated myself to dinner as well which, in turn was followed by finding suitable wrapping paper for the final work related present of the season.

I did turn the attic into a treasure trove of items that I collected through the years. (Lucky for me that the support beams were 2x8's, or else the attic would have landed into the upstairs bedroom. There was lots of treasure there.) This collection of valuables and near valuables was quickly becoming a symbol of my material success. I could fully sympathize with the Egyptian pharaohs who took everything with them. In one corner of my attic was a large garbage can filled with wrapping paper, both new and that which I attempted to recycle on occasion. With the third dive into the can I retrieved what I thought was the appropriate holiday wrap and headed down to the dining room, where I could take care of company business. The stuff that came packaged would get some bows or something, while the loose stuff — the bonus part of the present package — would get the recycled paper since that's what these presents deserved. I diverted from this operation for just a second to put on some Christmas music on the stereo, just to get in a better holiday mood, and proceeded to unroll the large, good quality, unused paper on the dinning room table. Unfortunately for me, Kiki saw this activity on the table and was intrigued to the point of compulsory investigation. From the chair unto the table it was a quick pounce right into the center portion of the good wrap. Nothing from either new wrap or recycled stuff on the dining room table looked salvageable after the quick shred. I took the Kik, put her gently on the floor, and rolled out another portion of new paper. Kiki was not deterred; up on the chair and unto the table again to make another direct strike.

There looked like there would be a possible run on wrapping paper. Half exasperated, half laughing, I took Kiki off the table and placed her in the back sunroom and closed the French doors. She stared unhappily through the glass but I had a job to do. I also had to do this job with less paper. I didn't feel like going out and buying another roll, so

I improvised with the stuff that looked somewhat salvageable after the cat attack. With ingenuity and adaptive engineering, the revised and adapted wrapping plan kind of worked, sort of. All well and good; I didn't want to waste even more time on this gift fiasco that wasn't my idea to begin with. With the two presents read to go, I placed them in a plastic bag by the front door so I wouldn't forget them — how could I? — on the way to work. And then I released Kiki from confinement and she immediate went back to the table and proceeded to shred the uncollected wrapping paper into even smaller shards. She probably had a better insight into this gift business than me. After this emotionally exhausting activity, I topped off the night with a brandy and then went to snooze land.

Another gray, early winter morning! I had to get up, though, since Tuesday held a tight schedule for me. Kiki, on the other hand, was only semi-awake on the bed. Went through the morning rituals quickly enough and proceeded down the stairs to breakfast. As I was finishing, I heard the thump, thump, thump of the Kik coming down the stairs. But she did not join me in the kitchen for her food but went straight to the dinning room to look for any paper remnants. After finishing my food, I put some stuff in her bowl and prepared for my takeoff to work, when I heard an unfamiliar, rustling sound. There she was, by the front door, with her nose in the bag, trying to get at the presents. Lucky for me I was a little too quick for that cat. I picked her up, removed her from the general presence of the presents, and forcibly took this delinquent to the kitchen to show her her breakfast food. Begrudgingly she ate and I escaped out the front door with the remnants of my custom wrapped and somewhat personalized Christmas packages.

Another uneventful weekday drive on 287 quickly brought me to that oasis in Metuchen, Lucca's coffee house. Because it was such a nondescript, flat morning with nothing faintly glorious about it, the streets allowed parking almost anywhere. There was simply no one around. Quickly I made my way inside the coffee house. The smell of fresh brewed balanced nicely with the holiday decorations inside. That same ol' Christmas music was playing, albeit unobtrusively, quietly in the background. Tawdry, pop music finally got its deserved place! Service was quick, complete with a salty bagel. It looked like my day was off to a good start.

I took the solitary bar chair in front of the steamy window and mindlessly gazed unto the sidewalk and the street. Without forethought, or near thought for that matter, I chewed and sipped, chewed and sipped, in a kind of unconscious, undulating rhythm, drifting off into thoughts of being pleased with myself and how good life was. I think I would have bought one of those "life is good" shirts if asked. My drift into the wonderful fantasy world of the unconscious was abruptly jolted into stark reality by the gravely voice of the artist who slide into the chair next to me. "Hey, hoe, are you ready for Christmas?"

Half startled, half dazed, half confused — I did not have my full cup of caffeine to get up to morning speed — I could only grunt incoherently in response. Initially she babbled on, but when I wasn't adequately responding to her needs, she gave me that cross look again and said, "You're too grumpy for this holiday season! Scrooge thought it was a humbug too." Then she chuckled to approve her quick retort. That was it; I quickly paid my final respects to her and left with a half eaten bagel. As I was departing, I turned back and said, "Have a nice holiday." But this wish lacked any deep sincerity.

"You too, Ebenezer," she chortled her response.

Leaving the coffee shop marked my time of mindlessness where my great thoughts wafting into the great universe would abruptly come to an end. Back to the harsh reality of work and what the day would bring. Hopefully it would be good.

Got into work more or less on time. Since I was close to schedule, I tried the side door and snuck in and went straight to the office cell.

Astride was already there; she was already in line for a commendation for industry or something. I never felt like being a corporate roll model or a roll model for anything else, for that matter. We exchanged morning pleasantries and with that I took my plastic bag with the absolutely last load of presents to the main office to place same officially under the Charlie Brown Christmas tree.

The walk down the hall was uneventful. I saw Janet but she was moving in the same direction way ahead of me. There was no possibility of catching up with her. It looked like she had a motor on her butt it was shaking so much . . . and at nine in the morning. I had to be satisfied with greeting others on staff. When I got to the main office, the pre-holiday buzz was already evident. In the background, their traditional Christmas muzak was on, the ladies were wearing red and green stuff with buttons and pins noting the season, and there were cookies by the coffee machine. They brought stuff in, and the ladies in the front office could bake! I stuffed one cookie in my mouth and proceeded to take Kosnowski's gifts out of the bag. Before they could hit the table where the tree was, Rosemarie noticed the slight alterations that Kiki made with my gift wrapping.

"What happened to the wrapping?" It was loud enough for the entire office to stop and take notice.

"Oh, nothing much. Just probably rough up a little in the transportation process."

"Have another cookie," she shouted. "We're all looking forward to what you're bringing in tomorrow."

With everything else, it slipped my mind that tomorrow was the day that I had to bring in something homemade to share with the office staff. Names were written on paper slips, thrown into a hat and then pulled weeks earlier to determine who was providing holiday goodies to warm the heart during this season. Tomorrow was my turn. I've completely forgotten. Maybe I could slip some Entermine's cookies off as my own. But that was tomorrow. I had to get out of the office, after stuffing another cookie in my mouth, just to escape the interrogation of warm and fuzzy Christmas conversation and clawing sentiment. It was just too early in the morning. Went back more depressed than elated to the office cell.

As I came flying around the corner and into my penitential holding area, I ran into a brick wall, or was it the smell or should I say the overbearing fragrance of what had to be Kosnowski's perfume? It was overpowering to the point where it could have stopped a moose in its tracks. I tried to suppress a cough but couldn't. She noted my discomfort and responded, "Let's open a window. It's kind of stuffy in here in these close quarters." I could only agree. But as I got to my desk to look over my work assignments for the day, the cold from the outside was having its effect on my innards. I was beginning to freeze, plus I couldn't breathe because of the perfume. Even the attempt to concentrate with my mind solely focused on an evil desires toward making out with Miss Janet would be close to impossible. In the process of shuffling the mess on my desk back and forth I did look at my schedule for the day. There was salvation in sight, a luncheon meeting with two friends who were sympathetic to the plight of some of the financially hard pressed kids who attended the school. Salvation was in sight, but only after I had to endure another morning of personal affliction.

As usual, the morning dragged on like a nun lecturing on religion. The pretext of making three trips out of the office cell for coffee gave me a chance to gasp for warm, unscented air. It was a choice between the agency coffee and breathing or the suffocating confines of the penitential cell. This is kind of like your choice in departing this life: by drowning or hanging. No choice is really ideal. As I sipped my third cup of coffee in the cell, Kosnowski announced that the cell was very warm and decided to open the window again. The temperature inside quickly began to plummet from hot to warm to cool to freezing. But it was already past 11 and I had a lunch meeting around noon. So I made my announcement that I was going to my lunch date and leaving her in charge of the operation. Actually, I could have hung around longer but between the perfume, freezing temperature and the Christmas season, why bother? So I put on my coat and departed with a grin as large as the Cheshire cat's. After all, it was the season. And I could kill time just as effectively out of the office.

As I left the building and got into the BMW, the fresh, clean, free air was intoxicating. It had that holiday feel. I had a few minutes, so I decided to make a detour into the mall, the same place I was just hours ago the night before. There was something in the novelty store that fascinated my strange sense of humor and I wanted to see it one more time. If it was wacky enough, perhaps a purchase would be in order, perhaps.

I parked my driving machine in the approximate same area like the night before. As I got out and entered the mall, I thought it would be nice to see if the hostess from the bath, bed and fine smells shop would remember me. Perhaps I would be remembered. Perhaps I would get lucky. Perhaps . . . oh, no! I forgot something for my upcoming meeting with my dear friends and donors to the agency. The thought of all this bonus free time out of the office suddenly evaporated. I had to go back to the office and retrieve the missing item. This would be more annoying than embarrassing, and, to boot, I would miss the opportunity to see if the hostess would remember me and if I finally got lucky. So it was, back to the car and back to the office. In what seemed almost an eternity, I made it back from the mall to the agency door and went in. I kept my coat on, just in case Miss Janet would see me and how impressively a top coat could dress a man. Unfortunately, luck was not with me at lunch time, again, and I made my way toward the main office and the Christmas tree and the presents underneath. Inadvertently I placed their gifts under the corporate tree, a mistake made in the early morning hours since their gifts were not that large. I couldn't attend a luncheon date without bestowing some gifts to my friends. It seems that gifts before Christmas, even if they remain unopened, have a greater appeal and value than those given after the big day The value ages like a fine wine. That was one of my theories that I still hold fast to today.

It was approaching lunch time at the agency. With topcoat on and full of confidence and at maximum speed, I skimmed quickly through the halls. I thought that I would be able to get to the presents under the tree and quickly get out of the place, but that was not to be. There was a small crowd around the tree. Very strange, indeed! There was nothing that was worth that much attention or admiration. But as I got closer, Rosemarie saw me and shrieked, "Oh my, guess who's here!" The onlookers began to peal away from the tree, until Ferucci and Kosnowski remained. When she saw me she shrieked, "Oh no, we're caught." She was taken back. I still didn't have a full appreciation of what was transpiring until I saw Ferucci turn with an opened present in his hands. It took a stunned second or two to realize that it was the present that I earmarked for him. And on the floor was one of Kosnowski's presents, opened. Shocked and dazed, I could only exclaim, "What's going on here?"

Ferucci had an impish smile and, looking at Kosnowski, said, "We got busted. This was a great idea: to substitute gifts for the ones you gave us. Can you imagine the look on your face if we pulled this off? But we just got busted. You caught us. A good move!"

"You've violated the first law of Christmas. You've opened presents, unauthorized, before the big day. You're guilty!" With that outburst, I grabbed the gifts I originally came back for and stormed out of the office. As I exited, I heard Kosnowski say, "He looks really mad." To which Ferucci responded, "He'll get over it. He's got other problems."

As I blew down the hall, oblivious to everything around me — Janet could have been there and I wouldn't have noticed — a smirk came over my face. Nothing for nothing: I finally had Ferucci where I wanted him. The ultimate payback was coming, right after I finished my luncheon engagement. He tried to pull the proverbial fast one on me and he got caught. Not only did he get caught, but I got Kosnowski, the interloper, in the bargain: two for the price of one. It doesn't get better than that. I would have some two hours to plan the revenge of my counter attack. I intended to make it very much worth my while. But first the luncheon date, which now I would enjoy even more, because Ferucci's head on the proverbial corporate plate would be the best dessert. The proverb says something about vengeance belongs to the Lord, but today the deity would be sharing some of this get even stuff with me. It felt good leaving the building and letting those with guilt stew!

I met my two delightful friends at the Cheesecake Factory. My association with them began because of a funded grant that required me to get some sort of collaboration with an outside group. But after the project took its course, I still remained friends with them and periodically would meet for whatever reason. I smiled throughout the entire lunch. I don't know if it was more pleasurable because of their company or just the thought of sweet revenge upon Ferucci. The smile slightly faded when I picked up the bill, but that was OK. No, I didn't even think about having the agency reimburse me, although my friends gave me very generous gifts to take back for the kids. Just something about the spirit of the season would make it tawdry in getting money back for an act of kindness. For my way of thinking, it would diminish the quality of the gift. So I went back to the agency with a full trunk and a plan for derailing Ferucci. The smile quickly came back even larger.

When I arrived at the agency, I immediately went to the social worker's office and deposited the gifts. She was also impressed. It's one of those ironies of life, I guess, when strangers or those who have no direct connection to a particular cause prove the most generous in terms of reaching out and offering kindness. This was a good deed done solely for its own sake, with a bonus of a luncheon out of the office. And a simple thank you is reward enough. On occasion you just have to admire the magnanimity of the human spirit.

Well, my sense of wonder and warmth quickly ceased when I left the social worker's office. I flew back to my office, with the intention of dropping my coat off, and then to proceed, without appointment or anything else — I really didn't need one — to HR to file a formal complaint against Ferucci. As I blew into the office, my sudden appearance, again, startled Kosnowski. When she turned around, she could only blurt out, "I'm sorry but Ferucci made me do it. I'm so sorry."

"You committed the unpardonable sin. You ruined the surprise and magic of Christmas. I'm on my way to O'Leary's office to file a formal complaint. Hopefully, you grinches will get a formal reprimand and it will go on your permanent record. Then you could go humbugging down the hall together." With that I flew out of the office and made my way down to HR.

Reagan O'Keefe pontificated over the entire HR department and tried to do the same over the entire agency. She was famous for her memos. These were bureaucratic works of art, and I'm sure will go somewhere into a place like the Smithsonian or the Library of Congress to be archived for all humanity for all time. Either she went to school to learn the art of the memo or had a *Memo for Dummies* book someplace from which she borrowed frequently. We would be all in dread in receiving one of these epistolaries. A shrug, and then a sigh, would most often be followed with a "What's next?" on staff's part. Not that O'Keefe was a distant relative of Glinda and the rest of them east of Oz. To look at her one would get a rather different impression. She was half maternal (somewhat buxomly) and half idiosyncratic looking, the latter because of the shock of curly red hair. And every time she was in my presence I would be treated to a smile, perhaps a mark of some condescension towards me. Maybe she was somewhat taken with me. I never knew for sure. So it was with this underlying ambivalence that I entered into her palatial lair with the overriding determination that I was going to put the screws into Ferucci.

You would not believe the O'Keefe office, though, especially if you had ever experienced first hand the paradigmatic corporate American working environment. This office was a mix between visions of sugar plums dancing around in your head (it was Christmastime) and HGTV's home remodeling makeover. There were always candles burning (fire code violation?) and the lighting was subdued. How she was able to lessen the output of the same fluorescent lighting system that was in the entire building still remains a mystery beyond me, even today. In addition to make matters complete, she had one of those small waterfalls in her rear bookcase that sometimes made a jingling sound in addition to the peaceful sound of water falling over some phony rocks. It also smelled perfumy. How she managed to get this entire package past the overbearing scrutiny of Rigatoni remained beyond me. Nevertheless, if I were looking for a place to have a good time with anyone on company grounds, this office would be the theoretical idea. All I would need would be a wine cooler — and she probably had that hidden away too!

As the perfect storm blew in unannounced upon her idyllic paradise, she tried to placate me with her customary greeting and warm smile.

"This is not going to be a pleasant visit, Ms. O'Keefe," I said. "I am hopping mad and this time you're going to have to do something about it. Ferucci is out of control and I'm pressing charges."

She kind of smiled and grimaced at the same time as she bade me to sit down. I sat, she sat, and then I began my tirade. "He has ruined Christmas for me and everyone else!" And with that I slammed my rolled up fist on her desk. Nothing shook especially; I just wanted a dramatic effect. I think I got it since her smile ceased.

"Why are you so upset? And how can he ruin Christmas when it's just days away?"

"He and his minion, Kosnowski, were caught by me, with the entire administration office as witnesses, opening the presents that I got for them, prior to the assigned time when they were supposed to open the presents. These gifts were not formally presented to them. This is a pure and simple act of theft. Breaking and entering! Therefore, they are crooks and must be prosecuted. Not only have they violated my personal property space, they have violated the spirit of Christmas. I want heads to roll, all the way to hell."

My performance must have had some effect upon this captive audience of one because her body language seemed like she was jolted to the back of her office chair. (By the way, in keeping with the entire ambiance of her office, this was not the ordinary run of the line agency chair but a deluxe, cushy model.) I must have made some impact upon her tranquility. This was good! She paused, looked at me without any smile, and then paused again. Finally she said, in good HR/company form, "I will have to investigate this further. There are procedures in place for grievances."

"Do I have to put this complaint in writing?"

"No, you have already begun the first step. I will take care of it from here and get back to you."

"When?"

"You can't put a stopwatch or a timetable on any procedural thing like this, especially if it involves high-level administrators, but soon."

"Thank you for your time and courtesy." With that I walked out of O'Keefe's oasis of tranquility with a smirk on my face, knowing that she would be under some kind of pressure to do something to appease me. And I knew that she would have to run this grievance complaint by either Rigatoni or Ferucci. Good! She probably would also have to get more scented candles and a more soothing, bigger and mellifluous waterfall to steady her environment. Some herbal tea would have done her wonders too. As for me, I glided down the hall, back to my cell, and looked forward with piqued delight to upcoming encounter with Kosnowski who must have felt like Eve after hooking up with that most famous of snakes and the most expensive, in the long run, fruit in the entire world.

On those wonderfully but infrequent instances in life, fate deals you four aces. Then you are playing the game just the way you want it, knowing that no matter how bad you are or how good your opponents are, you are going to win. The outcome is never, ever in doubt, like a cat beating up a poor defenseless mouse. With the outcome most certain, you can torment the opposition to death. The possibilities are delightfully endless. Thus with this assured state of mind I entered my cell, coat opened and flowing, like Count Dracula ready to pounce on the next intended victim.

The grand entrance was not made quietly. This was for effect. Kosnowski turned around quickly — half startled, half embarrassed. The litany of profuse apologies began immediately.

"I'm so sorry. I didn't mean to ruin your Christmas. He made me do it. It was his idea, not mine."

I paused for a moment, to heighten the effect, and calmly said, "You could have just said no. You're an adult."

"You don't understand. It was the magic of the moment. And he is our supervisor."

"He may be your supervisor, but I would not follow bad leadership."

"I'll make it up to you somehow. What would you like me to do? I will do anything not to wreck your Christmas. Would you like a hug?"

"No, the damage has already been done. I'll just have to limp through this holiday season as it comes to its sorry conclusion." With that I proceeded to hang up my coat and looked forward to the remainder of a deliciously quiet day. For once I felt I was in control of the asylum. The remainder of the day went by deliciously quiet but all too fast. I reveled in the quiet. It bathe me in a serenity of true piece. There were no visitors to the office. No phone calls. Nothing. Just quiet. The day came and went. Just like that first Christmas Eve, I suppose, there was a stillness that was a prelude to a much bigger event. This was my quiet before the final days, culminating with Friday the Santa that I found, or who found me, would arrive and put me out of my corporate gun sites and my misery. It would be just for a day but I've learned to relish victories of every kind.

As I left the office I did bid Kosnowski a courteous, perfunctory good night. Of course she was required to respond and did so with a meek response. She was suffering. This was good. I wonder if my punishment went too far. I paused, then decided to enjoy the complete victory on my way home, with no mall stops, directly to be with Kiki. I felt good about myself, but at the expense of others? So what! I didn't start the fire. I just didn't know or care to think about it at this time. But the deity always seems to have a way to balance things out in the long run and all perpetrators of ill will pay for their respective crimes in the end. But I didn't feel religious at this time, just peaceful. And that was more than enough! Overall, today appeared to be another good day.

Wednesday was my day to share my culinary skills. In addition to buying a gift for the Secret Santa, every office member volunteered to bring in some holiday treat to share with the entire office. It was my turn to show off and shine. The only problem was that I lacked any enthusiasm to do great things for the office crew. In fact, I was hard pressed to be anything more than civil since they took it upon themselves to be unequivocally critical of everything. Daily I felt like a moving target with a permanent bulls-eye plastered on my back. Maybe I should be wearing a Target vest? It was a loosing assignment even before I started, so why bother to do anything but the most minimal?

I remembered a holiday drink a fellow neighbor made several years ago. It was a nonalcoholic mixture with powered ice tea and Tang, spiced up with some ginger, nutmeg and other stuff that I could not remember, a grander variation that I tried to concoct a few nights before. So I went to the butler's pantry, pulled what I thought were the essential equipment and ingredients and started mixing . . . in small numbers first. The first sampling of half a glass did not taste too good. So, if you don't succeed, try and mix again. This time I added more nutmeg. The second sampling was even worse. Undaunted I decided to go the other way: less nutmeg and more ginger. The third sampling had a little more snap, but still something was missing. It came as an epiphany, at 8:45 in the evening that perhaps a little brandy would do the trick. A shot of brandy went in, and then the entire concoction went into the microwave to render, hopefully, the finished product of a hot, mulled holiday drink. Well, sometimes success is allusive as this drink was proving. It smelled good coming out of the microwave, all steamy. In fact, it could have doubled as a pretty good substitute for a potpourri burner for the winter holidays, but as a drink it could have used more brandy or something. So I redrafted the secret holiday recipe and added more essential brandy. It tasted somewhat better but the mix was still lacked something. That prompted a creative change: scotch would replace the brandy. Another run in the microwave and the stuff came steaming out. Another taste, another failure. Back to the brandy, but this time it would augmented with more nutmeg and ginger and more brandy. As the stuff came steaming out of the microwave, my anticipation quickly turned to disappointment. It was like taking your good looking sister to the prom; it just doesn't quite make it. In the midst of all this experimenting, I was getting a headache. It could have been the failure of creativity or just the brandy meeting up with the scotch and other secret ingredients. At any rate, it looked like I would never, ever have a career in the food processing industry. My only recourse was to go to bed early, meditate upon what may have gone wrong with perhaps things would be better in the morning.

The morning did come, in the nondescript way that is so typical of early winter. Not even the slightest hint of the sun. All well and good since my head was a little stuffed from the previous evening's experimentation of supplements to the grog creation. Getting cleaned up and dressed was particularly plodding and laborious and almost painful, but one must do what one has to do to get to work in a timely fashion. The anticipatory tension of going down stairs and viewing how the grog weathered the overnight hours grew and grew. The knot in my stomach began to push the limits of what boy scouts had to know to make tenderfoot.

I immediately went to the Dutch oven pot that I left on the stove overnight. Lifting the top led to a ghastly sight. Unattractive pieces of detritus floated all over the place. Looks could be deceiving so I got a spoon just to taste a sample, with the hope that overnight the concoction would age gracefully. The taste was not good. I wanted to call it wretched but I made it myself. Evidently, its golden years were passed as the whole thing needed some kind of life support to resurrect it to taste sensation I once remembered. I had to think but not on an empty stomach. Breakfast would definitely help.

The breakfast experience was hasty. Kiki was not around and I had to resolve this culinary conundrum before going to work. With palate purged and with restrained enthusiasm I went back to the pot for another taste. My goodness gracious! — the whole mess seemed to have gotten worse in just a brief ten minute period. I had to leave early and the bad taste would not go away. The only solution, on the spot, that I could think of was more alcohol. I had bottles of gin, vodka, brandy and the like around, but I really did not like scotch. So retrieving an almost full bottle of the stuff, I proceeded to dump the entire contents into the elixir of Christmas. With this problem solved, I grabbed a ladle and bounded out the door for Shop-Rite for any pastry on special, just in case the liquid magic of Christmas would possibly be fatal to those at work.

The visit to Shop-Rite was quick and lucky enough. I was able to find some (day old) cookies at half price. With that purchase, it was a quick run into work. There was no stopping that day at Lucca's.

It was quite a challenge trying to get everything out of the car and into the office in one trip. I wouldn't have it any other way, although I did look like some refuge from a Dickens novel. I think the ladle sticking out of my pocket gave it away. Balancing everything perfectly and not wanting to spill any of the precious liquid in the rather large pot, I gingerly made my way towards the executive office. Rounding the corner, there was Miss Janet with a kid in a wheelchair. She looked at me and started to giggle wildly, and I think that she also encouraged the kid that she was whisking to therapy. I felt like Ichabod Crane or something akin to one of his county bumpkin relations. But, undeterred and eschewing Miss Janet's gaze and any further interaction with her for the moment, I continued undeterred unto the main office.

For one of those singularly, extraordinarily, once in a lifetime events, my arrival into the main administration office was greeted with some degree of enthusiasm. But I honestly knew it wasn't me but the holiday treats that I was bringing to that group of domestic vultures. Rosemarie was the first to blurt out, "What surprises do you have for us?"

"I have some cookies which will be complemented by a holiday (I dared not call it Christmas in respect to the importance of the event) grog from a recipe that I obtained from an old acquaintance."

"We can't wait," she said as she got up from her chair and moved towards the table where I placed the large pot down, followed by the cookies and the ladle. With that, I did an about face and was proceeding to leave, while Rosemarie began the collective snoop for the entire office. Her holiday smile started to fade when she saw that the cookies were from Shop-Rite.

"These are store bought. You didn't bake for us?"

"No, they are not the main treat. All my creative energies went into this once in a lifetime grog creation."

With that she lifted the lid of the pot and looked in. I could almost swear that her smile was now a full fledged scowl as she exclaimed, "It looks and smells awful!"

"Looks are deceiving, as you well know. When you heat the stuff up, it takes on a different, glorious life of its own. You'll see. At 10:30 then?"

She gave a rather unenthusiastic acquiescence as I finally escaped from the early morning inquisition. From there I proceeded to my cell where Kosnowski was engaged in some project or other. We exchanged quiet morning courtesies, and I went about my assignments uneventfully, waiting for the summons from the main office to sample my Christmas offerings. With the pedantic duties of the morning quickly eluding me, the call came in at 10:15 from Ferucci that the office staff was getting eager and restless to party and sample my holiday treats. In one of the very few instances, ever, I bounded out of the office and down the hall to give that undeserving crew my creative best.

I retrieved my Dutch oven pot from the administration fridge and proceeded to put same on the stove burner and lit a low to medium flame. After that, my Shop-Rite cookies were artistically placed on a serving tray that I brought from home, with the hope that the serving tray would add immensely to the presentation appeal and flavor. With the magic elixir cooking on the stove, I went into the main office and made a general appeal for glasses or stemware to serve my frothy treat. Rosemarie immediately shot up from her desk and offered to help because she probably didn't have too much work to do. Nevertheless, despite my efforts to dampen her enthusiasm, she was effervescent, until she snuck around me and pulled the cover off the pot. Her enthusiasm faded as fast as a snowball on the fourth of July. "It looks like sludge," she said with some dismay.

I knew from experience that confrontation never made a convert; so I agreed with her. "Yes, it looks like that now but when this holiday mixture is fully heated and warm, then it will be different. You'll see. Have faith in me."

Disappointed, she went back to her office desk. I, in turn, picked up the lid and looked in. She was right. It looked awful, but hopefully, some heat on the burner would bring my Frankenstein to holiday life. In my perplexed and agitated state, I turned the heat onto a higher setting and proceeded to watch, proverbially, the pot boil. To break the monotony of staring at a burner, I admired my artistic presentation of the Shop-Rite cookies on the tray and proceeded to throw away the box that had the half-off sticker. No prisoners: I didn't want anyone to know that I got these day-old cookies on sale . . . just in case the grog was not a universal hit. Just immediately after my da Vinci admiration, the office staff started to trickle in. The pot was beginning to smoke and a spicy, aromatic fragrance began to permeate the room. Holiday cheer was inevitable. Carol, or somebody, looked around and exclaimed that "We're almost all here! Where are the glasses?" With that she went to one of the cabinets and pulled some glasses out. Casually inspecting same, her facial expression slightly soured, evidently the glassware wasn't clean enough or the wrong shape or size or something. Nevertheless she placed them on the table. At that time a beaming O'Keefe came in, followed by Rigatoni. "We're about ready!" came the shout from the back. But before we could begin, Ferucci swept into the room and proclaimed for all to hear, "Because it's a special day, I'm wearing my holiday socks that match my Christmas tie. I can't wait to sample the doctor's holiday cheer." Evidently the enthusiastic office crowd was lifted to a fever pitch of joyous anticipation. With that, like an indentured servant, I turned the burner off, grabbed the mittens and moved the pot from the stove to the table to begin serving this crowd of unworthy disciples. I had that confused look because there was no ladle (I think I left in the cell) but before I could go to the drawer, Ferucci cast the first stone with "You need a ladle; you dropped the ball again."

"No epic problem," I responded as said ladle was found and placed into immediate service to fill each and every glass, each smoking hot and steamy. Everyone took a glass but before anyone could sample this holiday elixir, Rigatoni broke in and offered his own impromptu toast to all. It was something about the holidays or something. There was even more reason not to listen this time since I was on my own time. He was never at a loss to interrupt with a few words of wisdom and commentary. With that, all raised their glasses and sipped.

It's amazing how the holiday spirit is so superficial with some and could be over in a few meager seconds. I observed each and everyone's facial expression. It was the famous cascading domino effect. Smiles went to quizzical looks to something approaching scowls. Apparently I single handedly wrecked the holiday season for these unworthies even before it could begin. It could have been disheartening, if this bunch of barracudas were warm and fuzzy. Someone coughed, followed by the remark that "Perhaps I'll have a cookie." Then began the litany of resounding rejection and negativity. Rosemarie, never for a loss for words, was the first to blurt out "Something's gone terribly wrong." And that was the most charitable comment that began the negative verbal salvo. The intercessors became progressively worse; each sounding more negative than the predecessor. Some comments could have been taken even personally. It seemed like a crescendo of condemnation. The only two positives in this entire experience was that Regan O'Keefe, always trying to see the bright side of things or perhaps trying the placate me for the Ferucci affair, thought it was a good effort trying to get back to the simpler spirit of the season. And Rigatoni, who was never at a loss for words anytime or anywhere, just kept on coughing and clearing this throat. Maybe I inadvertently finished him off; this could have been a crowning, positive moment. The final result was that everyone returned to their respective desks, with a diminished holiday spirit, and I was stuck with a massive supply of grog and a sizeable number of one-day old, almost fresh Shop-Rite cookies. Somedays, you just can't win. Somedays, you just shouldn't even consider playing the game. Quite evidently, this was not my day to bask in the glory of a culinary triumph. The only recourse left open to me was to return to my cell, head bowed in the humility of defeat, and painfully await the very long time for the five p.m. dismissal. With the ending of the work day, I retrieved what was left of the grog (almost all of it) and the remnant of Shop-Rite cookies (most of it), slinked out of the building, loaded the BMW and sped hurriedly home. At least Kiki would welcome me. And she did, along with the almost filled pot of grog and a score of Shop-Rite cookies. All during that dismal evening at home I wrestled with the tangible remnants of my culinary defeat. I couldn't pour the stuff down the drain because of the potential of clogging and a massive follow-up plumber's bill. And if I dared to drink that stuff, at even a glass a day — well, I couldn't even consider that option. It would take months! It was kind of like having a radioactive waste product that you didn't want in your home. Like every other problem, if I slept on it, the solution would be readily apparent in the morning.

Thursday . . . another upcoming go-around with the agency with more stuff hanging on the line than resolved. The occurrence with Ferucci was still on a holding pattern with HR. It was just 24 hours away from my Santa visit and I still have not heard from him (did he get run over by a reindeer?), and I had a massive quantity of grog in the kitchen that defied disposal solutions. There was no way that I was going to put that stuff down the drain. The only options were composting it or inviting my neighbors over for some pre-Christmas cheer. But the day did begin, summoning me to my respective duties and chalenges, like it or not. The only positive was that Kiki was intrigued by the aroma coming from the grog pot in the kitchen. There had to be a solution somewhere. But I did find myself developing a sincere sympathy for those who have to dispose of toxic waste for a living.

My morning regime for work weekdays slipped into a nondescript routine, from saying goodbye to Kiki, to driving to Lucca's for that most needed cup of coffee before arriving at work more or less on time. The last Thursday of the work year, the last Thursday before Christmas, was no different. The mechanical quality of the whole thing kind of added a robotic reaction to everything else that sort of zapped feeling from the moment to moment stuff. Nevertheless, I was surviving.

I did my perfunctory walk through the hall getting to my office cell, greeted all those who by chance crossed my path (couldn't care if I saw Miss Janet or not), said a grumbled good morning to the secretarial staff, and proceeded to park myself at my desk. Astrid was already in the office. Her perfume wafted through my nostrils and out my ear drums. I was resolved to a day of quiet withdrawal and some paper shuffling and quiet suffering.

But this, too, did not last. At about mid-morning, the phone rang summoning me and Kosnowski to the main office area, where it was Ferucci's turn to share his holiday treats with us. With everything else, I practically forgot that the office lottery assigned him the next to last day to provide merriment for the office before the Christmas holiday recess. I mumbled something to Kosnowski about the imminent festivities occurring in the main office but made no attempt to walk the halls with her together. The swing of the season found me out of step! So we walked separate paths that day.

I was the last one to get to the main office. The gaiety was already in progress with Ferucci leading the stalwart revelers. It was already loud and boisterous — all I needed at this early hour. He was carving up two of his culinary perfections: a rum cake and tiramisu, both homemade. With Rosemarie taking the first bit, the ranting and raving began. I was able (perhaps because I was somewhat sensitive) to glean from all the background noise that today was a vast improvement upon yesterday. My spirits sank lower. When I was given the tiramisu, I had to concede that the quiet little voice from the back was right. It was so good that I had to squeak up with, "What store did you buy this stuff from?" The response quickly came back, "He made it himself." This was followed by another with the derisive observation: "You could have used some lessons."

Admittedly, I was beaten by Ferucci's performance and there was still another sampling to be had. But I resolved not to go down with the count. I was going to take Ferucci with me. I awaited my opportune moment and targeted O'Keefe, as she was shoving her face into a rather large portion of the holiday desert. I wanted to share the suffering. She saw me, smiled and asked me how things were going. Just when she stuffed a rather large portion of tiramisu into her mouth, I asked about the status of my grievance against Ferucci and Kosnowski. "It's been a few days and there may be some favorable movement."

When O'Keefe smiled she showed a mouthful of tiramisu between her teeth and mumbled a response that sounded like, "It's a very sensitive matter since he is my boss, so I have to proceed slowly." And after a long moment's pause added, "Perhaps it wasn't so great an issue that you should be that upset."

"The issue was and is that my privacy was violated. There should be something in the agency's guidelines to that." With those words and not waiting for one of those administrative canned replies from O'Keefe, I turned away quickly and focused my attention on the homemade rum cake. There were pieces already cut and placed on paper plates. I took one and without ceremony quickly left the holiday revelers to themselves. They most certainly deserved each other. For my solitary part, I returned to my cell to sulk, engage in busy work and indulge in the rum cake accompanied by agency coffee. Hopefully, the rest of the day would pass without controversy and disruption. And the rest of the morning was quiet right up to lunch time. Kosnowski was not an irritant on this particular a.m. Serenity was mine and mine alone. This holiday treat thing was slipping into the past.

Religious writers and philosophers seem to be in agreement that nothing lasts. As far as my state of serenity and peace of mind within the protective confines of my cell, they were right. The intrusive ring of the phone brought an equally intrusive summoning from Ferucci to meet in his office. "When?" "Right away," was his response. Not even a chance to go to the restroom. This was one of his subtle cracks with the whip of authority. Evidently O'Keefe must have run my complaint by him, perhaps for the second time, and this was his get-even response.

As I got into his office, Ferucci was on the phone, in all likelihood again with one of his many family members. From what I was able to glean from the conversation was that his Italian Christmas Eve dinner would be held this year at his brother's and sister-in-law's house, with a starting time of 6 p.m. Normally, any word about Christmas would place me into an immediate festive frame of mind, but I lacked any modicum of spontaneity being abruptly summoned into this office. After the differential knock on the door and without waiting for a reply, I went in and proceeded to stand, my act of uncomfortable defiance, until being bade to sit down. I wasn't kept waiting that long as he concluded the phone conversation, but it was just long enough to make a subtle point regarding who was the boss and who was the hired hand.

"I'm pretty busy at this time of year so I hope this is an important summoning." Actually, this day had a comparatively light work load but one should never give any supervisor the feel good notion that his/her meeting is more important than your own work assignments. Humility is not always a good virtue to practice, especially in a cauldron of crooks.

I tried to gauge Ferucci's body language but, as usual, he was as easy to read as the faces on Mount Rushmore. So I stood in personal defiance of his subpoena, hoping to make a statement. Evidently this had no impact either. He began with the usual, dumb question which would eventually lead into a trail of complexity and intrigue. "Do you know what tomorrow is?"

"The day after today," I responded.

I thought my smart, spur-of-the-moment answer was good enough. But the look on Ferucci's face was one between disappoint and annoyance, evidently I was not playing the game well.

He repeated, "And what else does tomorrow bring?"

Since I always thought about finances and money, I retorted, "One day closer to payday . . . and oh, yes, Christmas and vacation."

"Is there anything else?"

"Not that I can think of. You kind of got me on the spot." Since I was standing during this verbal tennis match, I thought this allusion was kind of cool. Evidently Ferucci was not thinking metaphorically.

"Just in case your busy schedule has distracted you, again, tomorrow is the big holiday party for the children. A lot of parents will be here and your only job was to get us a Santa for a day, no, not for a day but for just an hour or so. So . . . can we count on you to carry the ball and deliver on time, or did you drop the ball again? At least, did you get in touch with him with a gentle reminder that tomorrow is the big day for the kids here?

"I called yesterday and everything seems to be on schedule." Literally, I was on the spot. So in these no-win situations, lying in a corporate environment is an acceptable recourse. The truth of the matter, known only to me, was that yesterday and the day before I called the number that was given to me but with no response. The phone rang and rang and there was no answering machine even.

"Good," Ferucci exclaimed with some degree of feigned enthusiasm. "Now I can concentrate on my important work. Oh, and just one other thing, if you can't produce this drive-by Santa, then you will don Henri's costume and be the agency Santa this year. One of us has to cover all the bases. I didn't get where I am today by not planning ahead. That's about all. Have a great afternoon." With that I was summarily dismissed out of his office. I took my time going down the hall and getting back to my office cell. I was on company time, and I was getting set up to get beat up the next day. So, let them pay, even if it was only a minute or two of company time wasted.

My first duty was this Santa Claus business. This albatross, Ferucci's ultimate holiday directive, was killing me. Tomorrow was the big day and I still haven't heard back. The phone calls from home — I must have made more than one attempt, I don't remember how many — were not successful. The phone number that I had just rang and rang continuously, with no answering machine or nothing. Perhaps I transposed the numbers wrong. So I began fumbling at my office desk for the original number. However, since I am so focused on my work and assignments and due dates, the office desk was not the paradigm of order that one would see on HGTV or something like a commercial for household organization. I had to hunt through piles of paper. There were papers in front of me, to the left side of me, to the right of me. There were mounds of important stuff coming in and going out. It was close to being entombed by paper. Yes, I pushed a lot of paper during the course of this past year and a lot of sequoias met their demise because of me. It was one of those accomplishments that garnered mixed reviews. But the project at hand was to find the file with the missing phone number. The more I looked, the more agitated I became and the more papers went flying about the desk. I don't know how many times the pile was moved from the front, to the back, and back to the front. And then the dance went on to move papers from side to side, and back again. Perhaps someone overseeing this entire procedure would have found it humorous; but my equanimity was upset and my temper was quickly going out the only window in the office cell and with that my very slight chance for candidacy for sainthood. Honestly, at that time, I would have rather found the telephone number than be nominated to have my statue placed in the vestibule of some church or out in some courtyard. Beyond a doubt one of the many laws in the universe, which serves as a curse, is specifically designed to hamper and impede good people trying to accomplish good things. The missing phone number was not for a hot dating service or something like that, it was to help kids out. I certainly wasn't getting anything out of this ersatz Santa visit. No, I could not find the stupid number. It was then that my temper got the best of me and I may have started banging things around. My antics must have been either irritating or attention gabbing because the usually forthcoming Kosnowski interrupted my distress with, "Can I be of some help?"

Normally, under usual circumstances, individuals are very receptive to solicitations for help. However, this was not a normal circumstance. Kosnowski was an interloper who took away any chance of me having my own office and with that corporate respect. And this Santa Claus thing seemed like another nail in my career coffin; I had to get this thing straightened out by myself to save myself. Thus I responded to her abruptly, perhaps uncharitably, I just don't know, except Ferucci had me on the ropes again. I kept shuffling and searching, but a half hour of this futile exercise produced nothing but a bad temper. A coffee break was called for; caffeine was needed to sooth my troubled soul.

With cup in hand I went around the corner to the secretarial office. They were always pleasant and cheerful during my dalliances and today was no exception. After a half a cup of the agency's worse, some unremarkable chatter and I bestowed my blessings on the lot of them and left to continue my joyless treasure hunt. The cell was most eerily quiet. Kosnowski did not look up or anything upon my return. Perhaps she was working, perhaps taken back by my upsetting disposition. Who knows what goes on in other people? I've got a litany of my own challenges and problems.

I decided to take a mental break from the phone hunt and do a little work for the company. I was able to focus pretty well since the cell was as quiet as a tomb. Kosnowski was not exactly cowering under her desk, but . . . . My pretend assignment did not take that long, but the afternoon session of purgatory was half finished, and I was still where

I started: no phone number. I needed more air and time to think, so I took a leisurely stroll to the bathroom. The hubbub of the kids' afternoon dismissal was almost finished and a kind of peace was settling in on the building. This exterior peace did little for my inner turmoil. The critically essential stuff in this life is never readily available when you need it. One is always left shifting gears.

Returning to my desk, I resigned myself to the futile but safe busy work; more shuffling of papers. I spent some 20 minutes as a pretend executive, after which things got even more tedious. So to break the monotony of afternoon boredom, I pulled out the little metal box that held all my business cards. I intended to call my architect friend on alleged business to find out the correct time for Christmas dinner held at his house when to my amazement, the lost Santa number fell out. Evidently the Post-It stuck to the back of Carmine's card. With relief and excitement I dialed the alleged Mr. Claus' number. With every ring, I became more perturbed since there was no answer; not even after 10 of them did an answering machine pick up. Nothing! Just a nonfunctioning number? I could have been called a phone booth for all I knew — most disturbing, to say the least! The parents were coming in tomorrow for the real holiday party and Rigatoni would be there with his ominous presence lurking in the background. Compliments he would let go by the board, but complaints, he would register each and every one to use against you at a later date. This is what I needed at this time of year, another nail for my corporate coffin.

Just as I was mulling over my sorry situation, the phone rang. It was Ferucci with his impeccable sense of timing . . . which seemed always at my expense.

"Where you able to connect with your Santa for tomorrow? A lot of parents will be here. Mrs. Wojohowitz always makes it and if she's disappointed in anyway, you know how she can complain."

He had me here: either lie, and get off the hook, or tell the truth and get nailed. I had to make one of these split-second, executive decisions to save my sorry career and anatomical parts or risk loosing my soul to hell for all time since I would be not telling the truth to administrator Ferucci. Where are the Jesuits when you really need them? What to do? The best compromise solution I could think of, under work environment duress, was to take care of the immediate problem and let eternity take care of itself much later down the proverbial road.

"No, I didn't talk with him personally (this was the truth), but I left a message" (this was kind of true since in my heart and spirit I did cry out "Help!" but there was no immediate or discernable answer).

The voice on the other end of the line said that "We're all looking forward to tomorrow, where you can prove me right or wrong in trusting the course of this agency to you. Until that time, we'll see. I'm leaving early to do some shopping for my family. The coupons expire today so I have to get cracking. See you in the morning, earlier than normal, or at least on time, I hope."

I never knew of anyone who could deflate a person in so few words. Nevertheless, I was determined to stick my heels in and hold my ground, even if events were to prove a loosing deal.

The rest of the afternoon went by with the kind of eerie silence that one would experience going through a graveyard at dusk. Kosnowski and I said very little to each other, save for "Good night," and that was all. As I headed home on 287 at the end of another work day, I could not help but think just how stupid this whole situation was becoming, how I could be taken in on the carpet again because of something as dumb and out of my control as a drive by Santa. What a big deal over nothing of real consequence! Just give me anything in a red suit tomorrow. The kids would never know the difference? Would the parents see any difference? And the staff? In all probability they were counting the hours down to begin their long holiday break. Why did I have to be in the middle of all this turbulent nonsense anyway? It seems that the most trivial things produce the most monumental crises.

161

When I got home, Kiki was waiting for me in the window. And that was the high point of that evening. There wasn't much going on that evening in terms of concerts or other activities that close to Christmas, and TV wasn't much better. I felt that I was plunged into a vacuous emotional limbo with nothing to do except wait. If all this holiday stuff were important, my emotional time bomb would have long exploded. So that evening I had both time, brandy and a book of poetry in my hands and just resigned myself towards waiting until the last final days of the work year would inevitably come and go of its own accord.

Friday morning had one of those inauspicious starts: cloudy and gray, with the sun struggling, but not successfully, in trying to bring some light into a winter's day. I was doing everything mechanically that morning, from dressing, eating, feeding Kiki and getting into my car to go to work. Since I was marginally early, I gave in to impulse and stopped at Lucca's for coffee and something buttered. There were a few people in there, but none of the regulars, mostly Rutgers students or people about to catch the train to New York for some holiday excitement. I thought about and then agreed in principle how the prospect of their trip into the city, for any reason, was more exciting than the day ahead of me. With a few sips of coffee in me, and with a state of mind that bordered on the morose, I drove toward the center with a resigned spirit to endure whatever the day was going to throw at me. With cup of coffee in hand, I walked through the school toward my office cell. I was struck, though, by the contrast in attitude of staff and kids; they seemed to know that this was the last full day of school. They all seemed to be infected with a joyous effervescence that was in striking contrast to my frame of mind. I guess that the old saying is still true that the one wearing the crown, or doing all the work, knows no rest or peace of mind. Whatever!

Kosnowski was not there that morning, a clear departure from her routine — perhaps a sign signifying something? But since it was the last full day of school and work at the agency, no one would be too concerned.

I wasn't. I did enjoy and revel in the quiet. I stared at the wall like Bartleby. At that moment at that day, I seemed like a spectator watching my own life unfold. I didn't seem to know what mattered or what was important or what should I really care about. I merely stared at the wall, my thoughts meandering like some river on a summer's day, lost in the riparian twists and turns of life's flow. Time stood still until I was wakened out of my somnambulation by a loud bang; Kosnowski arrived. I didn't know whether to thank her for waking me out of my lethargy or be angry since I was so abruptly startled. But Kosnowski had a way of smoothing everything over; the more she schmoozed, the more ingratiating she became. Since I was a little on the snoozie side, she schmoozed me rather well. She mentioned something or other why she was late but, as usual, she did not have my full attention. I nodded and smiled and withdrew back into the world of my own thoughts, conditions and problems. This state of semi-euphoria lasted for a few more minutes until I was awakened again, this time by Ferucci's jolly voice on the other end.

"Good morning, my champion! And how are you on this, one of the most glorious days of the school year?"

"Fine," I said. I didn't want to give him any opening. But already I did not like the tone of his greeting. His MO was to place a Persian rug down in front of you and then give it a quick jerk when you thought it was safe and walked two or three steps. I was right, because his next remark was, "What time did you say your Santa was coming?"

"Around ten, I think, that was the deal." The tennis match begun, and with a cryptic response, I thought I could placate him without giving away too much incriminating information. But he didn't get to be an executive manager for nothing. He could glean a conviction from even the most minute pieces of evidence. I couldn't live like that but I had to live with him in this work environment.

"What do you mean 'thought'? Didn't you call him just to touch base and confirm?"

Another corporate lie was quickly coming. "I left a message on his answering machine."

Of course there was no answering machine or any telephone contact since I was unable to get through to this guy for days. I needed to breathe for air and had to get Ferucci off my back if even just for the moment. After all it was still early morning and there had to be a rule in the book forbidding nagging at an early, inauspicious hour, even by a spouse, not to mention a work supervisor. I wasn't even married since I doubly did not want to be under the gun. Not now. And the hour was coming. If Santa came, I would be off the hook, and if he was a no-show, then I would worry about it then in a half hour. So, I just wanted time. And I got it, Ferucci hung up and me and left me staring at the wall.

Kosnowski, of course, who had even keener hearing than a cat and was slick in her own right, added, "I can't wait. Everyone tells me that this is the best day of the year here. I hope your Santa knocks 'em over in their tracks."

"We shall see. Personally, though, I can't wait for this day to be over. It's just too much stress for a simple farmer like myself to endure."

"Oh, common now!" And with that, the office fell into a quiet silence as the clock made its climb up the hill towards the ten o'clock hour. Just before the top of the hour, I proceeded to the secretaries' office to get a half cup of coffee to settle my nerves. Caffeine could have medicinal effects. The secretarial office, fortunate for me, was quietly abuzz and paid little attention to my coming, mooching and going. As I was about to reenter my cell, I heard the vice principal's voice on the PA summoning classrooms 1, 2, 3 and 4 to begin their respective treks to the auditorium for the holiday festivities. It gave me just enough time to plop into my office seat and glance at the clock. The magic hour of ten was past. The kids and staff were marching towards their holiday destiny and I was alone without my Santa. What I needed now was Ferucci on the phone. Within seconds my holiday nightmare was answered; it was the voice of you-know-who on the phone with the least appreciated question: "Is your Santa here?"

Stalling for time, I replied, "Not yet. Let me get away from my desk and look down the hall." Without waiting for an answer, I dropped the receiver on the desk and went for a look-see. It was an abrupt, instinctive reaction, but hopefully it would prove annoying enough. And I kept him waiting just long enough for him to stew ever so slightly.

Picking up the phone after the contrived delay, I responded, "No, not yet! He must be delayed feeding his reindeers or something."

"Call me back in five minutes. It looks like you have a crisis on your hands." With that he put the receiver down in a non-discreet manner. Immediately after, I heard the PA announcement summoning classrooms 5, 6, 7 and 8 to go the auditorium. The exodus was now half complete and all I had was a promise or a good intention or something, but nothing concrete. I needed a presence. I got the voice of Kosnowski asking me if indeed Santa was coming.

You can't take anyone's head off for a seemingly honest question. But this crisis situation was not the time for any questions that would belabor the obvious. As I muttered quietly under my breath, "I don't know," the PA summoned classrooms 9, 10, 11 and 12 to the auditorium. It was long after ten, and I noticed that my blood pressure was rising and my pulse was quickening. Maybe it was the agency coffee. I got up from my office chair and went to the main hallway. I peeked in both directions and saw only the kids and staff moving to the auditorium. I went back to my cell, plopped in my chair and looked for Santa's phone number. I had to do something. The idea was stupid, though. If he was on the way, he couldn't answer. And if he was home, then all was totally lost for me. I began fumbling anyway, just as the PA made the final announcement that the rest of the student body and staff were to report to the auditorium. Within seconds, my phone rang again. Guess who? My time had run out.

"Is your Santa there?"

I muttered, "Not yet."

"Then come to my office immediately. Is that clear?"

"Yes," I responded. With that, I began my long journey to Ferucci's office, dejected, broken in spirit and expecting a verbal beating when I got there. In this regard, you were never disappointed.

The first thing I noticed when I came into the office was the slight smirk. It was similar to the facial expression of an inexperience poker player who suddenly found four aces in his dealt hand.

"What time is it?"

I looked at my watch. "12 after ten," I said.

"Not really, I have fifteen after on my watch. And where is your Santa? Did the sleigh break down on 287 or something?"

"I don't know. There were no calls or nuthin'."

"Well, we can't disappoint the kids, especially at this time of year, not to mention their parents and our president. So, here." With that he reached around his desk and quite literally threw a Santa suit at me. It was kind of ratty looking.

"What do you want me to do with this?"

"Well, since you were in charge of getting a Santa and you dropped the ball, then you must accept full responsibility for this fiasco and step up to the plate and . . . ."

"No, not me! Why don't you volunteer fat man Bill for this assignment? After all, he's ideally suited — sorry for the bad pun — for this job. He's like a 100 pounds heavier than me and he likes kids more."

"No, Bill is busy with other assigned duties, and he's not the one who dropped the ball on this most important matter. So . . . you can get dressed here. We can't disappoint the kids, parents, staff and our president, can we? I'm leaving now for the auditorium and eagerly await your grand entrance."

With that he departed his office, leaving me with only my thoughts and the Santa suit.

What to do? Nothing, since this battle was lost. I had no choice but to follow his stupid order. I mechanically began by dressing myself. First the pants, then the jacket and then the vinyl things that look like boots from a distance. The suit immediately smelled stinky. I don't think that it was dry cleaned or washing machine cleaned since the first time someone wore it, which was probably 60 years ago. After stifling my olfactory senses, I went to the big belt with large buckle. That worked OK but I immediately ran into a significant problem. I wasn't as big, or call it fat, as Bill Brown or Santa Claus. In this instance, I was pathetically thin. The big belt, when fastened on its thinnest hole, fell from my waist to the floor. From all pictures that I've seen, Santa always had that belt. You couldn't have Santa without that big belt and buckle. Ferucci always had a cushion on his office chair, perhaps because he had hemorrhoids and/or shared same with others who had any business dealings with him. So necessity and invention and the situation being what it was, I took the cushion and stuffed it into my Santa pants. It wasn't exactly a perfect fit since even without any close observation since you saw the four square corners poking through the costume. Round would have been better. Next came the beard. It was ratty. But I counted my luck since there weren't any birds or other wildlife nesting in it at the time. Finally the hat. I looked at this thing for a while. The white tassel on the end wasn't; it had more of a yellowish or golden hew to it. Then I mistakenly looked on the inside. That was not a good move; my stomach churned. There was dark, caked stuff on the inside, like someone's hair conditioning stuff left over from the war. But what could I do. I prayed, briefly, for divine protection since I was doing this for others and put my crown of velvet thorns on. There weren't any Santa glasses, so I guess I was finished and ready for the big stage. Just at that time, Ferucci came rushing into the office, in an excited state. "Let's go. The kids and staff have sung 'Jingle Bells' three times through already and the place is about ready to rock off of its foundations. My, do you look . . . special."

"I would look better if I could disguise myself with some Santa glasses or something."

"Say no more." With that, he went into this office drawer and pulled out what looked like a pair of wire rimed reading glasses. He gave them to me and said, "Now you perfectly fit the part."

I put the stupid glasses on and immediately realized I couldn't see. They were his prescription glasses.

"I can't see."

"Just put these glasses on the end of your nose and I will lead you down the hall."

"Great! I feel like a steer being led to slaughter. Thanks for the offer, but I'll find my way to the auditorium by myself. If I can't see, then I will follow the sound of the noise."

"Fine, then I'll see you there and soon." With that Ferucci left and I reluctantly decided to follow some ten to 20 seconds behind him.

With my time expired and heeding a call that I could not refuse, I began my slow shuffle to the auditorium. The administrative office was between an eighth to a quarter mile away. You went straight for a while, then made a sharp left and walked until you came to the very end of a long hallway and then made another left. At any rate, it gave me plenty of time to sample all the random thoughts that went through my head, all pointing to the fact that I was indeed one of the greatest jerks of all time. Why did I let myself get suckered into this type of situation anyway? I trusted humanity too much!

As I rounded the first corner and made the left turn, I began to experience what would be called in the trade mechanical problems. Given my lack of rotund size, Ferucci's pillow, which was originally to be my stomach stuffing, began to sag. It wasn't secured inside and just a few steps were causing it to succumb to the laws of gravity. Undaunted, I grabbed the thing, shook my frame and brought the pillow back to where it belonged. The shuffle continued but the cushion did not stay in place. This time it was really bad since it went to my knees. I couldn't even shuffle. I bent over to make another style adjustment when Ferucci's glasses fell off and broke on the tiled floor. Before I was able to use bad language, the kind that one would not normally use before kids, I heard uncontrolled laughter. I turned out Miss Janet came back to her office for something and caught sight of me at this worse moment of my life. I knew immediately that her derisive laughter was really the nail in our relational coffin. So I snapped back, "What's so funny?"

"You . . . in that outfit. You look pathetic, like a Santa from a concentration camp or something. It's hysterical. You look like a bean pole with a pillow or something hung around the middle. I don't even think our kids are going to buy it." She continued laughing until she had tears in her eyes.

I looked at her and could only say, "Thanks for the opportunity to brighten up your day." But what I should have said was "Janet, Janet, heart of granite, wish you were on another planet." With that, I continued my shuffle down the hall of infamy. All the months of tactical flirtations and any promise of a seductive sampling of a delightful future with Miss Janet was lost. I went down the hall knowing that my imagined social relationship was finished, and I did not want to think about my work career at this point. No woman wants to be hooked up with a refugee clown who escaped from a third-rate circus. My only option was to accept the nadir of my life, make a public spectacle and fool of myself in front of an incredulous and unsympathetic crowd, and get the thing over with and go home.

With head hung down, I proceeded to the gym for the final curtain call of my life. But as I got to the middle of the school building, I heard another laugh but one that was more gentile. It was Joe with an entourage.

169

"Sorry I'm a little late but I got held up."

Just when I didn't expect it and needed it the most, salvation! I perked up. Things changed in a moment. The frown went 180 and vanished.

"Where can we change? It'll take us just a minute."

I pointed to the deserted office right by the entrance. "Let me take this stupid suit off and I'll be back in a minute to pick you guys up and lead you to the auditorium." With that, they headed into the office and I hustled back to Ferucci's office to get rid of a uniform that was so dirty that the moths wouldn't even think to touch it.

As long as the time seemed to get me from Ferucci's office to the middle of the building, it was in a comparative instant that I returned, dumped the Santa suit and returned to the middle part of the building where I left off the real Santa and helpers. Just as I got there, Ferucci came rolling down the hall with a none-too-pleasant look. Just as he was about to get a heart attack, share it with me, and excoriate me about being out of uniform and late for the auditorium party, Santa and his entourage came out of the office, ready for business. I don't know if it was the moment or what, but he looked more real than the real thing . . . and Ferucci just shut up . . . didn't say a word. He glumly led this unexpected retinue down the hall and made the left turn into the auditorium. His gloom was my glee, all the more so! I was saved by the real thing. Santa, Mrs. Claus and the Snowman all were dragging rather large bags filled with presents down the hall. Both Ferucci and I stepped aside as Santa and entourage entered the auditorium to a resounding scream from kids, parents and staff. The place literally was rocking off its foundations. With that very successful entrée, I ran back to my office and got my camera, just in case there were to be decent photo opts.

Teachers and therapy staff were with their respective classrooms. And there were big, black plastic garbage bags, all with name tags, filled with presents for each child. These presents came from a variety of sources; some that I hustled from groups and individuals, some from the outreach efforts of the social workers, some from staff — a nice collection of gifts that came from the heart. This was one of the few times that staff was in agreement that no kid should be forgotten at Christmas. The only philosophical disagreement pitted practicality against fun: should the kids get clothing, which some needed, or toys (what's Christmas for kids without toys?). But it looked like the disagreement was over before it even started; the kids were getting both. Santa went around and greeted each kid personally. He even called them by their first name — evidently he was reading the name tags on the garbage bags. Gifts were flying out all over the place. Mrs. Claus and the Snowman followed behind the fat man and pulled stuff out of the canvas bags they brought (no plastic here). Their presents were astounding! Clock radios, watches, remote controlled toys and other good stuff followed, inexhaustibly, one after another. My camera was firing away, burning up roll after roll of film. The din of the entire proceeding overwhelmed everyone, well, almost everyone. I cast a quick glance over and caught Ferucci who seemed more agitated than normal, perhaps things were a little too loud and out of his control. And then there was Rigatoni who had a scowl like a kid who was forced to have a generous helping of caster oil. But everyone else was having a good time, so whose problem was it?

The festivities went on for about 45 minutes. Every kid got something very special from Santa and his helpers as well as the potpourri from the individual bags. But just as in life, nothing endures forever, good times or bad. Just before 11:30, things came to a conclusion. The kids, led by the music teacher, sang "Jingle Bells, again, as Santa and his retinue waved goodbye and departed the auditorium. I took a final photo as they all waved goodbye and then accompanied them to the middle of the building to change clothing and get back to civilian life. Santa became Joe in less than a minute. As the kids and staff streamed by, I thanked Joe and company again for their gifts of time and toys for the students. Since I took lots of photos, some of them had to have turned out pretty good. I asked, "Would you like some photos of today's event?"

"Thanks, but it's OK! Just to see the smiles on these kids faces is enough."

"The photos are our nonprofit way of saying thanks. And I've taken plenty of shots. How can I, on behalf of our agency, thank you enough?"

"You already have by letting us be part of your holiday festivities."

With that, the entourage quickly swept out of the building and toward the parking lot. I was too flummoxed to see what kind of car they were driving or anything else. In the midst this farewell, the kids were returning to their respective classrooms, and their rush swept me away from the front door like an autumn leaf being taken downstream by a strong current. In the process I tumbled into Ferucci and could not help but ask how he liked the Santa show that I brought in, saved the day and was the best Christmas event ever in my tenure with the agency.

"It was OK but the gifts probably fell off a truck somewhere."

Sometimes you can't even get credit for a clean and clear cut victory. I let it pass, since to me the event was an unqualified success, and made my way back to the office cell. The continuing procession of kids and staff were still emptying the auditorium. A "Thank You," or two, would have been nice, but nothing like that was forthcoming in this place. I had to be contented with the smiles on the kids' faces; and that's enough and that's all that could ever be expected.

Kosnowski was already back in the cell when I got there. When she saw me she nearly exploded with congratulatory remarks. "Everyone was right. This is the most spectacular day I've ever had in any work environment. The kids, the Santa, the sharing of the gifts, the festive music . . . ." With that gushing, understandably she began to cry.

"Next to my wedding, this was the second nicest day of my life."

I didn't know what to say or do, except keep a stiff upper lip. I never quiet knew how to handle a gushing female. So I said, with a slight laugh, "You'll get over it."

"No, this moment will stay with me forever."

I didn't know about forever but I was still on an emotional high. Since the adrenaline was still flowing, I didn't feel like working on anything. Lunch time was approaching, but I didn't feel like eating either. So I decided to wander over to the secretarial office and mooch a cup of the world's worst coffee. The shock of it certainly would bring me down to earth and help me gain some of my equilibrium back. So, with mug in hand, I inflicted my presence on the secretaries. They were all busy, evidently getting stuff out of the way before the Christmas holiday break. This was kind of perturbing since I just came off of an impact, roller coaster event and no one seemed to be interested or affected. I took my half a cup, sipped it a little, and quietly departed. I could have been invisible as all they cared. Went back to the office cell, sipped more coffee and stared at the wall. Work probably would not be an option. Since it was approaching lunch time, I decided to ponder my options: eat out in celebration or go to the cafeteria and mooch whatever was left over. The real question was whether food would taste better, the same or have any appeal upon my taste buds after this morning's event. But what the heck: I was too wound up to care, and to save money I went on the mooch route. Besides, it would only cost me a dollar and dessert would be basking in the glory of my latest triumph. So I shuffled paperwork and played pretend busy for a few minutes until I finally cracked and headed off to Dora's kitchen for leftovers. For one of the few times in the many years that I worked in that place, I even smiled. I could be approachable.

Dora's kitchen was always abuzz, especially during the narrow window of only an hour of lunch for the kids. It was into this caldron of activity that I entered, wearing my festive, victory smile. This small area was crowded with teachers and aides getting food on the carts for the kids in their respective rooms, and poor Dora, diminished but not defeated by the heat, quickly dishing out salads, entrées, drinks and desserts for each and every kid. I patiently waited on the side until she finished her daily duty. All during that time, I was kind of ignored or overlooked. Perhaps I was just invisible. The glory of the morning was gone and forgotten. No one said anything. Perhaps they were too busy, too caught up into the routine and regimen of their own lives, perhaps too overwhelmed by other stuff that they forgot what happened just a short while ago. I was stunned. My disappointment quickly grew and my smile, which bloomed for day just once a year, faded away.

It was only when all staff members left the kitchen area that I asked Dora for lunch leftovers. I was always lucky with Dora since she always gave me extras; today, I got a double helping of macaroni and cheese. The stuff looked great but had absolutely no taste. I had to heavily salt the stuff down, and I never salt anything since it's bad for the blood pressure. In the process of salting food, tray, table and floor, Dora remarked, "It was quite loud in there this morning."

"Both me and the kids had a great time of it. I don't know about the staff."

"Oh, they had a great time too! They just are caught up in the excitement of today, that's all. This is the last chance they have with the kids because of the vacation break. You know just how attached and devoted they are to these kids."

"Yea, you're probably right. But my head is still spinning from this morning."

"You'll have a chance to come back down to earth with the break. Are you taking the entire time off or are you coming in to catch up on work?"

"I haven't decided yet. We'll see what happens."

"Well, in case I don't see you again, have a wonderful Christmas and New Year's." With that, Dora came up to me, and I still had a rather large mouthful of pasta in my mouth, and gave me my first Christmas hug. It was great, although Dora was very short and I towered over her by a foot and a half. I finished my meal, salt with some macaroni thrown in, and left the quiet of the kitchen area. With lots of time left on my lunch hour, I decided to grab a book and read in the corner of the atrium. Perhaps one staff person would come up to me and congratulate me on the Santa experience.

So I hung out in the atrium, halfway through the book, read and watched staff come by. Perhaps I was too scrunched up in the corner because only about a third even remotely acknowledged my presence. No one said anything about the morning. It was as if nothing happened. After about 45 minutes of this curious inactivity, I packed up the book and headed back to the cell to finish up the last full work day of the year.

Kosnowski wasn't there, so I had the insular kingdom all to myself. No need to shuffle papers or do anything, just stare at the wall like Bartleby. Normally my Puritanical upbringing would begin nagging me not to dawdle but I was both physically and emotionally exhausted and tuned out. So for the longest time I just stared at the wall until I was shocked out of my miasma by an energized Kosnowski who returned from an impromptu shopping trip at the mall. By contrast, she was very energized. She began her prattle about her successful luncheon shop with presents for her family and wacko friends — since it was Christmas and everything — and I was the captive, catatonic listener. There was nothing else I could do; I was on the verbal receiving end. But it was the holidays, who was I to dampen anyone else's spirit of the season? So I listened, smiled and nodded my head in agreement, and she went on. My mind began to wander during this lecture session, but before I went off the deep end, Kosnowski's phone rang. She politely excused herself and the interruption — I honestly didn't mind — and answered. The smile slowly left her face. When she put the receiver down, she turned to me and said that the president wanted to see both of us later in the afternoon.

I said, "You still should be smiling and basking in the holiday spirit. Scrooge probably wants to shake our hands for a job well done during the course of the year and probably give us some kind of end-of-year bonus."

"I don't think so. He mentioned that we both should bring some note pads or something to take notes."

"It's probably a holiday ploy."

And with that, we both tried to engage in busy work until four when our meeting was scheduled.

A few minutes before four, Kosnowski jumped up like a jack-in-a-box and was ready to bound down the hall for the meeting, the last one of the year. The thought could have been Christmas bonus enough. I glanced at her smiling countenance, gushing with holiday grace, and asked, "Where are you going in such a hurry? It's fashionable to a little late for these meetings, then he would respect you more. You could claim that you were working on an important project or something. Pretend."

"Come on! The sooner we start, the sooner we get it over with, and then we can all go home."

Kosnowski led me down the hall. If this were a race, she would have beaten me out significantly. But this was one race I didn't care to win. Seemingly with every passing day, I would loose just a little more desire to coddle up to Rigatoni. Just could not get into that groove anymore. For the sake of my job security, I hope my disaffection just didn't show.

Kosnowski was already seated and spinning her note pad when I walked in. Rigatoni had his holiday puss on; evidently this could seriously impact my anticipated Christmas bonus. As I took the only other available seat, he began with his introductory rite of clearing his throat. He always sounded like someone on life support. Perhaps I should have fastened my seat belt for this meeting.

He began, "I've called this meeting at the last full day of the official work year to briefly recap your activities (he looked at me with that one) of this past year and set your goals and marching orders for next year. The agency is growing. Everybody wants our services. But no money, no mission. The supplemental funding that came in last year was inadequate (he looked at me again) to meet expanding expectations. This is an agency that is on the move."

With a knee-jerk reaction I found myself blurting out, "But I brought in more money this past year than last. I've added, if memory serves me right, three more funders to the agency donor pool." What could I do? The truth of the matter was that I brought in more in an economy that was in a downturn. I had to defend myself against administrative bullying and incorrect assumptions. Evidently, I must have hit a nerve or something or Rigatoni did not expect one of his paid servants to talk back. He winced slightly and said, "A senior development officer, like you claim to be, should be pulling in much more, from what I read in all the trade journals. This holiday program is just one .example where you spent too much time in getting donations that don't directly benefit the agency. We would be better served if it were dollars going into programs."

"But people give what they want to give. And it makes them feel good at this time of year to play Santa to our kids."

Rigatoni cleared his throat again and looked at me, without any approving smile, and said, "It's your job to make them feel good about supporting this agency. The vacation break is coming up and during that time I want both of you to be busy thinking about aggressively going out, making each and every donor feel good (I know that he was talking to me on this one), and getting more support for this agency. The excuse that these are tough economic times just will not cut it with the board. Daily they ask me how you are doing. I don't want to report failures. I want to report success. Thus, when you go back to your office, I want you to formulate an action plan for the next three months for next year. I want this in writing on my desk the day you come back from the break. And with these marching orders, I wish you a good holiday and hope to see you with renewed vigor, enthusiasm and initiatives for next year. Any questions?"

I looked at Kosnowski and she looked at me, and then we both looked at Rigatoni. Kosnowski asked how long should this plan be and Rigatoni retorted, "As long as it takes to be effective and working. The agency counts on your efforts and the board is watching all our moves closely."

With the dismissal we schlepped back to the cell, nearly speaking a word. What a day: going from the exultation and high from Santa in the morning to Rigatoni's edict in the late afternoon! Every emotion that I could have experienced was felt during that work day. One could not imagine what could be next? But one thing was sure, no Christmas bonus.

Back in the cell, I turned in my chair to Kosnowski and asked her what she intended to do about the action plan. Evidently she wasn't too concerned. She was just going to write some things down and give it to him. "Nothing to worry about." I felt less confident as I started racking my brain for some kind of strategic plan that would save me or at least put Rigatoni off for a few months. I knew that the beginning of a new work year was the worst possible time for raising money from donors. People were financially tapped out by December and needed time to recover, both financially and emotionally. It all seemed like a dead end. What to do, what to do? A dead battery needs recharging. But that takes time. I wondered how much time Rigatoni would give me.

So I started scribbling some random thoughts on how to get more donors and more money. But I've been doing this stuff for years, and got to know the ebbs and flow of money, both incoming and outgoing. The months of January and February were about as productive as finding water in a desert. Stuff was just not readily available and no amount of executive whining or bullying was going to change anything, except perhaps my status with the agency or giving me a nervous breakdown.

I scribbled a few disconnected thoughts on paper. Nothing was very incisive or earth shaking. Since foundations were finished for a couple of months, I noted some corporate visits and some pandering to social service organizations and groups. It was all words, nothing of substance. Perhaps Rigatoni would buy my lame action plan or perhaps not.

At any rate, the way things were going, it was almost time to go home. So I packed up my stuff, put on my jacket and paid farewell respects to Kosnowski and headed out the door. I had the film from the morning shoot with Santa and the kids and headed to the photography shop for processing. I had my excuse for an early dismissal as well as an accompanying headache. What a day!

Dropped off several rolls of film at the local photography shop. Since it was the weekend with Christmas around the corner, the stuff would not be ready until the following Thursday, at the earliest. Sometimes — more often than not — things are out of your control, so why worry or even think about it. After that, I went home, and as I pulled into the driveway there was Kiki waiting impatiently in the window for another of my late returns. At least, by day's end, I had one vote to the good. The rest of the evening was nondescript as I marked time for the new day to finish off the last full day of the work year at the agency. A brandy after dinner, while listening to some baroque Christmas music, was the way the evening was going. But after half-an-hour of sipping and swirling the stuff in the snifter, a strange idea suddenly popped into my consciousness: why not put up the Christmas tree? I hadn't gone through that seasonal ritual in years, not since the ex walked out because she had to rediscover and reconnect with her feelings. So, after one more sip and getting rid of the slower paced music for something a little faster in tempo, I began the marathon of ascending and descending the stairs, from first floor to attic and back again, with boxes of trinkets and treasures to put on the fake tree. Actually, the tree wasn't too bad; it did look better than most real trees. Placed in the front bay window with all the white lights, the house certainly got that needed boost for the holidays, all in less than two hours time. It could have been a little quicker, but I had some problems with Kiki who had to explore each and every string of light bulbs, and then decided that the fake red apples placed on the lower boughs of the tree were not to her liking. Several were batted around the living and dining rooms. So despite the disciplinary problem with the cat, all eventually was set at the homestead and looking pretty well to boot. Privately I was celebrating Christmas for the first time in years. I was almost proud of myself.

Monday, the final day, or rather half-day, of the work year began with a glorious sunrise through the east window. Hopefully, this was a sign of god things to come. With moderate enthusiasm since it was the last day of the year with those people, I got out of bed, got dressed and went downstairs for some food. Kiki was already waiting impatiently for me and her share of the morning attention. Everything seemed to move by in a flash. So before I knew it, I was on 287 heading for Roosevelt Park. Since the day began so gloriously, nothing would be more appropriate than a stop at the coffee house to wish anyone there whom I knew a joyous few days (without me). But with a sparse number of cars taking up valuable spaces outside, the crowd inside the shop was even more diminished from the norm. Festive music played quietly over the counter din, the Lionel train in the rear of the store was not running, and there wasn't anyone I knew, save for the hostess. I gave her a little holiday tip, and proceeded to drink my coffee while starring mindlessly out the window at the town's decorations and people walking by the shop's window. It was an effort to pry myself away from this hypnotic trance, but the inevitability of bringing the work year to a conclusion drove me into the duty of a less friendly reality.

The parking lot was full, as I approached the school building. But the first oddity was the total lack of school buses in front. Then in a few seconds it hit me: no buses because there were no children. I made my grand entrance, through the front door, late as usual but the second oddity was that no one seemed to be around. Walking down the deserted halls to the cell, I passed the secretarial office where only light work accompanied by some heavy conversation was going on. Holiday music wafted between the breaks of work and conversation. It seemed so out of sync. When I got into my cell, Kosnowski was not there. It seemed that I died, became invisible, and then came back into a world that neither saw, heard nor needed me. All I could do to try to return to normalcy was to attempt some kind of work activity. So I went to it, although I had a hard time trying to focus on what seemed to be a meaningless activity. My mind wandered here and there, time was irrelevant and I was accomplishing nothing. My hiatus in limbo was abruptly broken by the Kosnowski's energetic arrival. Before I could even turn around, she blurted out, "Almost Merry Christmas!" Her joviality was matched by her very rosy cheeks — a sure sign of the season — and several tattered shopping bags overflowing with presents. I was jolted back into a reality of sorts. And even quicker as this shock expired, she abruptly bounded out of the office with one of the bags, leaving the others behind. It happened all so quickly that I couldn't quite remember if she even took off her coat or not. But what was obvious was that I was left, alone, in silence that was somewhat eerie. All I could do was ponder the wall; things were too discombobulated for any work. With the passage of time that was only a few minutes but seemed like a veritable eternity, I could not longer stay in the office cell any more. I had to go out and explore and try to establish some logical sense of this disconnectedness.

I passed by the secretarial office; they were still chatting and still oblivious to my presence and that of anyone else. Walking by the classrooms and some of the therapy offices, and the population was slight, at best. Where did all the drivers of the cars parked in the lot go? Finally made it to the main administrative office and only half of the staff were present. No Rigatoni, no Ferucci and no Kosnowski; none were nowhere to be found. I exchanged morning pleasantries and was told that around 11:30 everyone would be gathering to exchange holiday cheer and presents. With that pleasant bit of information, I returned to the office cell and waited. My only recourse was to watch the clock painfully and slowly tick seconds away. It was during this mind wandering time that I was jolted back into reality awareness by a knock on the door. There was Regan O'Keefe with Rachel, one of her HR assistants, with a squeaky wheeled cart wishing me a happy holiday or some sort of similar tiding. Both were wearing holiday smiles, red sweaters and assorted holiday paraphernalia, e.g., buttons and pins. Either they could pass for refugee elves or the holiday spirit did get the better of them. Rachel reached onto the cart and picked up a candle, which in turn she gave to O'Keefe, who in turn gave it to me along with a holiday greeting from Rigatoni wishing me and my family the best for now and the coming year. They also gave me another candle for Kosnowski who was some place floating around the building and asked me to extend the same generic, schmaltzie wish for her. I said I would, but under my breath I asked if this was my Christmas bonus. As O'Keefe was leaving, I asked her if she had any follow up regarding my complaint about the Ferucci situation and those opened presents under the office tree. But she bounded out of my presence faster than the last pork chop on the boarding house table, yelling out that she would see me in the front office at 11:30. That was the official time for present exchange. Until then, I was put off again. And alone in the office cell. That gave me time to meditate some more, this time on O'Keefe's handling of these holiday gifts. The candles that everyone was getting measured about three by four inches, and could cost up to five dollars at any retail store. These were replacement gifts for the poinsettias two weeks ago that had aphids. Some three hundred plants were handed out to staff that were plague infected with those little white puffy bugs. So I did the math. The flowers must have cost five bucks apiece, the candles five bucks apiece. That totaled ten bucks. For ninety more dollars I could have had my Christmas bonus and they could have kept all that useless stuff. But instead the agency gave me, and then recalled, an infected flower followed by a fragrant candle that I would probably re-gift since I had no practical use for it. What was next, aromatic cream lotion? So I continued to meditate and stew about the injustice of it all, staring at the wall. My tranquility was abruptly interrupted by the brisk and enthused re-entry of Kosnowski who was filled much too much with the holiday spirit.

"Are you getting ready? We've been summoned to the main office at 11 for celebration, cheer and presents. I can't wait!"

"Thanks," I muttered and proceeded to do something that would cover up my lack of enthusiasm.

Kosnowski then proceeded to unbag and rebag her collection of presents, and this was done rather loudly for my sensitive ears. How in heaven's name could packages make that much noise? But I didn't complain since this was the season for merriment and I didn't want to be called a Scrooge or a grinch or something of that ilk. When I thought she was ready, I asked Her Majesty if she, indeed, was ready to make the grand stroll down to the administration offices. She was. She was packing two rather large bags, along with a smaller one. I had nothing since my stuff was already under the tree. I could have offered to help, since I was carrying nothing, but I figured it would have detracted from her joy and the spirit of the season. At any rate, it would be a chuckle seeing if she could manage everything all by herself down the hall. I must admit, though, no chuckles since she was pretty good at managing the teeter-totter of all that she was carrying. As we passed on our journey, some staff person gave me one of those looks since I wasn't helping matters, but I was more confused than anything since the holiday period made things progressively more confusing minute by minute.

Certainly Kosnowski's arrival in the main administrative office was greeted by those shouts of joy that you would mistakenly think that she was some returning war hero or something. I quietly snuck in behind her. The environment was certainly set with over played pop Christmas music in the background quietly droning on, holiday pastries were in visual abundance, and everyone was wearing those festive colors of clothing that so typified the holiday period. Oh yes, there were smiles galore, like the kind that would have greeted a reformed Scrooge on Christmas day morning. What was I missing in all this? I needed feeling. The spirit of the moment did not capture me, perhaps the individuals of the moment never did. This was a work environment, and thus the friendships weren't really friendships but solely business associates ultimately forced on you. It's hard to get warm and fuzzy when you know that there are only a few dollar bills holding up the relationship. So be it; I'll be a fraud and try to maximize the moment, but it couldn't guarantee that my future happiness was dependent on this group.

The festivities themselves were certainly acceptable. Among the food items for the feast, Rosemarie brought in some homemade Hungarian cookies, the ones with the copped walnuts, and Ferucci brought in some of his rum cake, which seemingly had equal parts of cake and rum. Everyone ate and exchanged pleasantries. Off the record, this was the same group that engaged in some nasty backbiting during the remaining 11 months of the year. The no-win situation was such that I deferred to the spirit of the season, their alleged conviviality notwithstanding. But I could not help but feel like an outsider looking in. Anyone passing by the front door would assume that I was one of the accepted insiders of the agency. Appearances can sometimes mislead.

Presents were finally exchanged. There were "Ohs" and "Ahs" and other expressions of delight and surprise as the recipients received their rewards for friendships built up during the year's course of a work environment. They couldn't be more delighted. I got stuff too, but the spirit of the occasion was taken from me when Ferucci unceremoniously and without permission pushed the unofficial date of the present openings earlier in the month. Oh yea, there was nothing that I really needed or anything the marketing people would have me hungrily lusting for. I got nothing that I had to have.

With holiday muzak filling the ears, presents in their respective wrappings satiating the eyes, it was now time for even more holiday pastries to assault the palate. There were home baked cookies, chocolates and more Hungarian kifli. With all this, who needed lunch? With all this commotion going on, Rigatoni came out from his presidential cave. He wore a kind of smile that reminded me of the pope pontificating over the faithful during Easter. He evidentially approved of the lot of us unworthies partaking of the merriment of the season, but apparently preferred to be slightly detached, the curse of being a president!

After offering us the approval of his presence, Rigatoni asked, "Would anyone like a cup of Irish coffee?"

The lot of us responded in the affirmative. He proceeded to return to his office and began the brewing process. In a short time he returned, carrying a cup in each hand. The women had first service, and they began their holiday sipping. Ferucci and I were last. Sometimes the wait is worth it, though, since he did brew a mean cup. This was especially ironic since it was Irish coffee prepared by an Italian. After the rave reviews by office staff, Rigatoni did confide that his special secret was using Jameson whiskey, lots of it, to enhance flavor. Between the rum of Ferucci's cake and the whiskey in the coffee, we were all on that elevated road to holiday cheer.

The banter and chatter continued well past lunch time. This option was somewhat better than work. But things come to an end — good, bad or indifferent — nothing does last, so too with any office party. The ladies started talking about their respective preparations for Christmas Eve and Christmas Day, while they started collecting their respective treasures for their departure. I picked up on this not so subtle hint and began to collect my gifts prior to making my quiet exit. It was at this time that Rigatoni motioned for me and Ferucci to come into his office for this formal holiday farewell. I dropped my stuff and followed Ferucci in. Rigatoni bade us to sit down (I think it was sit down because he said it in Italian and Ferucci immediately plopped down in the first chair he could find.) And then he began about the agency, about a year of challenges, about moving forward, about his vision for the future and about other stuff. Normally, I always had a hard time giving his discourses full attention. This time I had some holiday spirits in me of the liquid kind long before lunch. All I could do was wear a dopey smile and nod along in approval at what I thought were the salient high points. In the back portions of what was left of my sober mind I started thinking why am I here listening to all this? I just wanted to get out of there, more than ever, and he was going on and on. For once, though, there seemed light at the end of the proverbial tunnel. Rigatoni reached to the side of his desk and proceeded to give Ferucci and I envelopes accompanied by a handshake and a commendation for all that we've done for the past year. I could hardly believe it: a sealed envelope for me! I felt like Ralphie in *The Christmas Story* when he finally got his Daisy rifle. It's not that an extra hundred bucks would make a huge percentage wise difference; it was the principle. I got blood from a stone; I got money from Rigatoni. It was like getting something from a pre-spirited Scrooge. This was anther victory for the true meaning of Christmas!

After the handshake, Ferucci and I made a hasty exit from the presidential suite. He didn't say much; he was going somewhere and I was heading back to my cell to collect the good stuff and depart for home and the quiet of the Christmas holiday period ahead. Both office staff and agency personal seemingly dispersed like quail. The entire building was quiet and vacant. When the kids left, they took the spirit of life with them.

The return to the office was quicker than normal since there were no distractions in the hall or rooms. When I got back, there on the desk was still another present. A small box was nicely wrapped with a red bow tie accompanied by a note. I didn't open the box — that could wait until Christmas Day — but curiosity did get the best of me because I had to read the note. It was from Miss Janet. I apologized to myself for ever thinking that she had a heart of granite. Evidently all the party activity in the administration office wasted any chance of encountering her until the long holiday break was over. I was chagrined. I did open the envelope — it was not perfumed — and read the cryptic message: "Enjoy your quiet time with this gift just for you." It was just signed with her first name, no love or best wishes or anything leading like that preceding her name. But the delayed gratification part of me reaffirmed that I would not open the gift until Christmas Day in the quiet of my own home. My spirits were boosted for the second time within a one hour period. How lucky could one person get?

I got my stuff assembled, put on my coat and headed for the door. The building was eerie by its quiet and lack of life. I couldn't say good bye to the secretaries since they were gone. As I got to the final door, there was Billy. The custodians, I guess, stayed with the building like a captain on a sinking ship. He wished me a good holiday season and my response was in inquiry if he paid all of his gambling debts to me since it was year's end. You gotta love the one line zingers. I think he kind of liked the camaraderie, though.

I opened the back door of the 528 and put the presents in the back seat. With that door closed, I got into the driver's seat, started the engine, took off my hat to get comfortable and began the final drive of the year home. I was filled with the gratification that I did all that I could do to make the kids' lives just a little better. My final thought, with the school and center in my rear view mirror, was that Rigatoni was so far off base about the kids having too much attention and toys and stuff for the season that he deserved a ton of coal in his stocking. Each and every kid there deserved a break this time of year, and hopefully I was one of the individuals that gave it to them. A kid can never have enough toys, especially during this time of year. And I was on my way for a break too, for about ten days, wherein I would not have to deal with the office population. The drive home was quick and uneventful, primarily because it was early afternoon. When I got home, there was Kiki waiting for me in the window. The Christmas vacation period could now officially begin.

It was early afternoon when I got through the front door. With this unexpectedly early arrival, I couldn't tell if Kiki was surprised, delighted or annoyed that I messed up her schedule. I did come with two packages of Christmas goodies which I placed on the living room floor. She circled the packages a few times. They were items of significant interest to her. In the meantime, I went upstairs to change into more comfortable attire. When I got back down, Kiki had knocked over one bag, and all that I could see was her backside and tail sticking out. Something got her attention. I hope it wasn't the left over holiday food that I snuck out of the office. In fact, her posture was rather funny. The backside and tail were stiff as proverbial boards, while the front of her was probably sniffing and poking around. After about a minute, she finally came out but proceeded to bat at the interior contents. Enough was enough and I pulled her away, after all the snacks that I snuck out still would taste pretty good a day or two later. Annoyed though she was, I placed the cat in the bay window and proceeded to survey and clean up the damage. To my surprise she did not get into the bag of purloined pastries but into the one that had Miss Janet's gift. And it was opened. There strewed all over the bag and on the carpet was my Christmas gift: some shredded but most intact tea bags. I didn't know whether to be mad at the cat or just laugh. This all too curious cat wrecked my plans for delayed gratification. I was now on clean-up detail. The brunt of the pussycat damage was to the tea; the other damage was just minimal. The laborious process began, with the unscathed tea bags being placed back into their gift container, while the damaged ones thrown into the recycling bin for composting. Kiki just watched and the condemnation of "Bad Pussycat" had no appreciable effect on her disposition. There was the remnant of the homemade, hand tied red bow that was prepared just for me, now in shreds. With a grimace I glared at Miss Kiki and exclaimed, "I hope you're happy with yourself now!" There was no response. She couldn't care less. She was having a good time exploring new additions to her empire.

I got a container to gather the remnants of Miss Janet's Christmas gifts, muttering bad cat on several occasions. But during the collection process something very interesting with the tea bags. These were not teas of the ordinary kind but strawberry tea. A light kind of went on. Wasn't there some kind of Elizabethan literary reference that linked strawberries with a sexual innuendo? This was very subtle but I think I got it. What a nice way to spice up my Christmas holiday although I would not run into Miss Janet for two whole weeks. This made me forgive the cat's intrusion. And while I was at it, I might as well open up Rigatoni's Christmas card. After all, why have Rigatoni's money easily available where the cat could shred it as well? It took me a whole year to wheedle a hundred extra dollars from him. In quick order I found the sealed envelope. In my haste I just tore at the seal; I didn't have recourse to the finesse of a letter opener. The suspense built to a climax as I pulled out the card. I opened it. That was it! Nothing fell out. The card contained nothing except his hand-written wishes to "Have a great holiday." Was this a mistake? I looked again at the inside of the envelope. Sure enough, nothing inside. I was duped. How far can anyone go with only good wishes . . . and these were probably not too sincere anyway? Money would have made this card honest and more palatable. I had a whole lot of well meaning nothing. As one of my Christmas traditions, I hung all the Christmas cards around the door hallway. Would this one make the cut? After all, it did not even arrive with a stamp or anything. It cost him nothing to send. Was this kind of a cheap joke? After some thinking, I decided to hang the card on the very bottom of the archway. From a distance it made it look like I had more friends than I could count. And if the cat started to play with this card, so what! Nothing lost. The card was posted on the bottom most part of the hallway and I proceeded to take care of the other presents strewn on the floor. Kiki watched me, perched on the arm of the couch, seemingly amused by the whole thing of her personal servant cleaning up after a play session. I was moving on, getting ready to enjoy the Christmas break in my own quiet way with real friends, not work associates, and family.

Everyone has his or her Christmas traditions. I had mine, a Polish one. Christmas Eve or the Vigil, "Wigilia" in the old language, began it. After sundown and with the appearance of the first star, the family would gather around the table for a meal that was ritualistically prescribed. Under the four corners of a table cloth pieces of straw were placed. Soup would be followed by the main course of an odd number of seafood dishes; there was never any meat. There was a goodly amount of wine available to wash things down. One strange custom of my family was that the wine served was Manischewitz, a kosher Jewish wine. The reason I was given was that they liked it. This never appealed to my taste but I suffered in silence — it was the family — and drank it . . . a lot of it during some gatherings. But the most memorable part took place in the beginning with the offering of the wafer or the "oplatki." Tradition held that the oldest at the table would offer the next eldest the wafer, and offering him or her a wish for the coming year, and breaking it would then pass it down to the next eldest at table until the youngest at the very end. Only then would the meal begin, marking the official beginning of the Polish Christmas celebration.

That year, this meal was held at my godmother's house. My mother died recently, so my father being the host for this event was not even a remote possibility. My father was lost around the kitchen. Rumor had it that he once defied the laws of physics and actually burned water.

So Eileen cooked. One thing was certain; all the food was good and there was plenty of it. The only curiosity, if you were purely Polish, was that Eileen always slipped in an Italian pasta dish or some olives. She had an explanation for it, so much for the adherence to a pure, Polish ritual. But I didn't care since the food was always good and I was not doing one iota of cooking. So we broke the wafer, ate and drank, and then ate and drank some more. It was almost always wine; only the dissidents drank beer. Curiously enough, Eileen got this fixation with Manischewitz cream dry Concord. It wasn't even red wine, and it went down with much difficulty. Because it cut down on drinking, it had to have a minimal impact on the fun as well. But no one ever complained about our Polish/Italian/Jewish Christmas Eve gathering. I guess a little borrowing from all over makes this the best of all possible worlds.

After stuffing ourselves to the point of pain, the entire crew retreated into the living room area. Here, Eileen would serve us cordials and proceed to put on the record player with 33 1/3s to support the spirit of the season. I think it was Lawrence Welk and one of his Christmas albums. I kind of remember somewhere that the authentic Polish traditions would have the family sing some "koledy" together. But our group was either one or two generations removed from those who just came over on the boat, so another tradition was corrupted by acculturation. But we didn't care. We were half plastered by this time and so stuffed that we couldn't get up from our chairs without tremendous effort. The vinyl on the record player made things so much easier.

Of course, the living room area meant presents. And stuff came out from under the tree, from adjacent closets, from under the sofa, wherever there was a hiding place! Not that the presents were Gucci stuff. The wrapping was more exquisite and deserving of "ohs" and "ahs" then what was inside. For me it was always a shirt. For my father, it was a shirt, slippers and a sweater. In an exceptional year, he would get gloves or a scarf, which he would never use anyway. And with every opening of every present, there was the background chorus exclaiming just how wonderful and appropriate each and every gift was. The irony was, especially to the casual observant outsider, that the wrappings were better than the gifts.

The wrappings had to go somewhere. The sad truth of the matter was that each and every bow, tissue paper and exquisite wrap all landed into the large black, plastic bag and unceremoniously and unlovingly thrown out into the trash. The hours of careful preparation discarded in a wink of an eye! But the family remained in the living room, talking and drinking. It was at this time Eileen got up from her chair, looked at me with a smile and told me that she would be right back. Maybe she was going to the bathroom? I wasn't going anywhere. I had my father in tow and he most definitely would be the last to leave anyway. He had a strong bond with his sister and although words were never spoken, they had the deepest affection for each other. I never recalled even one argument, and that side of the family was very argumentative.

When Eileen came back, she was carrying a large cardboard box. It was unwrapped. She placed this thing at my feet and said, "This is for you. I wanted you to have this and thought tonight was the best time." I looked at this old box, unwrapped, and got the feeling that I got short changed again by family in particular and life in general. Didn't I at least deserve wrapping? I was judging this book by its cover. Some things never change, and some people never learn, and some people are too quick for their own good. I nodded and gave a forcibly polite thank you. Eileen said, "Aren't you going to look in the box?" I gave some kind of excuse, on top of a smile, claiming that this was not the right time to rummage around. Eileen said, "Just look inside. I think you'll like what you see." Reluctantly I acquiesced. I was not the one to argue with my godmother, especially on Christmas Eve, in front of the entire family.

Sometimes it is most prudent to keep your mouth shut and have your own stupid thoughts reserved only for yourself. This was one of those instances, either out of respect or fear for my godmother. So I kept my big mouth shut and reached into the box. If I had thoughts about speaking, they were completely obliterated now. I was speechless. Inside the box was my late Uncle Charlie's American Flyer train set. Many Christmas' ago, my parents and I would make a post-Christmas day visit to Eileen and Charlie's for dinner. I don't remember the meal but I vividly remembered the train set. Every year it was a different scenic motif that took Uncle Charlie weeks to set up. Talk about the second coming; this was even more important to a kid. My eyes would be as wide as saucers as the engines came around the circle chugging and puffing that cedar incense smoke that smelled better than any expensive perfume that women wore, including my mother. Charlie would laugh as his nephew was spellbound in amazement.

When Charlie died, it was my understanding that the train set was sold lock, stock and barrel — my astonishment, again, as I looked into the box and pulled out one of the green passenger cars. Memories came flashing back to me. Charlie seemed to be still there in that living room and laughing at his stunned nephew. For a brief moment, time went backwards. Everything that was good with the past was still there.

The rest of the evening was nondescript. I sat in the chair, catatonic, just staring at the box. My father and his sister rambled on talking about past matters of importance to them. The other family members were just there. After a few more cordials for Floyd and family, and one more brandy for myself, the party began to disperse. As expected, we were last to leave. My father always had an additional word of advisement or three to impart on any captive audience and his sister Eileen.

I wish I could say that the remainder of the Christmas holiday was as memorable as Christmas Eve. I guess it's a Polish tradition to pull out all stops and make that one evening the most magical and special for the year. It certainly worked for me.

Christmas Day came and went. I did attend the mandatory church service. It was a lot of glitz and glamour and hoopla. As usual, I still cannot remember the sermon. Evidently the clerics, still with their collective noses in *The Summa*, cannot fathom or even partially convey the feeling of the season. Sometimes it's better to be slightly off and incorrect, even at the expense of keeping your discourse short.

There was an entire week to kill. I could never make any effective plans between Christmas and New Year's. This time of year it's kind of still and quiet. So I played the hero-martyr and went into work for a couple of hours for a couple of days. Ferucci was there as well as most of the office faithful. I don't know how much work they accomplished; I didn't get much done but looked corporately good in the process. Most of the chatter was on how I spent my Christmas vacation (best ever), not to be confused with how I spent my summer vacation (best ever) — almost the same scenario, just a different season. I added nothing to the conversation but enjoyed the diversion.

Of course, during the holiday season, the dreadful New Year's Eve date arrives. The ritual requires you to get dressed up, waste your hard earned money on overpriced food and drink, pretend to be happy for a few hours and then if and when you wake up the only remembrance of the past evening is a crushing hangover. It's kind of the prom for grownups who now ought to know better. I guess I did not graduate with that part of the class so once again I passed on these festivities and spent the evening at home watching TV with Kiki. The next day, I took my father back to his sister's house for the traditional ham dinner. All was low key. The food and alcohol were less in quantity. The conversation between my father and his sister went back again to the past and memory lane. I was kind of an outsider looking in and this was my family and history! Nevertheless, the layback spirit of the day was kind of welcomed, given the other events of the holiday. So this was how I ended my Christmas vacation. Nothing of the excitement that great novels or movies are made of, except for Uncle Charlie's train and the memories of Christmas past.

PART SIX CONCLUSION

It was almost a welcomed blessing to get back to the regularity of the work grind, even though this was a Tuesday at the beginning of what looked like cold winter; an uninviting, foreboding sky put the damper on anyone who would even think of carrying the cheer of the Christmas vacation into the beginning of a new year. Evidently the joy and spontaneity of the season was officially finished, taken over by a regimented monotony of work and winter. I skipped Lucca's this morning and went straight in to the main office for a pretend check in and get a cup of coffee — I had an ulterior motive — I was early for once and wanted to let them know that I was there and on time. But what did it matter; it was such a long time until spring that even counting the days was pointless. The administrative staff dribbled in, one at a time, in an unenthused, spiritless, an almost robotic manner. It was hard to believe that this was the exact same crew that celebrated the Christmas season so heartedly just two weeks previously. Was I in the right office? So I passed them, and they passed me, like ships in the night, as I returned to my cell to dutifully go through the vestiges of work until my five p.m. dismissal time, which was closer than the arrival of spring. My cellmate came in, we exchanged courteous pleasantries and idle morning chit chats and then went about the unremarkable business of the day. Then dismissal came. That was that! That was the first day of the new work year!

Ideally one would hope that the following day would be better. Statistically, or with a casual flip of the coin, there had to be a better than 50/50 chance that the sun would be shining bright in the sky and staff would be arriving perky with blazing ear to ear grins. As life and our best intentions go, this was not the case. Gloom and glum continued to hold court, ensconced and intractable. And as the day wore on, the overcast sky surrendered to flurry participation to put even a further damper on the mental state of those trying to lunch. But the precipitation almost always occasioned a humorous upside. Evidently the (female) staff was so conditioned to any form of precipitation and ensuing adverse driving conditions that they wanted, and even demanded, the proverbial early dismissal. This was one request that Ferucci would adamantly refuse to consider. In fact, more often than not he would not listen to such "hysterical, emotional, gold bricking foolishness." "If I don't have a problem driving in this weather, you should not have a problem driving in this weather. No one should have a problem driving in this weather!" The outcome was always the same: the staff was dismayed as the request was summarily dispatched and Ferucci was exasperated but victorious. The staff stayed until the bitter end of the day's dismissal. And his four-wheel drive Jeep was ready to undertake anything Mother Nature could dish out. That day, as always, I stayed until the bitter five p.m. end. The flurries continued unabated. The drive home was uneventful but a little slow — New Jersey will slow down if not stop for any precip on the road — and by the time I did get home it appeared that the precipitation picked up a bit. No worries though; I was safely home and Kiki was in the window waiting to welcome me. All was well. The almost religious routine of feeding the cat and myself, in that order, for dinner, followed by book and brandy and bed was upheld, waiting with anticipation for the exciting events for a better day to come.

Yes, the next day did come. Not with a breathtaking sunrise but with a ring of the phone. It was Ferucci's voice at six in the morning with an annoying abrasiveness telling me that I should go back to bed because the entire agency was on a delayed opening. If there was additional news he would let me know. The logic escaped me at the time but why call me that early in the morning to tell me to go back to bed when I was sound asleep? In retrospect, it was kind of dumb. But I couldn't go back to sleep. I was so startled from being awaken from a very deep sleep that all I could do was stare at the ceiling. Not that I could see anything since it was still dark. What to do at six in the morning, besides curse Ferucci? I refused to get up and do something constructive, so I put on NPR and listened to the news, hoping that I would doze off sometime as I passed in and out of reality. This intransigence continued for two hours until I finally forced myself to get out of bed and face a day of uncertain boredom.

All things are relative, or so they say. It seems that when you face a day of complete boredom all activities flash by instantaneously and all that is left is that massive clock with intransigent hands that do not move. Getting dressed, feeding Kiki, having breakfast and reading the morning paper all no time at all. All that was left to do was to watch the snowflakes pile up outside and make plans for lunch. The latter was going to prove difficult since I just finished breakfast and it's hard to put an effective culinary plan into effect while still satiated from the previous meal.

Unlike purgatory or that other place, time does eventually pass. This was helped by the ritualistic two shovelings of the snow in front of the house. Between shovelings, a call was recorded on the answering machine that the agency would be closed that day. From shoveling until lunch, the morning was taken. By one in the afternoon, the snow stopped. The skies showed no semblance of a breaking sun, however. I was too agitated to read, especially after having two cups of tea and four coffees. I wonder what prison is like if I felt this trapped in my own home. My only recourse was to pace, from the living room, through the dinning room, into the kitchen and the adjoining hallway, and then back into the living room. As I made the rounds, the observant Kiki became increasing perturbed with me, her tail began to vigorously swish from side to side. After a dozen or more sorties on my part, she bolted from my site much annoyed. What could I do? I needed but did not have a plan. I always wanted to live in Vermont, that beautiful, peaceful and serene place. But what if it snowed there? But what if became housebound for a day or two or a more? So if living in the frenetic state of New Jersey made me half crazy? I needed to call Ferucci.

I placed the call in early afternoon. He picked it up after only three rings. This was a good sign since it meant that he was just as bored or crazy like me.

"What's happening?"

"Not much. I went over to mom's and shoveled her out after the snow stopped. I'm thinking about going into work to get caught up."

"If you finish early or get bored, give me a call. No much going on here either."

"Will do."

That was my conversation with Ferucci that afternoon: short, sweet and to the point. No messing around with perfunctory prattle. I got my message across and planted the seed of restless discontent. I just had to wait and hope that I would not go cocoa puffs in the process. Usually he did get back to me. The percentages were in my favor, although he did suffer from memory lapses or something akin to that kind of disorder. The waiting for him to make a decision, one that would benefit me, was always a killer.

But for the interim, I had trouble with time and clocks. Everything seemed to stand still. The hands froze on the downstairs grandmother clock, and looking out the window and seeing the same stillness of the fallen snow only added to my irritation. Time and life seemed to place me on permanent hold. My options were limited: I could pace to and fro in one room or from one room to another, have a cup of tea, or read a book or something. The necessity of a brilliant idea had me do all three: pace, tea, read. The idea may have been theoretically great but its execution and end result left much to be desired, just a few hours of remaining afternoon daylight and the evening meal and more tea. I had to stew in my own juices of a lack of direction and make some attempt to like it.

The evening meal did come, much sooner than the later. In fact, there was still some light in the winter western sky, but this didn't matter because the repast was just beyond mediocre in taste. A phone call would have improved the taste. This was not forthcoming either. The only option was to wait with a cup of caffeinated coffee in hand. And wait I did.

There comes a point wherein you have to choose between the righteousness of your ways or getting what you want even if it means — forgive me for inserting that most foul word in the English language — "compromise." What will it be: rectitude or pleasure? Being strong or caving in? Staying home looking at four walls or a wild night on the town? Yes, there were two problems: snow was still on the ground and Ferucci did not yet return my call. Did he ever, truly and honestly, intend to return my call. The reality of the situation became bleaker by the minute. I had to be a big boy and face the harsh fact of life: I was getting stiffed. This reality prompted me to a desperate reaction plan. After a cup of coffee, I would break down and call him. This was a severe compromise of my ethical position based on very high standards, formulated by discussions with many wise, educated and somewhat ethical sages, but sometimes one must force the situation to affect beneficial outcomes. Amen!

It was barely after six when I called only to catch Ferucci in the midst of his evening meal. He proceeded to give me a discourse on the quality of Italian food and how everything tasted better with a martini or two, no olives needed. He couldn't make a commitment until he finished everything on his plate and in his glass and how he felt after. He promised to get back to me soon. Evidently this was a mission in the failure mode. If I were smart, I would make plans for a house-bound evening alone. The consequences of this thought was staggering: an evening of pure boredom. Imagine eternity if you were snowed-in in paradise.

I shuffled and putzed around, until that unexpected call came in at around seven. Mr. Ferucci announced that the roads by him were clear; what did I have in mind. The suddenness of this unexpected and joyous good news took me back . . . to my youthful days of stuttering. I hemmed and hawed and finally blurted out the Yellow Rose. This was a country and western bar in Manville that Joe, my Santa Claus, tended. And this was the bonus of my quick thinking: we could thank him personally, perhaps get a free drink — after all he was Santa Claus — and perhaps get an easy score on any of the desperate women who would come out on a night like this. Ferucci took the bait, hook, line and sinker, and would arrive at my house at eight. We would go together for adventure to salvage a lost day.

Hours later he arrived at my doorstep. It was a sight to behold: snakeskin boots, a lanyard tie and a feathered cowboy topping off the ensemble. Ferucci looked like a refugee from a very long and hard cattle drive. The Marlboro man would be agast from this competition. Stunned already, he threw me another curve ball when he said, "You can't go looking like that into a country bar."

"But a plaid, flannel shirt should be enough, especially on a night like this. If there are a dozen hardy soles there, that would be capacity for a night like this."

Then he proceeded to lecture me, in my own home, on fashion, fashion statements, appropriate attire and the importance of making that first initial impression. Not wanting to argue but just to go out, I went upstairs and changed. When I made my grand reappearance coming down the stairs, he noticed my boots.

"Not western enough! A rounded toe doesn't quite make it. You need a style like these." With that he pointed to his own foot ware. "Six hundred dollars, that's what it costs if you're going to do things right!" I thought that six hundred dollars was too much an expense to impress someone who was looking only at my feet. But I just smiled in silent agreement and nodded my head, after all, I kind of won by bringing him out post snowfall to go to a dive country and western bar.

It was decided that I would drive since the Yellow Rose was in my neck of the woods and I theoretically knew the back roads and such. We got into the Beemer and fishtailed out of the driveway and onto the open road. I was somewhat effervescent and I imagined that he was kind of glad to get out too. I even dared to take the back roads, snow and all, since it was a shorter route. If the gods of luck were with us, there would be nothing to fear. Plus this trip was blessed with the best of intentions, since I was personally going to thank Joe, the Santa Claus who saved my rear end the past month. En route, I chatted and Ferucci babbled. Neither paid attention to the other. It didn't matter since we were out, free and happy. This is what long-term relationships are about.

About a dozen cars were in the Yellow Rose parking lot when we pulled in. This was a good omen, indeed, since we were comparatively early and more barroom revelers were most certain to come. We were both happy with our decision to escape from our snowbound confines. As we were entering the bar I mention to Ferucci that I would like to go to the bar immediately, order a drink to warm up and thank Joe for coming out and making Christmas so special for the agency's kids. Ferucci seemed excitingly receptive to the first option. He loved his martinis.

As cool as can be we sauntered, text book style, up to the bar and took our seats. Sometimes I wonder why we go through these posturing motions and affectations, even when no one is apparently watching. Maybe it's just a question of style, maybe it's because of who we are. We took our seats and what seemed a very long minute the barkeep came over to attend to our order. It wasn't Joe and he was the only one behind the counter. I ordered the house draught and Ferucci ordered a dry martini with no olives. Ferucci then went off on a tangent about the lack of quality and quantity in his recent martini orders; I, on the other hand, strained over the bar to make absolutely sure that Joe was not there. This trip of thankfulness would be a complete failure if there were no one to thank. I was perplexed by this unforeseen invisible obstacle. Why do I consistently get these curveballs in my life?

In the due course of time — the order was filled neither exceptionally fast nor exceptionally slow — the drinks arrived in front of us. Ferucci was intent on examining and sampling the contents of his martini but I had another issue on my mind. Discretely I began my interrogation of the bartender with a seemingly innocuous question.

"Are you here by yourself tonight?"

"Yea," he responded. "This appears to be a slow night, so I don't think I would need any additional help."

"Isn't there a Joe who also attends bar here?"

"Not any more."

"I hope he didn't get fired or anything like that. We just came here special to thank him for helping us out during Christmas."

"Well, that's going to be hard to do since he failed to show up here Christmas Eve for work."

"Was there a problem or anything like that?"

"The only problem was that he just didn't show up for work. Until that time he was a good worker and the people around here liked him. He got tips like crazy. He just didn't show for work. I tried to call him but I couldn't get a working phone number. He just disappeared. Are you looking for a job? Can you tend bar?"

"And he just disappeared? And you never saw or heard from him again?"

"Just vanished into thin air! Maybe he had a credit problem or just couldn't pay the rent. I don't know. All I know is that I have to fill this position since business will pick up in a couple months. Like I said, if you or anyone you know is interested in a job, just come on in and apply."

Well that was that, another lesson in life's futility. I tried to be thankful and went out of my way to express the same and what did I get, another cold, blank trail. I glanced over at Ferucci and was anxious to see his reaction to this whole affair but he was apparently oblivious. He was more concerned about the quality and quantity of his martini. He digressed and I had nothing more to say. He talked, the music started and a handful of dancers took the floor. We both turned our backs to the bartender to face the music. There were two striking similarities shared by all the dancers: they knew their stuff on the floor and they all wore those western cowboy boots. If fact, they were all so good that it would be an embarrassment for either of us to even think of venturing onto the floor. So we ordered another drink. With the second martini, Ferucci began rambling about his past life in college wherein he was pure country, knew the music, knew the players, all the dance moves, and then proceeded to show me the six hundred dollar boots he was wearing, again. I did all I could do to tune him out. As the music got loud, he got louder. But he was effective. I had to get another drink. What did I care about his past college life in small town in Pennsylvania and who or what he knew about country stuff? All I wanted was to say thanks to this Santa Claus guy. Where did he go and why? It's frustrating in this life to be denied expressing the most rudimentary of social courtesies. What is this world coming to . . . country and western music?

As the evening wore on, Ferucci became even louder and more animated and I became more withdrawn. What happened to Joe my Santa Claus guy? Slumping over the bar with my supplementary beer supply, some woman came up to me and asked me to dance. Evidently the pathetic, hound dog look does have some effect in attracting desperate women. I politely declined, claiming truthfully that I couldn't do that stuff. She was willing to teach me, but I told her about my war injury that made ambulation difficult. She left disappointed. The bar tender said something about rude, un-neighborly patrons and turned his back. Ferucci simply got louder and went to his third martini. All I was able to focus upon was where was Joe and what really happened to him?

The rest of the night was pretty much nondescript. A few more patrons came in and I had to struggle to get the bartender's attention for another Bud. Ferucci was decided happy with his third martini since I was driving. Things came to a non-conclusive end since we had to be at work the next day. We quietly left among the din of music and some dancers on the floor.

Although the drive back was less than four miles, it seemed much longer as Ferucci placed his snow laden, melting boots on my dashboard and began the discourse, again but in more detail, about his college days and his absolute affinity and expertise with country music, dancing and its overall life style. He was disrespecting my BMW, which is rightly known as the ultimate driving machine. I could not drive fast enough to get home and rid myself of this discoursing passenger as well as lessen the impact of melting snow on my dash and subsequently on my floor. As it always happens, I hit every possible traffic light home. By the time I did get in my driveway, my dash was awash with gallons of melting snow. My cheerful passenger bid me adieu with the farewell message of "See you at work tomorrow, and on time, I hope." I was less jolly. My best intentions of paying a personal thank you to my Christmas benefactor failed, I was scolded by the bartender for being an unfriendly sort, and Ferucci trashed my car. Talking about striking out on three straight pitches! Thinking ahead, since this night was a disaster, the prospect of getting up on a cold mid-January morning to go to the purgatory of work was not uplifting to my depleted spirits. Sometimes you don't win, no matter how good the effort and intentions

I am just incapable of recalling any piece of literature, whether great or on a Hallmark card, that extols the virtues and beauty of January. This is a month that is cold, oppressive, depressive and 31 days too long. It's a grind. Even the Catholic Church has no holy days of obligation for this month. The only day in red on the calendar is Martin Luther King's holiday. They gave that day to the Afro-Americans because every other good day during the year was taken. Who is willing to march up Fifth Avenue in 20 degree weather and buck a 30 mile per hour head wind to boot? Just go shopping — big deal — to take advantage of a white sale! Something is wrong here!

The rest of January passed with a monotonous, uneventful repetition that dulled the senses and the spirt. To buoy my sagging spirits I began counting down on the calendar for Ground Hog Day. That seemed to be my only alternative, or succumb to the extended drear of a winter depression that only January can bring. Admittedly it was a mind game, but . . . .

February brought to my mind the nominal end of winter, Ground Hog Day. This holiday came and went, overshadowed by the prognostication of a fat, furry, mindless rodent. My next milestone for hope and happiness was Valentine's Day. With the 200 or some women who worked at the agency, the odds were with me that I would get something — cards or chocolates or candy — to bolster my sagging spirits. Maybe Miss Janet would finally come through this year. But even the best plans, hopes and aspirations are seemingly given a detour by life. Two days before Valentine's Day a large sealed envelop made it across my desk. This was an expected surprise. And when I opened it, its contents were most unwelcomed. After a decade and a half working for the agency, I was given a "year end" performance review, orchestrated and signed by Rigatoni, or should I have said President Rigatoni. This was the first one I ever got. Among other things the contents read that I did lousy work over the course of the past year and there was a meeting scheduled that would include Ferucci and the head of human resources. So it looked like it was going to be three against one. If there was a problem with my performance, why not take me aside and discuss inadequacies one-on-one? Why wasn't this nipped in the bud months previously, if there was a performance concern? Why all this hullabaloo now? Something did not smell right in Italy, and it wasn't the cheese. I had two days to prepare a defense, if anything could prevent this travesty of a kangaroo court. What was I to do?

I had a hard time remembering anything in the days leading up to this meeting. Things were just a jumble. Time seemed to be moving inordinately fast toward this confrontational assassination. There was one thing for certain and that was I did nothing much in preparation. Given the circumstances, why bother? It seemed that the results of this meeting were preordained. It would not be a trial; it would be a sentencing. I did pull my file folders out and took some notes about the past year's accomplishments, but would it really matter? What does anything matter?

Needless to say, it was a depressing time leading up to this appointment which promised to be laced heavily with acrimony. The presence of my beloved cat would have given me solace, but I was enjoined into going into this arena of conflict alone. There was no chance. The seething anxiety and feeling of helplessness leading up to this meeting was traumatic enough. The sad irony was that the cat could not come and be an advocate in my behalf. As the Kingston Trio once sang, I had to walk down that lonesome road all by myself. It would be comforting if I just could see some being there, something from another dimension there, just for emotional support. But I had nothing but the thoughts of a furry, purring cat and a BMW in the driveway. I was alone, a vulnerable and a hapless target, playing a game with their rules on their home playing field.

The morning of the trial and subsequent damnation came. The meeting was scheduled for 11 — very late or me. This inconvenient time was intentionally positioned into running and ruining my lunch hour. But this was a typical Rigatoni move. If nothing more came out of it, I would be punished by overbearing inconvenience and a certain degree of intimidation. The two-hour wait between arriving at work and this appointment was punitively interminable. I can't remember the number of times I felt that time was standing still. I don't know if I was in hell or purgatory or limbo. Ultimately it did not make a difference. The anxiety, discomfort and angst were present and real and now. The future was inaccessible and not within my control.

The dreaded hour finally came and seemingly went as the big hand touched 12. Nothing happened. No one came for me. The tension and anxiety levels dropped. I breathe a sigh of exasperated relief. The trial would be at another date. I began to think about escaping for lunch.

"No such luck, turkey!" as some philosophers would say: Nothing lasts forever, especially good times or a reprieve. Ferucci was at my desk with the: "It's time." With those words I felt my blood, once warm, happy and flowing, turning to ice. The inevitability of the situation was hitting me square in the face. There was nothing apparently I could do but to stoically face this farce with a hanging judge and a loaded deck with skewed evidence. My previous good works and accomplishments would amount to a giant nothing. All I could rely upon was me. I would have loved and appreciated if the deity would have sent me an angel in this hour of crisis, even an incompetent one like Clarence in *It's a Wonderful Life,* just to know and have some semblance of friendly support and comfort. Unlike the Bible, these helpful spirits, just like the police, are never around when you need them. But there was nothing in the board room that even suggested warm and friendly. Rigatoni was there with a pile of paperwork in front of him, sitting in his usual presidential position at the head of the table, Regan was there representing HR and Ferucci representing I don't know what, perhaps just to take notes, for all that mattered.

The proceedings began in Rigatoni's usual manner. He cleared his throat several times, kind of like having a vocal gavel to gain attention and bring the court to order, and then began his monotone diatribe.

Looking directly at me, he began, "As you have been apprised in my official memo to you as president, there have been increasing concerns about your performance this year as director of development. We are gathered here this morning to formally alert you that your lack of an acceptable grade of performance over the past year is directly affecting your future with this agency. You are hereby formally placed on a probationary status, which will last for 90 days."

No one there said anything to interrupt. All were stone faced; no one dared offering another option. This was the trial wherein Rigatoni was prosecutor, judge and jury, all efficiently rolled up into one being, a kind of unholy trinity. You would think that with almost two decades of employment and abject servitude things could have been orchestrated differently with a more humane, respectful, or sensitive touch. He presented me and all there with a Lutheran list of my inefficiencies and delinquencies; these were three pages long. I silently accepted this documentation but only glanced at it and did not respond. This was not the time to be inquisitive or confrontational.

The immediate and most unfortunate aspect of this orchestrated inquisition, lasting for over an hour, effectively intruded into and wrecked my lunch time. Its conclusion was somewhat interesting since he additionally gave me, in writing, a five-page list of directives, goals and objectives that were to be met. The most onerous of all was that everything I would do must be submitted to his office for prior approval, save, I guess, for going to the bathroom. The conclusion of this meeting with this Angst committee put all on notice that there would be a follow up interrogation in less than a month — no set date yet — to see how well I could conform to his list of immediate directives.

Since I was totally stupefied with no objections or comments or questions, the meeting was declared officially concluded. I was the first to leave — just couldn't wait to get out of that stuffy, claustrophobic room. Who stayed, how long and what transpired were questions that just did not interest me. It looked like things were definitely over; not just if but only when. I looked at my watch. Lunch was unofficially late too.

When I returned to my desk I imagined a sense of an ominous quiet that placed a kind of funeral pall over everything. It seemed that those who spoke to me were very deferential but lacked the usual spontaneity, humor or warmth. I felt spent and naked, if I had any feelings at this point. Nothing seemed to make sense anymore or have any feeling. Everything was gone. Trying to help special needs kids as a central focal point of my life simply did not have any relevancy anymore. All my past efforts and accomplishments seemed meaningless. What then?

Lunch was taken alone. Following that, the rest of the day wore on. When five came, I departed quietly and quickly. Did it matter?

The rest of the work week rolled on, leading to the weekend. I lost any desire for even making plans for anything. I felt like a candidate for an Edgar Allen Poe tale of someone affected by the semi-demented. I became transformed into a mechanical man during the intervals between evaluation meetings. I sincerely tried to meet the goals and objectives that were set forth by Rigatoni, but failure was becoming an option turned into reality. Some of these directives were either contradictory or just self defeating. And there were just too many that an ordinary mortal could not meet. Most assuredly, anything handed to him for his approval would be met with suggestions, objections or just plain rejections. How could anyone be spontaneous or creative with a gun pointed to his or her head? Yet this was the imperial directive. I lived during this probationary period with the knowledge of certain, imminent failure. If this were a legitimate legal proceeding, at least I could offer evidence or throw myself upon the mercy of the court. But this wasn't the reality at hand. I became the walking dead, and I felt that my relationship with everyone there was now tainted. I was looked upon me as someone who contracted leprosy or AIDS. All I needed was a bell to announce my impending passage through the halls so everyone could conveniently avoid me.

Time melded into a continuous present, dull, throbbing and numb. A day or two prior to the next scheduled meeting of kangaroo court, there was another sealed envelop on my desk. Probably it did not strain the imagination or the stats of probability to guess that it was from Rigatoni setting up the game's playing field, on his terms, for the next joust. Of course, like everything that Rigatoni did, the entire format was very official looking. I had my full, entire name with my current job title, along with the notation, in bold letters "Personal and Confidential." To give this administrative love letter the full and proper respect it deserved, I pushed it to the side of my desk unopened. Life is so full of unnecessary flotsam and jetsam that's hurled upon us by the deity lording over us with unfeeling fate and emotions. I just couldn't, at this time, accede to this, another insult against my tottering peace of mind and emotional tranquility. So it sat; and I contemplated lunch. This was taken, as usual, in the kitchen with the custodial staff munching away at the leftovers that the absentee students would never eat. Waste not, want not. Could never beat the price nor the company of the custodial staff were always certainly preferable in character and kindness to anyone in administration.

But there is a certain fatalistic inevitability about our lives' cycle. Decisions and events do come upon us. Either we accept them or delay them or just ignore them, nevertheless they pop up like relatives during the holidays. Sooner or later, the inevitable faces us, square in the kisser. So when I returned from lunch, I reluctantly opened Rigatoni's envelope. Surprise, surprise! The meeting was postponed for a week. He had a scheduling conflict but noted in his correspondence that this would benefit me because it would give me additional time to get focused, my stuff in order, blah, blah, blah. This delay was not because of any love or affection for me; there was always an underlying ulterior motive that was so constructed to present him as totally benevolent. But I couldn't care less in finding the real cause for the delay. It just meant that my trial and the ensuing guilty verdict would be delayed by a few more days. It was inevitable, just the when was waiting for more exactitude.

I never found any spiritual benefit derived from waiting. I always wanted to get to the point and get things over with. Of course those with a religious bent could point to Carly Simon's "Anticipation" as just another example to support their mantra that some things are worth waiting for or are part of a necessary growth process or something akin to their respective spiritual ilk. Me, I just want things over with, especially if it's nasty or doesn't appear to provide me any apparent good. I'll leave the ascertaining of spiritual benefits for the religion people. I've always had at least one foot firmly planted on the ground because I've learned that a healthy skepticism goes a long way towards insuring my survival. My life would never be considered a fine wine that would benefit from a long aging period.

Needless to say, knowing the temporality of the reprieve just exacerbated the nervousness and apprehension of waiting for the next installment of "As the Rigatoni Turns." I was absolutely sure that he was boning up on his conclusively, indisputable case that would find me absolutely guilty without my position requiring mercy, pardon or parole. So I waited for the inevitable and it came. Unexpectedly — I should have known better — as I came into work on a spectacular, sun lit morning, his car was already in the lot. This was most unusual since normally he was never on the clock. When I stuck my nose snooping around the executive offices on some pretensive trip, his door was unceremoniously closed. I didn't put two and two together until Ferucci came to my desk some time later and informed me that my presence would be required, with notes, in the executive conference room at 11 sharp. Another lunch messed up!

When I walked into the conference room, I tried with a quick glance to give a slight smile to all there. This was not reciprocated effectively since they all looked like Easter Island stone(d) face statues. The portent was that this meeting was going to lack the minimal joviality of the previous one. Ironically, this was the only thing that I was going to get right that day. The good news/bad news for me was that Rigatoni was less boring and more to the point. He had paperwork galore which he distributed to all. Either he skimmed through the stuff or I wasn't listening too well until he got to his coup de grace: a new demand was that I was to generate three new ideas per day and hand over same to him in writing. I don't think that Jesus or Superman, on a good day, performed three outstanding feats in that kind in rapid order in a week, much less daily. Either I was being set up to fail or challenged to become the new messiah sans cape. I think that the former option was the safest bet. HR director Regan evidently tried to take the edge off and asked if I was up to the task. I replied that I would try, although I knew it would be a loosing effort. It looked like my tenure there was finished; all I could do was play for time and set my long term goals for my finances and personal life in order in a very short time. The boreathalon was mercifully short and concluded with the "save the date" in two weeks to evaluate my progress, attitude and full compliance to these additional requirements. I shoveled up the excess paperwork and proceeded to leave. Glancing back I noticed Rigatoni's displeasure since apparently I did not show enough of enthusiastic attention and response to his written directives and did not neatly place them in order prior to leaving. Neither did I say a warm and fuzzy goodbye or a contrite thank you for being verbally mugged. Inadvertently, I felt some degree of satisfaction since I, too, could be annoying, but with considerable less effort.

When the work day concluded, finally, I went home and after a light dinner looked at my finances. This included checking, savings and stock market accounts. These were more or less OK. When I looked at my plastic credit card statements, I grew progressively more concerned. There was some easy living in the fast lane, and, with continued employment, could be paid off in a reasonably extended and painless period of moderate austerity. However, it looked like the agency and I were getting divorced soon, and the short term prospects did not look good. Like a nagging toothache, this was a concern that was not going away.

My interim existence at the agency continued estranged. Seemingly I was treated with differential aloofness by all, except the kids with special needs. I guess I was becoming one of them, an individual with special needs although mine were not physical but of emotional origin. I was an outsider but still working on the inside. The walk through the halls felt different, except for the interaction with the kids. It was kind of being diagnosed with a terminal illness; you and everyone else quietly knew that you didn't have long but no one did not want to contract your disease nor make any long term plans with you for the coming weekend — the fish or cut bait syndrome. I guess I was the dead mossbunker.

The inevitable two weeks came as scheduled. On that morning I gave Kiki a big hug for the little luck that I hoped it would provide. Light breakfast notwithstanding, my stomach was still upset a little, but I could not help but stop at Lucas coffee shop for a cup of support. I spent the remainder of my time there slowly sipping the cup and staring out the window. The artist did see me and berated me for being unsociable again. It was the same repetitive litany that I failed to listen to in the past. The only solace was the probability that this would be the last time I would encounter this harpy. When time came and I had to leave this oasis, I did not look back. I would retain fond memories of this place, although her rasping voice was still buzzing in my ear as I drove off in my car.

My assigned parking spot was still available at work; no one, not even the custodians, took it over as yet. I do wonder, though, even to this day, whatever happened to that sign. It certainly would have made a great addition to my collectables in my study hall of fame area. In retrospect, I should have absconded with it. The sign would have been part and parcel of a fair and equitable severance package.

The morning at work lolled on. I performed pretend work. I took a break and got coffee from secretarial office to break the iron rigidity of boredom and see if there were any feelings of sympathy for me. They were courteous but this did not supply the ointment for my impending psychological wounds. When I returned to my cell, the office mate mentioned something about the weather or something innocuously similar and inoffensive and of no particular political import. If this were an omen, things were shaping up to be bad. Does it pay to listen and be verbally responsive?

The time came. I did not go to the administrative conference room on my own; instead, I had Ferucci come and get me. It was a kind of last symbolic act of defiance on my part. Why make their dirty work easy? Are feelings and conscience the same? I wonder if anyone in that room felt bad or just was writing off this day as the end of a bad business experience.

When I entered the room, I did a quick glance at all their faces to see, unlike a poker game, if anything could be forthcoming. Rigatoni, who was a dark, southern Italian, rumor had it from Sicily, seemed to have a reddish glow to his face. Either his body was being taken over by Satan, overstayed his time at the tanning salon or was on the verge of a stroke. I suddenly had a flash of hope for the latter but as it panned out the former would prevail. A second flash gave me an epiphany of some comfort; he was not as attractive as he thought himself to be — tan notwithstanding. As cruel as it is, some are born, are and will die unattractive. With this bit of sardonic humor bouncing around in the back of my mind, the meeting began, as usual, with the clearing of his throat as his way to call the proceedings to order with all eyes and ears focused on attending to his every word and movement. The loyalists in attendance would be taking voluminous notes. I only catatonically stared over his left shoulder. Perhaps I could see his familiar. At any rate no one who witnessed this trial from a distance could accuse me of not paying full and proper attention to all the pronouncements. If they only knew better! I couldn't care less and just wanted to get this thing over and get out of this place.

Rigatoni had even more paperwork than before. With a sardonic insight on the current state of affairs this new mound of paperwork would justify, at least to his mind, his course of action. And so it began as he shuffled though his stuff and picked something up from the middle of his mountainous pile of paper refuse and began with a clearing of the throat.

"During our last meeting you were given, both in writing as well as verbally, a list of criterions that you were obligated to meet. These were not suggestions. These were not pick and choose from a list. These were objective goals. You have failed to meet completely what was expected and required of you and your position here. To that end I have been in continual contact with our corporate attorney, Mr. Stark. He has concurred with me that these and other failures on your part constitutes insubordination and are grounds enough for immediate dismissal, notwithstanding your dismal performance and unprofessional decorum in other matters. So, in conjunction with legal advisement and approval from the executive members of our board of directors, I am hereby informing you that your employment with our agency is terminated." He pulled out some paperwork from the pile and flashed it about like a bull fighter with a red cape; evidently, that was a sufficient bit of supportive evident. It could have been his dry cleaning bill, if he ever had anything cleaned besides the agency treasury. With his usual glare he turned directly to me and asked, "Do you have anything to say?"

I shook my head and said nothing. The HR director interjected and asked me if I had anything to say in response. Perhaps there were extenuating circumstances or something else that could shed some light on the situation. I looked at her and shook my head no but then added that "My many years here have been good enough."

With that Rigatoni jumped in and gave his final directives. "I have directed our financial department to provide you with your severance pay for vacation days and sick days outstanding. Since there was a lot of time accrued on your part, it would be inconvenient to pay you the entire sum at once. Thus you will be mailed a series of checks when disbursement would not present a hardship to the agency. And lastly, you have an hour to clean out your desk of the items that are personally yours, leaving the agency properties behind. There will be no socializing or farewell attempts during your removal. You will have approximately one hour to clean and leave. Any questions?"

I shook my head no. What I really wanted was a few minutes to walk through the building and pay my final farewells to those that I garnered some affection through the years. This, evidently, was not to be the case. And no final lunch — a kind of agency last supper in the school kitchen — with the maintenance staff. Nothing, no account or consideration for my feelings or needs or concerns or appreciation for all the many years of service. The macadam was ending on this one-way street. As a final parting comment Rigatoni added that the agency's director of security would be summoned to be by my side during the process wherein I cleaned out my desk as I departed the facility to make sure everything was done in a proper and orderly manner, without any compromise to the agency. This was the final insult since the director of security was his son whose two claims to fame and immortality were that he had a black belt in the martial arts and his position with the agency was the first time in his life that he was able to hold down any full-time job for more than a year. Give anybody a title and they become instantly respectable.

There was no request for any final comments on my part, nor was there any desire to communicate anything. Perhaps I should have taken the example of Rocky B. and came out swinging and threw a few punches. Perhaps one or two would have landed. Perhaps I, too, would have enjoyed an upset victory. But for some unexplained reason, I opted for silence during the proceedings. Thus in stunned silence I left the room and left my history with the agency. I gave a final glance at Rigatoni. It was not a stare, just a glance. It was my hope that in his constantly machinated mind he would take it as a stare and a sign of disrespect and disregard to this entire process.

As I exited the room, the son of Rigatoni was at the door. No words were exchanged between us as I deliberately walked the halls slowly for the last time as an employee. He lurked behind me like some predatory animal waiting to make a kill on a wounded beast. Like my feelings, the halls were vacant. It was close to lunch time and the staff and kids were preparing for meals. Not even a last change to say good bye to anyone. You would think that a merciful deity would grant me a minimal amount of comfort to just look a Miss Janet for the fleeting moment. The last female I would see would be the roommate. As I came into the office she got up and expressed some words of disappointment and regret. I kind of felt like a living corpse at my own funeral. Some comfort! I don't think I was listening or very responsive at that time.

I began the tedious task of packing my stuff into the provided boxes, all under supervision. There really wasn't too much. The six-drawer desk had some correspondence, scrap paper, pens, pencils, scissors, rulers, paper clip holders and a yarmulke — you must always be prepared for any special event. You don't have to be Jewish to be prepared for special events. The debris from the desk took up about a box and a half. I intended to take each box individually to my car but the director of security stopped me at the door and informed me that I would be making only one trip to the car; once I exited the building that would be it. With most repressed smile, he pointed to a hand truck that was conveniently waiting outside the office. So I loaded the first box. From the top of the desk I took my dictionary, thesaurus and familiar quotations book and pen holder. I left paperwork in the file rack since I suspected that someone would go through anything I left behind. I also did not do anything to sabotage the computer. Weeks ago I pulled important critical stuff of the work that I was doing. Let the agency or whoever was following me start from square one as I had to do. Thus the second box was filled and somewhat heavier. That went on the hand truck. Finally, I went to the communal book shelf to retrieve whatever was meaningful or important to me. Not much there, with the exception of a dusty coffee mug. Didn't that Santa Claus character give me took loose leaf binders of PR stuff? Where was it, or did I give it to Ferucci or something. This was my property too and I would like to have that as a memento of one of the good times, but that was gone too. I would have liked to have called Ferucci but the director of security was getting somewhat annoyed and impatient since I wasn't moving fast enough. But that was that. Two and a half boxes. The last thing I grabbed was my sweater that was always on the back of my chair. I said a curt farewell to the office mate, threw my sweater on top of the boxes and began to push my personal stuff down the hall to my car. The director of security was officiously behind me the whole time but offered no help at all. All during my exodus I saw no one to say a final farewell. You would think that a benevolent deity would grant a dying man a last look at an attractive, sympathetic face. All I got was the director of security and a long row of concrete walls. I loaded the boxes into the trunk of my car and strategically pushed the hand truck away to let it roll a little. Too close and it could have scratched my BMW, too far and it may have provoked an incident with the director of insecurity, but just enough to get him slightly annoyed and thinking that this was another act of disrespect. I got into the car, locked it from inside, turned the key and backed out. My final vision was the director retrieving the hand truck. After all, we all must do something to justify our keep, no matter how humble!

The drive back home on 287 was quick and nondescript. There was no traffic to speak of since it was midday. As I pulled into the driveway I happened to just glance up at the bay window and there was Kiki, waiting for me or just enjoying the faded sun for mid-winter? When I got out of the car, the first thing I did was grab my old beaten down sweater. I guess that was my most prized possession. Entering the house, Kiki didn't move, so I decided to empty the car of all the contents. After three trips, the living room was filled with boxes. Before going through the final ritual of unpacking, I decided to make myself a cup of tea, something hot, refreshing and soothing. After the kettle finished its song, I grabbed my cup of Earl Grey and dropped into the rocker, ostensibly to rock, calm down and try to get one foot back on the ground and reality. As I rocked, I looked at Kiki, calm in the window surveying her estate, and then back onto the boxes that were littering my living room floor. Then I saw something rather curious with one of the boxes. Maybe it was the tea or just my stressed out, demented mind. Took another sip and got up. There on the top of one of the containers of collected debris was a candy cane. Not the usual one but an Italian one with both green and red stripes. Although I never was a candy cane aficionado, I kind of knew that this one was somewhat larger than the average one, plus it had the dual colored stripes. I picked it up, twirled it around a few times and placed it on the coffee table. Then I started laughing hysterically. Of all the things I salvaged from this job was a piece of candy. All the years, some individuals get a watch or a clock; all I got was a piece of Christmas candy. Then I stopped laughing when I thought that this possibly could have been Santa's parting gift to me? Or maybe this was in my drawer at work all the time and I never realized it since I never was a clean freak or someone who was super organized. Then I returned to the rocker, sipped my tea and thought that if it were Santa, he came to me and not to them. Why me? Was I more vulnerable than those people or more gullible? I rocked, sipped more tea and looked at my placid cat in the window. All that was left on my schedule was to wait for the mailman for the promised checks that would one day come. But for now and forever, a kind of peace came over me, knowing that I did the best that I could with no regrets for anything. As I looked back at my cat in the window, the snow began to gently fall. A quiet peace came over me. Nothing more could have been done.

Made in the USA
Middletown, DE
26 December 2019

81963045R00139